THAT MAGIC MOMENT

McFearson draped his arm over the back of the seat behind Tessa's head. With his other hand, he caressed her cheek. His touch electrified her, sent warm currents of desire through her body. His darkly handsome face, with its high cheekbones and silvery eyes, seemed to reach inside to her soul.

The evening sun cast a rosy glow inside the coach. She saw the bow of his lip, the shadow of hair that had grown since his shave that morning, and she had a sudden urge to run her fingertips over that roughened skin, to feel the supple lip mixed with the masculine scrape of beard. Then he lowered his mouth to hers and she had her wish.

Other books by Gloria Harchar:

ENCHANTED BY MAGIC
KISSED BY MAGIC

Endangered by Magic

Gloria Harchar

LOVE SPELL

NEW YORK CITY

To my mother, June Adams.

LOVE SPELL®

August 2005

Published by

Dorchester Publishing Co., Inc.
200 Madison Avenue
New York, NY 10016

ISBN 0-505-52618-2

The name "Love Spell" and its logo are trademarks of Dorchester Publishing Co., Inc.

Printed in the United States of America.

Visit us on the web at www.dorchesterpub.com.

Endangered by Magic

Prelude

The hallucinations hovered like dark spirits waiting to take him into a world of madness.

Desperately, he held onto his sanity, to simple, pure reality—taking a brisk ride in Hyde Park, swimming in the clear waters of Lake Neba in the Highlands, fox hunting with his favorite hound, watching Selena in ecstasy as she climaxed. That was the real world, the world he loved.

In desperation he tried to ward off the swirling mist that hovered around him, turning his head to focus on Selena as she slept. She lay on her side facing him, one hand tucked under her cheek, her dewy lips parted. Even in the moonlight, he could see the healthy glow of her complexion, the shimmer in her blond hair. One petite leg was hooked over his, a possessive, trusting gesture even as she lay in slumber. Selena, his steadfast, adorable wife. She loved him, believed in him, was forever reassuring him that he was *not* going mad. Merely watching her, thinking of her faith in him, caused the debilitating haze to momentarily retreat.

1

But the spirit world darkened, billowed in gathering power before rushing at him, as thick as tar, enveloping him in blackness. His determination to stave off the assault went unheeded as the strange darkness reeled him into the soulless tunnel he had begun to call hell.

Images spun around him, and dank smells from the wet pavement infused his senses as he materialized on the street in front of his townhouse. Voices swirled, faded, then sharpened.

"Kill . . . knows . . . kill now. . . ." Were the voices in his head a part of this abnormality he had begun to suffer more and more frequently? Were they thoughts or words? His? Or someone else's?

Darkness sipped at him, threatening to swallow him whole. The images continued to rush at him, disjointed, familiar, terrifying. Madness. Surely he was mad to envision such a horrific chain of events—bloody, insane scenes that made no sense. Then eternity consumed him in a black night with no stars.

Wakefulness came with the sun beaming through the window of his chambers. A lark trilled nearby. Lying on his side, he couldn't seem to open his eyes. A paralyzing heaviness held him down as fatigue sucked his energy. It was the usual aftermath of the mental attack. Selena's leg still covered his. The reassurance of that comfortable weight calmed him. The dreams that had flickered through his mind were only that—dreams. Not real, not this time. As he inhaled with beginning relief, a metallic scent invaded his senses and he suddenly stilled.

The sickeningly sweet smell caused his stomach to churn. At the same time he became aware of a cold stickiness on his hands. Dread seized him, making it difficult to breathe. Suddenly he wished he could fade away into the dark passageway again. He would rather face the darkness in hell, keep the nightmares in that black tunnel, than let hell visit the world he'd tried to cling to.

With considerable effort, he managed to pry open his eyes. Selena lay on her side exactly as he remembered. Her mouth was still slightly open with her hand curled under her cheek. But that once rosy cheek was now ashen. And she lay so still. Glancing down, he saw gashes on her neck, her chest. Horrified, he recoiled. Blood was everywhere—on the once-pristine bedcovers, on her gown. And on his chest, his stomach, his hands.

Her blood stained his hands.

Dear God in heaven, Selena lay dead, and by his own hand. His worst nightmare had come true.

He truly was mad.

He truly was damned.

Chapter One

A long time ago in a place far, far away, the country of Jubilant thrived in its heavenly clouds high above the land known as Great Britain. Maestro's rule was strict, but tempered with benevolence. The pixies under his reign prospered—tending their fields of faerie dust, ensuring love matches between the humans, brewing their powerful elixir, studying at the University of Coda, and living in harmony with the world. That was, until staid, straitlaced Allegro Soprano surprised everyone—including himself—by disobeying a law that broke the lock on Sedah, the Underworld.

Evil poured from Sedah, threatening to throw the whole world into darkness and despair, which would keep love from budding. Without love, the faeries would die and Jubilant would become a faint memory. Ostracized for his lawlessness, Allegro would have been forced to face the dangers outside Jubilant alone except for his loyal friend, Largo, who refused to abandon him. With his strong right arm, the mighty Largo shielded gentle Allegro as they set out through the dangers of the lands, beginning their adventures to restore goodness in the world.

At least, that was the way Largo Bass told the tale. He sat on a wildflower and absentmindedly swirled the last bit of elixir in his flask as he wrote in the journal he'd begun to keep on a periodic basis. Since the adventures had begun, he decided he had better record all his reflections. He was making history.

A puff of wind caused one of the petals to droop, forcing Largo to shift his weight more to the center. Most of the bluebells had already wilted as the last warm days of summer left the rugged Welsh hills, and he'd been lucky to find this one.

"Or perhaps I'll say . . ." He sat straighter on the petal and cleared his throat, imagining the audience with his girlfriend, Dulce, in the center. "Ostracized, his loyal friend, Largo, refused to abandon him to certain death, and ventured forth to defend timid Allegro from the perilous trolls."

As he wrote, he dreamily thought of Dulce's dainty features, beautiful violet skin, and pink cheeks, her expression filled with rapture as she listened to him. But when he heard a whirring of wings, he opened his eyes to find the narrow face of Allegro Soprano glaring down at him.

"Why do you insist on altering the facts to your favor? I am *not* timid. You know very well that it's been due to my efforts that we have managed to survive."

Irritation pricked at Largo, but he refused to rise to the bait. Perhaps Allegro's contrariness came from the high expectations the Sopranos always demanded. If Largo's family similarly insisted upon feats of heraldry, perhaps he would be just as grouchy.

Studiously ignoring him, Largo carefully closed the notebook and shrunk it small enough to put in his waistcoat pocket. Then he dug into his pack and withdrew a tomato, savoring a juicy bite of the delicacy grown by his cousin Staccato, who specialized in cultivating small vegetables just the right size for pixies. He took a swallow of elixir from his flask and gave a loud smack, knowing it would rile fastidious Allegro. He rather enjoyed stirring up Allegro's faerie dust.

Allegro still fluttered above him. "Well? Are you or are you not going to give me a little credit for our missions?"

"Ye tell it yer way, and I'll tell it me way. I want to know when we're going on another adventure."

Allegro slumped on the petal opposite him. "You're supposed to ask when we're going home. The harp's fixed and Maestro seemed pleased with our work. I would think my ostracism would be over and we could return to Jubilant, but he didn't mention it. Now it looks as if bad weather is coming on top of all this waiting."

With a frown, Largo glanced over his shoulder and saw a dark cloud rapidly approaching. "Only a wee thundercloud, nothing to fash yerself about. And mayhap Maestro was pleased—mayhap not."

Allegro had been studying the sky but turned at Largo's comment about their pixie king. "What's that supposed to mean? He gave us a feast and invited lots of faeries to celebrate, didn't he? For a very *fine* reason." Purposely, he glanced across the glen toward the magical harp, playing its mesmerizing music that kept evil creatures in their underground homes.

Largo hummed along with a particularly lively tune, then retrieved a miniature banana from his sack of food. "Aye, but that dinnae necessarily mean anything. It was all for the benefit of the political eye that he did it, for morale." At Allegro's worried look, he quickly continued, "Forget Maestro. I'm wondering what Diminish is planning."

Scowling, Allegro bounced to his feet on the petal, causing the whole flower to sway. "Uncle Diminish? Why would you be interested in what *that* degenerate is up to?"

Allegro's animosity toward his uncle surprised Largo. Although Diminish was known to be a rogue and a scoundrel at times, as well as somewhat eccentric, he was legendary. The faerie was a colorful figure whom Largo would be proud to claim as a relative, if he were in Allegro's curly-toed shoes.

"You didn't encourage him to include us in any of his harebrained ideas, did you?"

With deliberate calm, Largo peeled the banana. "Mayhap I did, although I dinnae know if he's ever planned anything harebrained. Why do ye dislike him so? He's yer flesh and blood, yer kin. Besides, he seemed nice. Why, he even left us lots of elixir, which was quite generous of him."

"Which worries me. Uncle Diminish never does anything without expecting repayment—in blood."

Putting a healthy portion of the fruit in his mouth, Largo chewed, considering his companion. Allegro had always seemed a little on the prudish side, but never unreasonable as far as judging others was concerned. His reaction piqued Largo's interest. "What do ye know about yer uncle that I dinnae know?"

"Never mind. Just mark my words—he's trouble, and you get into enough dangerous situations all by yourself. Home is what should be on your mind now. That cloud looks suspiciously familiar."

The sudden switch in topics stymied Largo for a moment before he glanced once more at the billowing cloud, his anxiety growing with it. "It isn't Maestro, is it?"

After a few moments of squinting, Allegro shook his head with a frown. "Alas, no."

Relief washed over Largo. Maestro represented responsibility and a seriousness that Largo didn't want to consider—at least, not now. Tossing the banana peel over his shoulder, he said with much feeling, "Thank the music."

Never known to sit still for long, Allegro once again hovered above the flower. "What's the matter with you? Aren't you homesick at all?"

Just watching his friend whir his wings with bottomless energy made Largo tired. Taking the last swallow of elixir, he smacked his lips, wiping them with the back of his hand before tossing the flask aside. "Home might be tedious after living on the edge for nearly a year."

"How can you say that with Dulce waiting for you there?"

The sound of her name caused both restlessness and guilt to surge inside Largo. Everyone expected him to marry her, which was fine because he wanted the same thing—didn't he? Who wouldn't desire the prettiest, sexiest faerie in all of Jubilant? And she wanted him. So why did he get this strange lump in his throat and the unerring urge to flee every time he thought of going home for longer than a brief visit? Why did he pause at the idea of going home permanently?

"Holy trumpets, that's no mere thunderstorm." Allegro was looking up to the sky again, his body still, his wings beating as fast as a hummingbird's.

Perplexed, Largo once again looked toward the rain cloud and was surprised to see the vapors had begun to swirl. Iridescent pink flashed quicker than the blink of an eye, looking oddly familiar but disappearing so quickly that he wondered if he'd imagined it. A roaring followed. Before he realized what the sound signified, Allegro yanked him off the petal just as the flower disintegrated in a blast of wind.

"Quick, under this rock!" Allegro cried, pulling him toward a cave beneath a huge slab of stone. The wind had whipped itself into near-gale proportions. Wasting no more time, Largo threw himself into the cave just as a tree came crashing down in the space he'd occupied a split second before.

The wind abruptly stopped, the stillness deafening.

"Allegro?" The voice vibrated like a hundred rusty nails scratching over a school slate. "Damnation, you sly dog, where are you? I know you were here just a few moments ago."

The voice sounded so familiar that Largo was on his feet again, peering through the branches of the downed tree that now covered the entrance to the cave. "Isn't that your Uncle Diminish? Hello! Here we are."

Even as he called out, Allegro shushed him, trying to pull him back into the cave. But Largo ignored his friend and wriggled his arm free, then fluttered through the bramble to see the legendary faerie. Nobody knew for sure Diminish's age—some thought he was as old as Maestro. Rumor also had it that the faerie had played a major role in the taming of the world before the harp, although some claimed he'd used unsavory means to do so. It was said his powers might even rival Maestro's. That he was a rule-breaker appealed to Largo as nothing else did.

Now, as he looked at the old pixie standing amidst splinters of wood, his skin as gnarled as tree bark, the fuzz on his head as substantial as a rainbow, Largo could well imagine all the talk to be true. The old codger mumbled an anti-troll incantation before throwing faerie dust over his shoulder.

A tingle zipped through Largo as he shook the faerie's hand. "Good to see you, *sir*. We were wondering when we would get a visitor, and I must say I'm thrilled that it's you."

"Why, thank you, my boy."

For once Allegro didn't seem to be in a hurry as he moved toward them. Instead he glanced around as he distrustfully sniffed the air, uncannily reminiscent of his uncle. "What are you doing here?" he demanded.

Through folds of skin, Diminish's dark eyes gleamed. "Is that any way to greet your favorite uncle?"

Hands on hips, Allegro glared. "Cease your prattling and tell us what you want—*now*. Is it a loan, a character witness, or another botched mission you want me to fix?"

Anxiety sizzled through Largo. He didn't want Allegro to offend his uncle so much that he left without entertaining them with a few tales. "Allegro, please. You mustn't speak to your uncle so disrespectfully."

Diminish sniffed in an obvious show of hurt. "What has happened to this generation of pixies I'll never know. But you seem to have avoided the rudeness of your age group, Largo, and I'm very appreciative of it. For your information, Allegro, I'm here on the Maestro's behalf."

"Oh? Pardon me for asking, but where's the proof?" Allegro's voice was laced with suspicion.

What was wrong with him? Largo had never seen his friend so agitated, so full of animosity.

Diminish whirled his hand in the air and a pouch with the Maestro's seal appeared on his palm. "Is this proof enough? I'm here with the Maestro's own precious faerie dust to remove your brand." With that the elderly pixie snapped his wrist, causing a spray of glitter to circle the scarred burns Allegro had carried on his wings for the past year. The light so blinded Largo that at first he feared for Allegro, especially when his friend cried out. Then the brightness faded, leaving Allegro standing where he was. Carefully Allegro reached behind himself and pulled the tips of his wings around so that he could see. Where the charred markings of the musical sharps had been burned now appeared a brilliant yellow color, full of vigor and health.

Marveling, Allegro stroked his newly repaired wings. "I—I'm whole again. I can't believe it."

"Yes, and your wings are ten times more radiant than when you lived at Jubilant," Largo replied happily, thumping him on the back. Allegro somersaulted in the air. Although Largo wasn't nearly as agile as Allegro, he still managed one flip-flop to Allegro's five.

After Largo finished his spin, the hairs on the back of his neck quivered. There was someone else nearby. Nervously he glanced around. The breeze rustled the leaves of the uprooted tree, but he couldn't detect anything.

When Allegro did his final flip and landed in front of Diminish, his smile faded. "All right, spill the rest of it. Tell me the conditions."

"That is all. There's nothing more—you're free to return home."

"What? No bloodletting? No dangling the carrot only to snatch it away?"

Diminish tutted. "Such cynicism in one so young."

"A cynicism I learned from you," Allegro retorted.

"You're still holding a grudge over that misunderstanding with C Major?"

"Naaaa. Just because you almost killed me in that Swedish avalanche isn't a reason to hold a grudge."

Largo threw Allegro an incredulous look. "Why would you go to Sweden?"

"Mayhap because someone gave me the wrong directions?" Allegro replied sarcastically as he glared at Diminish.

"I never guided you there, my boy. That was all your own doing. You should be grateful that I was able to save you."

"Your memory is faulty, Uncle. You did guide me there and it was Aunt Tie who saved me."

"Which she wouldn't have been able to do if I hadn't given her exact instructions. You are much too uptight about our past partnerships, dear boy."

Allegro turned to Largo. "The avalanche was only my uncle's latest catastrophe to involve me. I'm not going to mention the venture into Skull Valley or the calamity on Vulture Mountain, or even getting marooned on Ghost Island."

Amazed, Largo could only stare at him for several seconds. "Here we've been friends all this time, but you've never told me about these partnerships?"

"Oh, I would never claim past alliances with Diminish. I was roped into these harrowing situations all in the name of family. The Crevice of Silence was the absolute last time. I refuse to ever associate with him again, uncle or not."

Diminish sighed, his rugged lips turned down in regret. "I'm sorry you feel that way, Allegro. I've done my best to make it up to you. I've even been talking to the city council about the possibility of you becoming mayor of Jubilant and so far they've been very open to the idea."

"Oh?" The mixture of skepticism and hope on Allegro's face was almost too painful for Largo to look upon.

Diminish nodded sagely. "I warmed them up to you, but I've done all I can. The rest is up to you."

Fluttering back and forth, Allegro halted in midair to look at his uncle. "What does that mean?"

"Nothing . . . other than the fact that they are a bit concerned."

"Concerned?"

"They're anxious about your strength of character. Now heed me—I argued on your behalf until I was blue in the face."

"Why are they anxious about my character?"

Diminish sighed. "It's unfair since you've been ostracized for a year and have endured so much, but because you've been more or less an outlaw, they fear you won't adhere to the rules of Quelgheny. After all, you've become accustomed to taking on roles of harmonics and tadpoles, which is definitely the sign of a renegade."

Allegro worried his lip between his teeth, his brows forming sideways question marks.

Once again the fine hairs on the back of Largo's neck quivered. Someone was nearby. But try as he might, he could discern nobody else in the area.

Diminish's weathered lips curved in a reassuring smile. "But no matter. Your staid character will shine through, especially if you join me in the mission I'm about to embark upon, which will give you hero status for certain. The trolls are forming an alliance with the Morthdones, and I need your help in getting a Shederin back into power."

Although displeasure radiated from Allegro, Largo was captivated by Diminish's story. The Morthdones, those evil Shapeshifters in the North, had always been a threat to the pixies. Allied with powerful trolls, who knew what damage they could wreak? "But I thought the Morthdone clan murdered all of the Shederins, including everyone in the royal city of Aria, twenty years ago."

Diminish considered Largo, a keen light in his buttonlike eyes. "Actually it was closer to twenty-eight years ago, but I managed to save King Arroyl's heir, who was but a babe at the time. The Morthdones are on the prowl again, and I fear they plan to take over all of Britain and Europe. The Shederin heir is the only one who can stop them."

Allegro had crossed his arms against his chest and was scowling. "You're not telling Largo the most important part of your history lesson—that you botched the mission to hide the Crystal Tuners."

The Crystal Tuners? Largo knew from his studies at the University of Coda that the instrument was the Shederins' major pulse point on the future.

Allegro continued frowning at his uncle. "You didn't take the Tuners to Angelo Bandstand. Instead you tried to second-guess Maestro by taking them to the Crevice of Silence, which had already been conquered by the enemy."

"The Tuners would no longer be a threat if I had destroyed them in the Crevice. How was I to know the Morthdones had taken over the valley?" Diminish added defensively.

"You didn't have to know—you had your orders and failed to follow them. Because you went against Maestro's strict instructions, the Crystal Tuners were captured by evildoers, giving them the power to destroy the royal family."

"It seems as if mistakes run in the Soprano family. At least I didn't cause the lock to the Underworld to break by interfering with natural sequences," Diminish retorted, giving Allegro a significant look.

"At least I didn't cause a whole royal family and the royal city to be murdered."

Since it appeared as if the conversation was going to degenerate into an all-out argument, Largo quickly intervened. "Diminish, you say that you saved the Shederin heir. How did you do that?"

Diminish frowned a couple seconds at Allegro as if debating whether to continue his quarrel, but eventually turned to Largo. "I switched him for a harmonic child who died at birth."

"In which family?"

Not quite able to look Largo in the eye, he instead kicked at a tuft of grass. "I, uh, don't remember, and I was in such a rush that I forgot to leave myself a note. You see, the murdering Morthdones were hot on my trail and so after I hid him, I, ah, spelled myself with the forgetful chant so that I could never tell what I knew, even under torture."

Diminish paused, his eyes haunted. Had he been tortured? Was that the reason the old pixie seemed a little

15

offbeat? Because of the suffering he'd endured? Largo started to ask, but Diminish continued.

"Finding the last Royal Shederin is the only way the Morthdones can be stopped. I need your help—along with Allegro's—in locating him. Now, Allegro, my boy, don't look at me like that. I'm thinking of your welfare when I ask you to join. After all, it isn't as if I don't have several candidates who would love to participate in this most important operation. But the more missions you succeed in, the better your chances with the council."

Allegro tilted his nose in the air. "I would rather take my chances with the council now than go on another mission with you. No, under no circumstances will I ever align myself with you again, Diminish."

Rubbing one side of his rough-hewn face, Diminish sighed. "Ah, well, I suppose I'm asking too much. Both of you have your own plans, what with your future in politics and Largo's full of wedding bells and a passel of children."

The thought of marriage made Largo break out in a sweat. The additional idea of children caused his head to swim. No way could he go back. Not now, not yet. "I'll help ye find the missing Royal Shederin," he announced, not about to let an opportunity like this pass.

Allegro fluttered in agitation. "What? Have you heard nothing I've said? He'll lead you to your death. Besides, what about Dulce?"

"Ah, I mean, she's a bonny lass and all, but those wedding bells can remain quiet a while longer."

"But she's been waiting for you forever! You were supposed to get married last year, but she understood your decision not to abandon me when I was ostracized. If I return and you don't, I'm afraid the lass's feelings will be hurt. She just might find someone else."

With arrogant bravado, Largo lifted his chin. "I'm the best thing that's ever happened to her and she knows it. Dulce adores me so she'll linger longer than forever for me. That ball and chain can wait. That dull life can wait. Let me have some fun and adventure before I get harnessed."

From the brush something was hurled at him. Before he could dodge it, the thing splattered on the side of his face. Glancing down, he realized it was a tomato. Two more flew at him and he ducked; one caught him in the stomach while the other whizzed harmlessly by. "You pompous, ungrateful flat note!" Dulce yelled.

In horror Largo watched her rise like a wronged Venus from the foliage. "Dull, am I? A ball and chain? So grateful for your exalted presence that I can wait?" With each question, she threw another projectile, each one coming faster and harder. When a solid object hit him on the forehead, he realized she'd progressed to apples.

"Dulce, my sweet little songbird, I didn't mean it!"

His protest was met with another bullet, this time a grapefruit, which hit him hard enough in the stomach to make his breath whoosh out of him.

"I'm not your sweet little songbird anymore. You're the *worst* thing that's ever happened to me. No more pining for you. There are other fish in the sea!" With a magnificent wave of her slender arm, she threw a cloak of glittering smoke around herself, and was gone.

With an unsettling sense of loss, Largo stared after her for several moments.

"I've never seen her so angry," Allegro said, marveling.

Neither had Largo, and her fury bothered him. Damnation, he wished she hadn't overheard him.

"You had best go after her and try to make amends."

"If you do, you'll lose an opportunity for another bit of fame," Diminish intervened with a shrug.

True. To find the Royal Shederin and have a hand in banishing the evil Morthdones from Quelgheny forever would be the adventure of a lifetime. However, he might lose Dulce to someone else. Naw, he decided, she would never leave him. Dulce loved him too much. In the end, she knew a good catch. She was a smart Sheba. "Ah well, she'll get over her snit. It ain't natural for her to lose her temper like that—she'll come to her senses and realize her mistake." He turned to Diminish. "Now, what should I bring on our mission?"

"You'll need at least a month's worth of faerie dust and elixir, your guide note, a few spells and one of your inventions if you don't want to fly. Which one will be best for carrying the two of us?"

"I suppose the aerocar." As much as Largo tried to concentrate on the mission, his mind kept circling back to Dulce. She had been really upset. The flash of hurt, of vulnerability, that darkened her beautiful green eyes, made his stomach churn.

Allegro continued to stare incredulously at Largo. Then he threw up his hands. "It's your life. I've tried to warn you."

Uneasiness pricked at him again. "What do you think she meant by other fish in the sea?"

"I heard from Aunt Tie that Ritardando and Mezzo were bringing her gifts and showing her a lot of attention. But why be concerned? You've got your mission to occupy your efforts."

"Ritardando and Mezzo? Why, they're simpering fools. I don't have to worry about them."

Diminish hitched up his trousers, his weathered face serious. "All right, pay attention, lad. We'll travel by night and sleep by day, so the enemy can't see us as well. Oh, and in the unlikely event we get separated, rub this ring and say my name three times. It will only work once, so use the magic sparingly."

Mindlessly, Largo accepted the proffered ring, slipping it on his finger as he still worried about Dulce.

Continuing his pacing, Diminish rubbed his chin thoughtfully. "The faerie dust we'll preserve with the economy spell—"

"But what about Divisi?" Allegro interrupted. "He has said more than once that if you were ever out of the picture, he would do his best to win her hand."

Divisi? Now that was a different story altogether, enough to make him feel truly threatened. With his Herculean good looks, Divisi was known for his appeal to the females. What was more, the faerie didn't seem aware of his own popularity. He was unassuming and truly nice, which caused Largo to experience an instant dislike. If he didn't make amends with Dulce, but instead went on this adventure, Largo had a distinct feeling that he would regret it for the rest of his life.

Evidently Diminish decided to ignore the discussion about Dulce and any possible beaus because he continued to pace, his brows twisted in thought. "The Shade Lord is the one to look out for. After all, he's a wizard, half-human, half-shapeshifter, the mastermind behind the fall of the Shederins. Nobody knows what he looks like, nor have we seen the human form of any of his Morthdone brothers, but they change into wolves faster than—"

"I'm not going."

"—an eighth note. What?" Diminish halted in his pacing, his jaw slack.

"I said that I'm not going." As Largo made his declaration a second time, calmness suffused him. It was the right decision. Although he yearned for adventure, he knew that he first had to make amends with Dulce.

Incredulous, Diminish stared at him. "But you must."

"No, I'm going home."

"You're turning down the chance of a century."

A putrid smell of rotten food, dead mice and skunk wafted over his senses.

"Trolls!" Diminish cried out a split second before black smoke surrounded them.

Try as he might, Largo couldn't seem to move. As he peered through the smoke, his eyes watering and stinging, he saw that Allegro had also been rendered immobile. Diminish had disappeared.

Out from the fog stepped three huge green trolls with pointed teeth, long noses dripping snot and enormous warts that protruded from their hunched shoulders. Largo quivered with fear as they approached. Although the rest of him couldn't budge, he realized he could move his fingers.

"Diminish! Damn your hide, where are you? Didn't I tell you that he's trouble?" Allegro exclaimed, already managing to retrieve his pouch of faerie dust.

The stout troll drew back his arm and threw a laser beam, the swiftness of which Largo had never seen. The shard hit Allegro, causing him to cry out in pain and drop the magic dust.

"Allegro!" Largo cried, wriggling to no avail.

As he struggled against the invisible chains that bound him, the scent of charred flesh caused Largo's stomach to churn. Where Allegro's finger had been was a mere stump.

The stout troll curled his leathery lips into an evil grin. "You'll learn now that you cannot win against Morthdone's power."

Allegro's eyes rolled back as he lapsed into unconsciousness, for which Largo was immensely glad. The pain must surely be too great for any pixie to endure.

The slightly taller troll punched the stout one hard enough in the chest to make him fall. "Gergross, you fool! You mustn't harm the faerie. If you do, then he won't be able to carry out his errand for the Shade Lord."

Gergross lumbered to his feet and glared at his companion, fist raised. The third monster stood unnaturally silent in the background, watching the exchange. Then Gergross withdrew his arm with an ugly grimace on his meaty lips. "Kill-a-pix, Bilen, you didn't have to knock me down. I don't know why our lord puts such value on these stupid faeries. Their brains are so puny I can't imagine them finding anything, not even their own spit."

As Gergross turned bloodshot eyes toward him, Largo felt a sudden surge of pure hatred. The beast continued. "You will find the Royal Shederin and return him to me. Do this and you might live. Otherwise I will turn you into a whisper of an ash."

By now Allegro had revived, barely managing to shake his head because of the paralyzing spell. "Kill us now, because we'll never do your will."

"Don't listen to him. He's a little addlepated with the pain from his finger—ah, that is, from his stump," Largo hastily said to the trolls, wondering if Allegro's reasoning had been damaged when he lost his appendage. All they had to do was go along with the thugs, at least for now. As soon as the tormentors left, what would keep him and Allegro from simply returning to Jubilant? No sense in making the nasty trolls angry enough to sever another limb.

"You refuse to do as we command?" Gergross said aggressively, ignoring Largo and staring at Allegro. The gloating look in his beady eyes caused the fine hairs on Largo's neck to rise. "Not even when we hold a sweet little songbird?"

That was what Largo had called Dulce not a mere twenty beats ago. With sudden dread, he watched as Gergross motioned to the silent creature standing in the background. The mountainous troll, larger than the other two combined, shuffled forward, his hand conspicuously behind his back.

"Scaley, show them what we've caught."

The huge troll revealed a golden cage that he held by

a ring on its top. Inside sat Dulce, her violet wings drooping and quivering, blue tears coursing down her pink cheeks. Largo's heart sank at the sight of her, captured like a beautiful butterfly.

"Do our bidding, or your little songbird will sing no more."

With that, all three trolls disappeared in a swirl of stinking smoke, taking with them Largo's conscience, his future and all that made him good.

Chapter Two

Tessa Ballard, Baroness Whitley, resisted the urge to wipe her eyes, scratchy from lack of sleep. Her sleek barouche rolled out of the London Docks at a fast clip. She'd been awake for the past forty-eight hours as the ship tossed in the restless sea crossing the channel. As a result, she could barely keep her eyes open. Although the morning hour was early, she had told the driver to take her to the rendezvous. She'd sent word and knew the Special Committee would be at the discreet house by Cornhill.

They would expect an accounting of her latest mission. She was ahead of schedule, but she had a sudden urge to complete her information-gathering and return to Mayfair in time for Selena's birthday, which was today.

Fingering the glass faerie in her reticule, she was careful to cradle it in her lap. Selena loved whimsical, fantasy figurines, so when Tessa had seen the beautiful glass-blown pixie in the window of a shop, she'd purchased it immediately.

Chilled autumn air blew into the coach from the open window, fluttering the green curtains, but she didn't close the windows, knowing the brisk air would revive her. The weather had been so warm a mere six weeks ago, when she'd last been in London. The passage of time bothered her, touched her spine with a cold finger of dread. She was being ridiculous. She supposed the worry stemmed from the fact that she hadn't wanted to leave London, or *England* for that matter—too many crucial situations had been developing. Especially the conspiracy.

The change of seasons underscored how long she'd been away. A lot could occur in six weeks—or in one week, a day, an hour. Time was strange. It took a handful of hours to inaugurate Prime Minister Liverpool, several weeks or months for Parliament to pass a bill, and a lifetime to change attitudes, sometimes more. It took centuries to build Rome, and less than a week to sack it, utterly destroying a civilization. Nine months were required to create a life, a split instant to end it. To build, to create, took so much longer than to destroy.

What had happened in the weeks since she'd been forced to leave? What evils had been brewing in the ever-evolving city of London since her departure?

As the coach rumbled up Borough High Street toward her appointment, she couldn't help but focus her thoughts on the conspiracy. She'd discovered the plot from a very unlikely source—her childhood friend, Selena, who was more like a beloved sister.

They had spent four years together at Treleven Abbey, orphans both. Tessa had always been rowdy, a rule-breaker. She'd insisted on pushing the limits, living on the edge. Selena was the opposite, calm and focused, only wanting love, marriage and children on whom to dote. Perhaps she was with child even now. Tessa smiled at the thought, then decided that no matter how tired she was after her meeting, she would visit her friend, if only to see her radiant smile.

Although they had since taken different paths in life—Selena choosing a staid existence as the handsome Earl McFearson's wife and Tessa traveling a rougher road involving espionage for the Crown—they had remained close. Even though Tessa didn't know much about the earl, he'd made Selena deliriously happy, which was all that mattered.

But Selena's sudden interest in danger had been out of character. She had begun to speak of dastardly plans that were about to take place. It had all started with a prediction of a debutante's spiteful intention to ruin another lady's reputation. Tessa had scoffed at Selena's sudden ability to tell the future. It seemed ridiculous.

But when the lady *had* been ostracized, both Tessa and Selena had been amazed, and Selena became more confident in her so-called predictions. Next she predicted an heiress's kidnapping and forced marriage. Then she foresaw there would be a robbery attempt at the London Bank. All her prophecies had come true.

For the life of her, Tessa could never get Selena to reveal her source. Instead her friend made vague references to social gatherings from which she might have gleaned information. When Tessa tried to pin her down on exactly how she arrived at the predictions, Selena became infuriatingly silent. That wouldn't do. Not when the prophecy was an assassination attempt on Prime Minister Liverpool.

Although she'd told Tessa exactly where she would find the conspirators, Selena had refused to reveal her source, saying only that she'd had another premonition. Premonition indeed! Her friend was hiding something—probably naively protecting someone. That attitude of Selena's was about to change, come hell or the revival of addlepated King George III.

The slowing of the carriage told Tessa that she had arrived. The modest, four-story brick house gave little indication that it was the occasional host site for important dignitaries. By the time the neighbors began to suspect the place was anything other than the home of the elderly Lord Benson and his wife, they would be gone, off to set up another rendezvous place in another part of London.

With a wave to the gardener, who was actually an armed foot soldier in disguise, Tessa allowed the footman to hand her down.

The butler was there to meet her in the modest foyer, the scent of fresh lemon oil indicating the wood banister had recently been polished. "I hope your travels were relaxing, Baroness."

"Hardly that, Jacobs, but quite fruitful."

"Very good, my lady." He led her toward the drawing room, where Tessa knew the four Special Committee members would be waiting.

The low murmur of masculine voices floating from the chamber underscored their presence. As she stepped inside, Lord Tinsington looked up from his quiet conversation with Edward Perry, the fourth son of the Earl Grafton, a man she considered more of a father than her own. Bartholomew Carmichael lowered his teacup just as the Viscount Chumley lifted his bushy brows at the sight of her and rose to his feet. The others followed suit.

But none of them caught her attention as much as did Prime Minister Liverpool. As he rose from his chair to greet her, she was so surprised that she couldn't help blurting out, "Sir, you shouldn't be traipsing about the town."

"Is that any greeting, my dear?"

She ignored the slight heat in her cheeks as she allowed him to bow over her hand. "But you're forgetting the assassination attempt."

"We've caught the conspirators, dear Baroness. Thanks to you and your connections, all is well."

She didn't know how she felt about his cavalier treatment of future threats. After all, his predecessor had been murdered, and who knew what other threats were looming, especially with the continued unrest in France?

Many weren't happy with the generosity England had shown Bonaparte, exiling him to Elba with a small kingdom at his beck and call. Resentment was rife at the return of King Louis the XVIII to the throne.

And she hadn't been completely satisfied about the raid in which they'd captured the conspirators. Most of them had been simple cutthroats and criminals. She believed that someone else had given them their orders.

But she could fret no more since Edward Perry, the head of the Special Committee, approached her with a frown she'd learned to respect.

Dear Mr. Perry.

If it hadn't been for him, and his kindness toward a wild, abandoned girl, she didn't know what would have become of her. As it was, he offered her a freedom few women in the *haute ton* were privileged to enjoy. He'd established her as a widowed, flamboyant baroness, a woman of the world. Now, because of his connections, she could exercise her adventurous spirit through her secret work for the Crown.

But she couldn't dwell on her affection for him, because he still frowned. The source of his worry was most likely her recent assignment. He gripped her hand in his own. "Lady Ballard, what a pleasant surprise to see you so soon."

"Likewise, sir," she replied with sincere warmth. Slight in build, Perry's angular physique was emphasized by the lack of padding that other gentlemen tended to wear

27

under their clothing. The fact that he didn't enhance his build underscored his honesty. She was weary of the games men played at court, no matter whose court it was.

Perry led her to a high-backed Georgian chair directly across from him and Liverpool. Tessa was careful not to bump her reticule, with its precious cargo, against the wood arm, instead cradling it in her lap once more.

"Tea?" Not waiting for a response, Perry motioned to Giffen, the only servant allowed in the chambers during debriefings. The small man scurried to pour the tea with quick, birdlike movements.

After letting her have a sip of the brew, Liverpool leaned forward. "So tell us the news of political intrigue on the Continent."

Setting down her teacup, Tessa concentrated on the last several weeks in France and Austria. "Louis has already insulted the tsar, putting him in chilly chambers and having the audacity to be served before his guest at dinner."

Viscount Chumley tugged absent-mindedly at his already long earlobe. "Petty of Louis, to be certain, but surely nothing to worry about."

"Perhaps. Perhaps not. I think his actions merely underscore hatred at Russia for being the direct cause of Napoleon's topple from power. I was told that advisors counseled Louis to insult the tsar in an attempt to win over the populace. But he undermines his efforts when he squanders tax monies on his lavish living. The masses are not pleased."

"What else have you discovered?" Perry asked.

"Lately a group of soldiers, who are more like vigilantes, are terrorizing the countryside. They murdered Count Aigre and his family." She paused, allowing that information to sink in, knowing that the significance of the massacre would shake up the committee. Count Aigre was a known sympathizer to the British Crown.

Perry leaned back in his chair, a stunned look on his face. "My God, who are they?"

"They call themselves the White Sacrifice."

In his no-nonsense manner, Bartholomew Carmichael regarded her intently. "Who organized them?"

"Nobody knows his true name, but he is known as the Shade Lord."

Chumley slammed his fist on a nearby table. "Bloody hell, I'll wager Ney is behind all this."

"Or Junot," Lord Tinsington piped in with his squeaky voice.

Boney's former generals? Perhaps, but she didn't think the culprit would be that obvious.

Prime Minister Liverpool obviously had reservations, too. He shook his head. "I'm not so sure about either one. I heard General Ney himself say that he would rather bring back Bonaparte in an iron cage than allow him to return to power. And Junot was quite unhappy with Bonaparte's alignment with Austria and his friendship with Foreign Minister Clemens Metternich."

Metternich had instigated a love affair with General Junot's wife, practically under the man's nose. Discovering their liaison, Junot became the laughingstock of the French court when he'd tried to murder his disloyal wife and ended up scarring her with scissors. The general still resented Bonaparte for his alliance with Austria.

Perry tapped his rather pointed chin. "What does the name 'White Sacrifice' mean, hmm? I'm inclined to wonder if the Russians are somehow involved. After all, the tsar himself referred to the deaths of his solders as heroic sacrifices. And he has not been treated well. Perhaps he wants to make France a part of Russia."

"Unless that's what the culprits want you to believe." Carmichael's calm, intuitive observations impressed Tessa. He rarely said much, and when he did it was invariably something that gave food for thought.

Carmichael was a bit of a mystery. Nobody knew his origins, only that he was adopted at the age of sixteen by Sir Thaddeus Carmichael. Bartholomew came into a fortune when the old man died. Always an avid participant in Parliament, known for his levity and his intelligence, he was one of the top choices for the Special Committee organized by Liverpool upon his appointment as prime minister three years ago. At the age of forty, Carmichael had yet to be married and was one of the most sought-after bachelors in England, although he seemed little interested in the ladies.

Tessa sat forward. "I took the liberty of asking Andre Larousse and his wife to investigate further."

Liverpool rubbed his hands together, his expression pleased. "Good, good. They are our best operatives in France. In the meantime, I'll smooth ruffled feathers before the Peace Talks in Vienna. I've already invited Metternich, Tsar Alexander, King Louis and the others to my hunting lodge in Sussex in three weeks."

Tessa rose from her chair, cradling her reticule as she stood. "All right then, gentlemen, I will leave you with these problems of strife and turmoil and retire to my own home."

Perry gave her a curious stare, his gaze flicking to her reticule. "What, pray tell, do you have in your indispensable that you are treasuring it so?"

She smiled. "Merely a gift for the Countess McFearson. It is her birthday today, and if you must know, this momentous occasion is the reason I am dead on my feet now, having traveled all over France in record time so that I could return before the celebration."

Perry blinked, his blue eyes filling with . . . what? Regret? "Uh, Lady Ballard. . . ." Sandy brows furrowed, he turned toward the others, who looked everywhere but at her.

"What is it?" Sudden dread curdled in her stomach.

It was Carmichael who answered. "We are sorry to inform you that Lady Selena, the Countess McFearson, was murdered in her bed a month ago. Her husband is nowhere to be found."

Satisfaction flowed through Nolan Monroe, the earl of McFearson. The wheels of destruction were already in motion. If everything went well tonight, in seven days he would finally leave this world and enter the fiery gates of hell.

"Nice night fer a stroll," the burly driver of the hearse said dryly.

"As long as the bogeyman don't get you," Nolan answered, giving the appropriate response. Nolan had discovered the secret code during one of his dark spells of unconsciousness. The haze came more frequently since Selena's death—as if the absence of her anchoring presence had caused the malady to unleash its fury against him.

Since the unconscionable murder of his adored wife, he had no reason to live, except to act on the strange knowledge that he gleaned from his spurts of madness. Because of these dark dreams, he had discovered the extent of the sleaziness in the Regency underworld in which he lived. It was a perilous existence, which suited him perfectly. The secret code was ironic, a cruel mockery most assuredly thought up by Mad Jack, a real bogeyman against whom mothers warned their daughters.

For if Nolan cared to look inside the carriage—which he didn't—he knew what he would find: young women, girls really, kidnapped from their homes to be sold on the streets for prostitution. The hearse didn't carry the dead, although they could be considered the living dead, as drugged with laudanum as they were. Why their captors bothered, he didn't know. Nobody would help them in this godforsaken place, except for him, a madman who had his own agenda.

Tonight he would be Mad Jack's personal bogeyman. He was good at it—he had experience. A black vacuum of ghoulish, bloody nightmares hovered just behind his realm of awareness, the dark void that would soon take him over completely. He'd had ten debilitating occurrences since his beloved Selena had died by his hand six weeks ago. Each time he'd come to awareness in the same filth-encrusted alley in which the black spell had hit him. Since Selena's death, he'd been careful to remain in the disgusting alleys where even rats didn't dare to go. It was his only means of protecting those around him from his bouts of dark madness. If only he had been elsewhere when the black spell had hit him the night of Selena's death. His throat wrenched as he thought of her, a constant reminder of the monster he'd become.

At the most inopportune times, memories of her would surface—walking down Petticoat Lane reminded him of the last time they'd shopped together when she'd found the jaunty little hat she'd loved. Crossing the street in front of the library brought back memories of her making faces behind old Lady Harriet's back when the harridan had scolded Selena for laughing rambunctiously in the reading area. Passing by a vendor brought the image of Selena drinking a foamy concoction made of strawberries and cream, with him leaning over to lick the sweetness from her full lips.

Under no circumstance could he reside at the townhouse where memories ate at him, so he stayed in the stews, only returning now and then in the dead of night to grab a change of clothes. He purposely avoided Selena's rooms. The mere idea of walking into her empty bedchamber conjured up the memory of her peachy complexion turned ashen as she lay in death next to him, blood everywhere.

Selena. How had it happened? How did *that* recollection fit in with the memories of love and happiness they had shared? Nothing made sense to him anymore.

Nothing but the fact that he'd turned into some sort of evil being who killed without mercy or conscience, without memory.

If the dark vacuum didn't take him completely, then his guilt would surely drive him to madness. Soon the craze would fully consume him, unless he did something about it. He couldn't allow the debilitating, tarlike fog to dictate his actions. He couldn't be responsible for any more innocent deaths.

The driver of the hearse eyed the box Nolan balanced on his shoulder, which supposedly held the coins for payment. "Ye're alone?"

"As instructed."

Evidently not convinced, the villain continued to peer down Blue Anchor Road. Even in daylight upstanding citizens would never venture here. At night it was usually desolate, except for cutthroats and criminals with evil intent.

Nolan figured he fit right in.

The lack of light in the deserted street put his other senses on alert, magnifying the rancid smell of a dead rat, and the sound made by the claws of an animal, perhaps a cat, as it scampered against brick. A shoe scraping on stone? Was one of his more recent enemies waiting in the alley to stab him in the back?

Perhaps.

For weeks he had stalked five of London's most dangerous criminals. Last week he had taken the funds that Tom Spider had stolen from a banker in Pall Mall; before that, Nolan had thwarted Spider's attempt to murder a merchant.

In the past weeks, Nolan had foiled the body snatcher, Deadwood Dials, who killed for fresh bodies to sell to anatomists for dissection. Nolan had moved the dead from coffins to grassy unmarked slopes nearby. He had left his calling card in each coffin to let Dials know who was responsible.

He had frustrated others, too, in their lucrative underworld businesses, mocking them, enraging them so that there would be no chance of refusal when he issued challenges to duels.

A shoe sounded on the cobblestones. Which one of the villains lurked in the alley now, waiting to sink a knife in his back? Was it Deadwood Dials? If so, he would most assuredly be dissected—not that he cared, for by then he would be permanently in hell. Medical students would learn then of his black heart.

Ironic that he was now about to steal a hearse filled with live flesh for sale.

The driver continued to eye him suspiciously. "I don't know ye and I don't like it that I don't. We lost the last batch of merchandise and if this is a trick, Mad Jack ain't gonna like it. Come into the light so I can see ye better."

He knew the driver looked for the scar that Nolan had painted on his face a month ago when he had stolen the carriage full of women. It wasn't there now. The ruse had been a trick he'd learned from an actress, a combination of kohl, reddish-brown dye and bone glue to make his skin pucker around the line. The effect had been convincing.

After scrutinizing him with the lantern held high, the

driver nodded in satisfaction. "Now open the chest and let's have a look."

Too easy. The routine was becoming boring, the test next to nonexistent. Even when the criminal dug deeper than normal through the coins, Nolan knew he would never realize that the coins were counterfeit. The fact that he wasn't challenged anymore gave him all the more reason to leave this life.

"Ho, mate, the cargo's yours."

A sudden rustling in the back of the carriage told Nolan that the occupants weren't as drugged at their captors had hoped. "Help us," a feminine voice cried into the night, and he caught a glimpse of a woman's desperate eyes as she gazed through the bars.

No sound would come from his mouth. He couldn't answer her, couldn't give her the assurance that she sought. What sort of ogre had he become? How could he save her when he damn well couldn't save himself? When he was the one she should run from?

A strange weariness fell over him, making him want to curse at the moon that had just peeped out between ghostlike clouds. Bloody hell, how he hated this life. Nolan wasted no time vaulting up onto the driver's seat.

As he drove by the alley, the scent of jasmine wafted over him and he wondered at it.

"Discover his destiny and nothing else," Tessa Ballard whispered to Milo, a fifteen-year-old lad who looked years younger than his age. Worry wormed into her heart. She didn't like his insistence on helping her.

Two years ago, he'd picked her pocket, and had been shocked when she'd chased him, then taken him home with her. She'd enrolled him in Eton for a while but school and life with the *ton* hadn't suited him. Instead he had started his own business, a network of boys who did odd jobs for the Bow Street Runners and other customers—from searching for missing relatives and friends, to solving crimes. And one of his priorities was to help her. He never asked about her unusual activities, just as she never asked about his other cases. But she knew he'd reached his own conclusions about her life and had accepted them.

Considering himself a man and beyond mothering, Milo didn't always acknowledge her concern, especially when the other boys were present, but she knew he secretly adored being fussed over. She grasped his arm.

His dark eyes darted over her features and he seemed to read her mind, for he said gruffly, "Aye, Lady, I'll be careful." Gently he loosened her hold. "And we'll get the bastard," he added before bolting after the carriage.

"What?" she called after him, alarmed. Milo read her too easily these days. He had known of Selena's death—thus, he probably knew who McFearson was. Would he take more risks and try to bring McFearson to justice on his own? Or would he do as instructed—discover the holding place for the kidnapped women and report back to her? Scowling, she watched as he leapt onto the back of the moving coach and hid in the boot.

She kept her gaze on the hearse as it rolled out of sight. For a moment she considered going after the carriage and confronting McFearson, but then dismissed the idea. At least Milo could tell her where the abducted women had been taken; then she could arrange for the women's rescue. As much as she hated to let those captives go, she had much bigger fish to fry.

She intended to prove that McFearson was the mastermind behind the conspiracy to overthrow the Crown.

And rumor on the streets was that new plans were being discussed. She *knew* he was guilty, that he'd killed Selena because she'd discovered his perfidy.

Tessa had been following him for two weeks—ever

since she'd found out about her friend's murder. The extent of McFearson's knowledge of the network of criminals that ruled the stews astounded her. He associated with the likes of Deadwood Dials, Spider, and Mad Jack—not to mention Torch, who liked to set people on fire, and Rat Chaser, who enjoyed using his rapier to maim women. What manner of man had her dear friend married? Someone conniving who'd wooed Selena, deceived her, never showed her the ugly, rotted condition of his soul.

Selena.

Tessa's throat wrenched and the backs of her eyes burned as she thought of her friend. For years, she and Selena had fought each others' battles. Selena had been her confidant, her stalwart—always the breath of fresh air to help Tessa see situations in a different light, to make her realize that things weren't quite as bad as Tessa tended to think. Oh, how she already missed her.

Even now it was hard for her to accept that Selena was gone. Despite what her colleagues had told her of Selena's murder, Tessa had called upon her friend, expecting the reception she'd always received when she showed up without notice. But when she saw the dark windows, she'd known the truth of the committee's words. It wasn't like Selena, who insisted on sunshine flooding the house.

The housekeeper, Mrs. Campbell, had met her in the foyer. Her gentle face was wreathed in pain as she told of how Selena had been found dead in her bed, gashes in her fragile neck. McFearson had disappeared. Mrs. Campbell worried that he was in danger, too. Ha! The fact that he had been missing since Selena's death only added to Tessa's suspicion that he had done the deed. McFearson was charming in a brooding, handsome way, and women—servants and *ton* alike—saw only that appealing façade.

That was the reason Selena hadn't revealed her source—to protect him. Well, Tessa had been fooled by McFearson's act, too, but she wouldn't be hoodwinked again. Damnation, why hadn't she sensed his foul character? Selena had been so deliriously happy that Tessa had been swept up in their fairy-tale romance, but that didn't make up for the stolen years of Selena's life. Tessa had known herself to be the more cautious one; she'd *known* that Selena tended to be an innocent, never seeing others' faults.

Why hadn't Tessa investigated McFearson? The least she could have done was discover his habits. Now she would regret her lapse for the rest of her life. She would see that he burned in hell for his crime against her friend.

Very soon now, she would catch him meeting with his conspirators, whoever they might be. And when she did, she would avenge Selena's death.

An eye for an eye.

The Shade Lord sat in the shadows, a strange unease flowing through him.

He shouldn't have killed Lady Selena, at least not until he'd tortured information out of her—mainly to ensure that her source of information was her own. But Lady Ballard had been damn close to discovering everything that night she'd stormed the warehouse on Skinner Street. And since she hadn't gone willingly to her assignment on the Continent, he'd worried about her return and had killed the Countess McFearson.

No, he assured himself once again, he'd heard the chit talking at some ridiculous ball, telling others she was gifted with a psychic power. If only he'd known of her gift before she'd confided in Lady Ballard. But all was well, and now Lady Ballard pursued the Earl McFearson. How convenient that the husband was so accommodating as to draw suspicion toward him. Yes, Lady Ballard was emotionally attached to the victim. Therefore, she might very well avenge her friend by killing the husband. All the better.

Only one other person had a seer's power. Madam Chiartano. Already he'd exercised his control over the mystic, blackmailing her into cooperating with him. It was through her psychic powers that he'd discovered the Royal Shederin had survived, but the woman couldn't discern the Shederin's identity or location. Even now, the Shade Lord continued to visit her. If the trolls didn't find the Shederin through the captured faeries, and if his brothers didn't find their enemy, he was certain she would detect the truth about the Shederin.

If all else failed, her seer's eye would find his enemy.

Chapter Three

Tonight Tessa would catch McFearson meeting all five of his cutthroats. For the past two nights she had been unable to find the earl. He was a slippery devil, she would give him that. However, she had an unexpected break when two of Milo's boys had been the ones to deliver the messages from McFearson to his culprits, designating the time and place for their rendezvous. Milo himself was still missing. It had been three nights since the boy had stowed away in the boot of the hearse. Stomach churning with anxiety, she could only hope that he was all right.

As she stealthily trailed fifty yards behind McFearson, eerie light from old lamp posts cast watery shadows on the filth-encrusted street. With his black cloak swirling, he fit right in with the surrounding clime. He moved like the wisps of ghostly clouds that traveled over the round fullness of the moon. His tall, dark figure defied any light the moon might want to give.

Distant thunder rumbled as the recent storm left London to fall on villages farther east. The damp streets magnified the scents of human waste and decay. All was silent, deep and penetrating, amplifying the splash made by her soft-soled boots in an unforeseen puddle. McFearson turned his head. Heart pounding, she froze against a nearby building. He barely broke stride, but instead continued the ground-eating gait that carried him toward Butcher Alley.

Gritting her teeth against the cold dampness that seeped through her stockings, she dogged her quarry.

When he entered the alley, she hesitated. Even though she couldn't see them, she knew the others were there—she could sense their presence. Malignant thoughts filled with evil intent writhed within the inky darkness of the passage. Sweat dampened the palm that held the hilt of her sword. When McFearson reached the center of the alley, he stopped.

This was it. He was evidently waiting for his partners in crime. Soon she would hear of their new assassination plan.

Sure enough, five shadows separated from the gloom, a pair on either side, with Mad Jack in front. She involuntarily shuddered as she looked at the soulless degenerate. More monster than man, he enjoyed tormenting women in unspeakable ways before selling them, often as slaves to corsairs. She'd known that Mad Jack and the others would be there, but seeing them together in person was overwhelming. Despite her efforts, she trembled.

They were the worst criminals in England, and her dear friend's husband was an associate of theirs.

Something about their aggressive stances and the manner in which they circled McFearson told her that their intent was not to talk.

Mad Jack's bulbous eyes bore into McFearson. "Ye're a cocky bastard, Monroe, ta challenge us at once. Someone needs ta put ye in yer place."

41

"This is the last time ye'll ever mess wi' my business," Spider growled.

" 'E wishes death, and 'e'll get it," Rat Chaser added with a sneer as he closed in with his slim rapier.

What was going on here? Tessa struggled to make sense of what she saw.

The next instant, Mad Jack swung his sword. McFearson met the attack, stepping toward his adversary with an animal like grace, then sweeping down his sword to parlay. At the same time, Rat Chaser stabbed at McFearson's back. The earl seemed to anticipate the move, for he danced away from the rapier's lethal tip. Then Deadwood Dials and Spider lunged at the same time, from different sides of McFearson, the swiftness of the attack stealing Tessa's breath.

McFearson threw himself away from the foray, causing his enemies to clash swords with each other. Before he could regain his balance, Rat Chaser scurried behind him and jabbed again, which McFearson must have sensed for he dodged and parried. Although he managed to deflect most of the thrust, Tessa could see a dark stain on the tip of Rat Chaser's blade as he withdrew it.

McFearson's grimace of pain should have appeased Tessa. This confrontation was a falling-out among murderers—or at least that was what she would have thought a few moments ago. But what had Mad Jack meant about a challenge, and what had Rat Chaser meant about McFearson wanting death? Was it because he had double-crossed them and had been found out? Did they want more of the money? Had they disliked the plan that McFearson had devised?

Whatever the cause for the attack, the bloody bastard deserved it. *Play with fire and you'll get burned.* It was a just ending to the man who had deceived, then murdered, her dear friend.

But this rendezvous hadn't played out as Tessa had

anticipated. She'd expected to overhear plans of criminal intent, not witness a murder. For with such overwhelming odds it *was* murder. As she observed the others circle, waiting to give the lethal stab, she had the sinking sensation that she was going to have to do something about the assault if she wanted answers from the earl.

But that didn't mean she couldn't make him suffer a little before she got her answers. Heart pounding, already regretting her decision to interfere, she eased into the shadows under a partially fallen archway and looked for an opening to help McFearson.

Nolan watched the five degenerates circle him, their eyes evil slits. With a harsh laugh, he called to death, beckoned the Grim Reaper to take him even as he met an attack from Spider with a ferocious clash of metal. He darted to the left to greet once more the rapier's stolen kiss on his vulnerable skin. Pain pierced him as liquid warmth flowed down his side, close to the other wound. Nolan snarled at the Rat and snapped back at him, jabbing below his collarbone. Rat Catcher squeaked and fell away.

Before Spider had time to regroup for another swing, Nolan whirled, not even having to look at his adversary but instinctively knowing where to slash. The stab to Spider's gut reminded him that what goes around comes around. For all the helpless souls Spider had tortured, a gut wound would make him suffer as he had forced others to suffer. Spider staggered and fell dead.

Deadwood Dials, Mad Jack and Torch stood carelessly to one side, watching the exchange. Deadwood Dials's thin nostrils flared. "I smell Monroe's blood."

Mad Jack grinned, showing his rotten teeth. "Aye, and I love it."

The wounds to Nolan's side became a dull ache. He forced the pain to the back of his mind.

"We're goin' ta see you burn," Torch added, his red hair gleaming almost as bright as the fires he enjoyed setting.

They moved as one, closing in for the kill.

A rush of anticipation hit Nolan as he welcomed the yawning darkness of Hades.

Suddenly a swirl of black skirts hurled from a recessed threshold with a violent battle cry and flashing steel. Stunned, Nolan froze as he watched the woman whip her sword under and up, halting Deadwood Dials's thrust and forcing him to step backward.

"Guard my back!" she cried as she stabbed Deadwood Dials, then swiveled to clash swords with Torch just as Mad Jack jabbed below her waistline. That voice seemed familiar but her face was covered with dark netting.

No time for questions. He deflected the stab at her spine, jumping between her and her third adversary. He worried about her fighting skills, wondering how any woman could have acquired such talent. She had come to his rescue—would he be forced to rescue her instead? Why would she risk herself for him in the first place? Why would she interfere? Who in bloody hell was she?

A whiff of something exotic swept over him—*jasmine*—and he knew she had been his stalker. Then his attention snapped back to Mad Jack and Rat Catcher, who swung at him simultaneously.

He kicked a booted heel into Rat Catcher's thigh to unbalance him, arcing his sword downward to thwart Mad Jack at the same time. In a continuing semicircle, he disarmed Mad Jack, stabbing him deeply in the right shoulder to make him incapable of further attack, and watched him scuttle into the darkness.

Nolan turned to see his uninvited accomplice jab Deadwood Dials in the chest, then pivot to disarm Torch. With a yelp, Torch dropped his sword. Realizing he now faced her without a weapon, the villain disappeared into the night. Without a word, she twisted to come shoulder to shoulder with Nolan as they both confronted Rat Catcher.

Without his cohorts, his nose twitched and his eyes widened in fear before he tucked tail and ran. For a brief moment Nolan considered chasing the good-for-nothing, then decided he would wait for another day to finish him off.

As the silence of the night descended upon them, he turned to stare at his unlikely rescuer. He couldn't see her face through the dark netting, but as she stood in the alley, her eyes almost level with his, he could see she was magnificent. He knew she had long, strong legs by the way she'd moved with her parries. Her arms had a graceful strength, like a young tree. Her breasts were high and, most likely, perfectly formed. He could see her as a Valkyrie with a battle ax in one hand, a sword in the other, wearing a golden breastplate. "Who is this angel that dropped from the night sky to fight my battles?"

For a moment she stood where she was. He could barely glimpse her dark eyes and the curve of one cheek beneath her trappings. A frisson of extreme awareness passed between them, something similar to lightning. Had the storm returned?

She must have been aware of the strange magnetism because she couldn't seem to find her voice for several long moments. Then she backed away. "Me? Fight your battles? Ha. The clash was a little one-sided. I couldn't stand by and watch you get massacred."

Massacred? Yes, that was what he'd wanted—a situation from which he couldn't escape with his life.

It was then he fully realized he remained standing. Although he bled from superficial scratches, he was still alive, and it was because of this unwanted partner. All his weeks of planning, months of prowling, agitating, purposely harassing those five murderers so that they would kill him, had been for naught—wasted because this Good Samaritan had intervened where she wasn't wanted.

"Damnation." He wanted to howl his frustration.

She twirled the sword in her gloved hand. "Nice company you keep, McFearson. As I always said, 'birds of a feather flock together.'"

"You know me?"

"As did Selena, to her misfortune," she replied. She raised her sword, her right foot leading as she assumed her ready stance. "*En garde.*"

Familiarity washed over him again. Was it the tilt of her head, the manner in which she thrust out her chin, the defiance in her voice? Or the way she stood with one hip slightly cocked? He tried to peer through the netting—her widow's weeds—to see her features. "Who are you?"

"You could say I'm an angel . . . an avenging angel. I couldn't let them have you when I wanted you for myself." With that, she slashed her sword toward his midsection.

He defended himself purely by instinct, then wondered why he bothered. Obviously she wanted him dead, which meant they had the same goal. What did it matter if he died by her sword or by the hand of one of the worst cutthroats in London? But who in bloody hell was she?

Avenging angel. Her reference struck him and he knew. She was Tessa, the Baroness Whitley, Selena's closest friend. Although he'd known his wife had seen the baroness several times since their marriage, he'd met her only twice—once at the wedding and later at the wedding breakfast. The woman was an obscurity—all Selena had told him was that they had grown up together at the abbey and were like sisters. Lady Ballard traveled extensively and was considered a woman of the world, having had several liaisons since her elderly husband's death two years ago. He'd always thought Selena's friendship with the woman was unusual since they seemed such opposites of each other—Tessa as dark and mysterious as midnight and Selena as bright and open as sunshine. But Selena had been accepting of everyone—her kindness of heart would never allow her to see any faults in someone she'd befriended.

All right, being a best friend gave her the right to kill him. "Baroness, give me your best, then."

"Don't worry. I will, because you deserve to die." She thrust her sword over and down.

Making a pretense of meeting her parry, he allowed her sword to break through his defense and slash his arm. The sting was barely noticeable. He knew he deserved more pain than this for what he'd done.

She scowled. "You can do better than that. Don't forget, I saw you fighting for your life just moments ago. What, are you being gentle with me because I'm a woman? Don't be or else your demise will be that much faster."

Hearing the fierce determination in her voice, he knew she meant what she said, and applauded her. "Yes, you're better than most men I've met."

When she performed a fancy molinello close to his heart, he decided to counter the circular movement with a hanging guard. Although he would eventually let her kill him, he'd best use his skills if only to make her feel better about the results of the skirmish.

Her chest rose and fell with exertion. She circled him, her sword quivering for a chance at an opening. "What I want to know is why you were careless with your secrets? Surely you knew that if Selena overheard, you would be forced to kill her."

"Secrets?"

She parlayed again, heedless of his question, then withdrew when he met her drive. "I thought you had some affection for her. Why discuss the assassination in the house where Selena could hear, thereby endangering her?"

Startled, he froze. "What assassination?" he asked, distracted. He brought up his sword to deflect another lunge.

Apparently his surprise at her words didn't deter her. She continued her diatribe. "You bloody bastard. If you knew anything at all about her, you would have known that she was a loyal British citizen and could never keep still once she overheard your dastardly plans." With more skill than any of the cutthroats he'd harassed, she forcefully struck with a cut and plunge.

He scarcely had a chance to block the attack. "What are you talking about?" he demanded. *An assassination? Of whom? And what was Selena's part in it? His Selena?* He wanted answers!

Suddenly he was fighting for his life instead of looking for a way to die. Lady Ballard raised questions about situations of which he knew nothing. "What would Selena know about an assassination? Whose assassination?"

"Don't play innocent with me, you bastard."

"Me? Why do you think I know anything?"

"Because of the company you keep. Nice friends," she snarled before aiming for his face.

Chopping her assault aside, he considered her statement. Hell and damnation, he had no answer for that. How could he explain the black spells, and that his reason for the associations had been to kill and be killed? As he deflected her blow once more, he grimly understood how she could arrive at such conclusions.

She continued to hack at him. "You're a womanizer, a

charmer. Selena never knew the depths of your treachery—otherwise she would never have come within ten feet of you." She kept up her assault as she spoke. Suddenly she swung under and up to cut his trousers from knee to hip. A line of blood welled.

He'd always been faithful to Selena. But he didn't think the baroness would listen to his protestations of innocence. Did it even matter? The woman thought him an assassin. Frustration tinged with anger made him grit his teeth—not because of the stings along his leg and arm . . . or the wounds to his side. "Baroness, cease . . . your attacks."

"Had enough . . . have you? Well, I beg to differ."

In a closed stance, she slashed backward and down, then ended with the terza, a forty-five-degree angled move in which she held the blade close to her hip before striking. He struggled to maintain his balance, moving down with her drive, determined not to give her the edge. By now both were breathing hard.

"Tessa, I must . . . talk to you."

"Murderer," she panted. "Traitor."

"Baroness, cease."

"Turncoat. Wife-killer." She pounced again.

In skill she was a close match for him. Determination swept through him—he must stay alive if only to discover what she knew about Selena. But he didn't want to hurt the baroness. Finally he managed to duck and step inside her swing to grab the hilt. With a jerk, he pulled her weapon from her gloved fingers, yanking her against his chest. The sword clattered to the ground and her hat fell off.

"Now," he said, breathing hard as he held her against him, "you're going to stop trying to slice me to ribbons. You're going to listen to me. You're going to tell me what I want to know. What is this about an assassination and what was Selena's part in it?" Then he looked at her face without the netting.

And was lost.

That she was tall to his six feet, two inches—lacking no more than six inches—was unusual in a woman. Her mocha eyes held mysteries he could only guess at. Smooth hair flowed like the dark waters of Lake Neba. For some reason she made him yearn for home, for Scotland, a place he would never see again.

Blinking, he tried to focus on the situation. It was then he realized they were chest to breast, thigh to thigh, and that his body was reacting to the contact. Her exotic scent drifted over him. "Why have you been following me, Lady Ballard?"

Her eyes widened and she blinked. As she looked down to where he had clasped her around the waist, she seemed to recall herself, giving him a glare as she heaved against his chest to gain distance from him. "Because I want to discover exactly what kind of a monster my dear friend married."

Her words struck a nerve. She was right—he was a fiend. The dreams, the horrible dark spells that he couldn't control, they made him one. But he had to find out more about the conspiracy and exactly what Selena's part was in the mess. "What does Selena have to do with a so-called assassination attempt?"

Full lips sneered. If anyone's snarl could be described as pretty, it was be hers. "Ha! As if you don't know."

"I *don't* know."

"You're simply trying to discover how much I know of your perfidy. Well, let me tell you—you won't get away with Selena's murder."

No, he wouldn't, and he would be the first one to bring himself to a just end. But not yet. Not until he discovered exactly what Selena had gotten involved in, and if somehow, some way, her death was a result of that. How did he figure in the whole mysterious scheme?

During his black spell, had he somehow been manipulated to murder her? "And how are you aware of a conspiracy? What is your part in all this?"

"Let's just say that I'm a loyal British citizen with connections in Parliament."

"How would Selena be involved with anything that has to do with an assassination?"

"Your continued pretense of not knowing anything is becoming a bit trite, McFearson."

Exasperation swept over him. "It's not a pretense. I told you that I don't know anything about a conspiracy."

"You keep saying that as if your denial will make it true."

Damnation, he wasn't getting anywhere with her. But the questions had surfaced and he discovered he couldn't leave this world without solving the intrigue that suddenly surrounded Selena's death. If Lady Ballard thought his association with the thugs pointed even more to his part in the conspiracy, perhaps she knew of their involvement. He would start with Mad Jack.

With the tip of his sword, he retrieved her weapon by its handle and offered it to her. Warily she took it.

"You can kill me later. But first I want to discover all I can about this political stratagem you keep talking about and Selena's part in it." With that, he turned with the intent to visit a tavern he knew was rife with information about London's underworld. He would start there.

The cold prick of steel against the side of his neck had him hesitating. "Not so fast, McFearson."

Pivoting back to face her, he considered the situation. "Do you want to set a date for a duel? This time with seconds?"

"I would rather kill you now, skewer you in the gut

and hang you by your toes until you bleed to death. But unfortunately I cannot indulge in my fantasies right now. You are more valuable to me alive than dead. I want you to be the decoy to lure in all the other culprits."

"I assure you that I would eagerly assist you in that capacity. However, I don't think the assassins know I'm part of the club."

"Huh. Skewer you is what I should do, and forget using you as a lure." She brandished the sword, slicing the fabric of his waistcoat above his heart.

He supposed she did it to taunt him. The woman had spunk. Despite himself, he was fascinated. Confident and worldly, she fought like a man, yet for a moment when he'd pulled the sword from her grasp, she'd seemed vulnerable. Was she as tough as she appeared to be? For the first time in weeks, he was actually interested enough to find out, and to discover the mystery surrounding Selena's death. "Lady Ballard, are you going to skewer me with that thing or not?"

"Not yet, but I'm not letting you out of my sight—ever."

"Not ever?"

She haughtily raised her nose in the air. "You're difficult enough to find. Now that you know I'm aware of your nefarious activities, what assurance do I have that you won't murder me in the night? That you won't disappear altogether? I don't know where you've been sleeping, but from now on you're going to reside at my house. And don't get any foolish notions because I am very adept at knives." She reached within the folds of her skirts and withdrew a dagger. Faster than he could draw a breath, she hurled the weapon toward a door. It pierced the wood with a thud.

This encounter with Tessa Ballard was becoming more and more interesting. A woman adept with weapons was definitely unusual, and he secretly applauded her skill.

She obviously thought the worst of him, which was refreshing since he was usually the only one to see the evil within his own soul. As long as she continued to be on her guard, as long as she persisted in believing him capable of all kinds of atrocities, she would be more than able to protect herself against him if he ever fell into one of his dark curses. And she would have to be on her toes if she planned to stay with him as she had indicated. "So you're going be with me night and day? Hold me virtual hostage?"

She nodded toward the still-quivering blade handle. "There are several more knives like that, so don't be any more of a fool than you already are."

"Whatever will the neighbors think?"

Walking up beside him, she allowed him to feel the tip of the knife that she'd promised him—right in his posterior. "I'll discredit your manhood by telling the entire *haute ton* that I'm holding you prisoner to discover all your secrets."

Despite everything, he couldn't withhold the dark laughter that sprung to life at her audacity.

She scowled. "I fail to see what's so humorous."

"Come now, you have to admit the irony of the whole situation. Nobody will believe your claims. In fact, they will come to the opposite conclusion."

Her look of grandeur was refreshing. "And pray tell, what is that?"

"That we're having an affair."

Chapter Four

"What do you think you're doing?" Tessa demanded as she scooped her hat from the filthy street and ran after McFearson.

"I'm going to the first place I can think of that might have information about a conspiracy."

"Which is . . . ?"

"The Cock and Bull."

She knew of the tavern full of thieves and cutthroats since she also had frequented the place on occasion. As she maintained her pace, she fiddled with her bonnet, using any pins she could find in her hair to better secure it. She was aware of the way her scabbard dangled from her waist, hitting against her leg as she walked. The knives in their leather cases sewn between the folds of her skirt slapped against her thigh. All the while, she thought about his destination. The fact that McFearson knew of the cesspool and the illicit information that could be attained there strengthened her suspicion that he was one of the cutthroats.

The whole situation was untenable and she wondered

if she'd made a serious error in judgment when she'd interfered with the fight. Perhaps McFearson would have gotten out alive. Perhaps she'd needlessly exposed herself as his shadow. Now the tables were turned. He now knew she trailed him. She would have to keep her wits about her, for he could be leading her into a trap.

No hackneys passed so they continued to walk. The longer Tessa followed McFearson, the angrier and more frustrated she became. That he made no effort to match his pace with hers only irritated her further. If he thought he could lose her so easily, he had another think coming. She lengthened her stride to keep up with him on the deserted street, vaguely aware of the night sounds, noting her surroundings, yet focusing her attention on him. "Where are those women you kidnapped a few nights ago?"

The watery light from the street lamp briefly illuminated one high cheekbone and bold brow. The other half of his face was cast in shadow, giving him a sinister look. "I'll tell you what happened to them if you tell me everything you know about the conspiracy and Selena's part in it."

Under no circumstances would she tell him. "I'm listening."

"No, ladies first—I insist."

Avoiding an uneven patch in the walk, she scoffed at him. "Huh, so we're at a stalemate. I don't trust you and you don't trust me. Where do we go from here?"

"You can go home. This is no place for a respectable lady of the *haute ton*."

That he said it in a mocking tone made her grit her teeth. "You will not be rid of me, McFearson, so cease your *gentlemanly* entreaties."

He turned without a word and continued walking. The man was as arrogant and insufferable as any she'd known. When they rounded the corner and were finally on Blue Anchor Street, she spied The Cock and Bull's dingy sign. The hour was late. Several sailors stumbled through the doorway with two doxies in their wake, all singing a bawdy ditty.

Without a backward glance at her, McFearson walked into the dimly lit pub. Irritated that he had the upper hand in this whole scenario, she followed him inside. The smells of stale ale and body odor assaulted her senses as soon as she stepped over the threshold. Dirty sawdust covered the uneven wooden floors; unkempt, seedy customers occupied the rough-hewn tables. A subtle shifting of attention took place—where the room had focused on nobody in particular, the sullen, evil awareness now swung toward her. Not a stranger to the occupants, she heard several whispers referring to her as the Black Widow.

McFearson had wasted no time. He was already talking to a robust man she recognized as Skeet Egbert, the establishment's owner.

Mindful of the clientele, she concentrated on her object of interest. She hadn't heard what McFearson had said, but Skeet was already shaking his bushy head. "Pardon me, yer lordship, but yer bloody fit for Bedlam. I don't know what ye were thinkin' ta double-cross Mad Jack and the others but yer days are numbered if ye continue ta rattle cages." Walking away, he bent over to wipe off a table.

McFearson followed. "Why so skittish? Are you telling me you know who is planning another assassination attempt?"

Was McFearson testing the man's loyalty, or did he really not know anything about the identities of the assassins? Tessa suddenly wasn't certain. The demanding tone combined with the fierce intensity in his eyes could be motivated by either circumstance.

Skeet backed up with his hands in the air, the dirty

rag dangling from his grip. "Bloody hell, yer lordship, I don't want no trouble."

"Who, me? Trouble?"

"Leave me be. I don't know nothin' about no plans like that or who would want ta do such a thing. Ye already got me ta tell ye the business of the most dangerous villains in London. And what do ye do? Poach on their territories and now they want ta peel yer eyelids off and hang ye by yer thumbs."

McFearson held out five gold guineas. "A fortune won't refresh your memory?"

"No! Blast ye, McFearson, ye're a reckless son of a bitch who wants ta die young. I don't want ta follow ye ta the grave. Go on. Leave me be, I say." He turned and almost bumped into Tessa.

"Good evening, Skeet. How are you?"

Blinking, he glanced from her to McFearson. "Black Widow. Ye're not with his lordship, are ye? No, don't answer. But be careful. He'll be yer death if ye linger in his presence." With that, he hurried through a back doorway and disappeared from sight.

A frisson of apprehension rippled through her. Placing her hand over the hilt of one of her throwing knives reassured Tessa that she was far from helpless against any perfidy McFearson might direct toward her.

Narrowing his eyes, he crossed his arms against his chest. "Black Widow, hmm?"

The name had been coined two years ago when she'd begun her dangerous games of espionage. Ignoring the question, Tessa cocked her head at McFearson. "I must say, I need to study your methods of endearing friends and nurturing confidence."

"If you think you're humorous, believe me, you aren't. Come," he said and headed for the door.

"What useless plan is hatching in your brain now?"

"You aren't obligated to accompany me. Go home."

"Ah, but you're wrong because I *am* duty-bound. My devotion to Selena's memory compels me."

"Just remember that—always." With a probing glance, he left The Cock and Bull.

The remaining night blurred before Tessa's tired eyes. Tavern after tavern, she dogged his trail, with neither of them getting any results. Did he go through the motions of searching for the assassins to convince her that he had nothing to do with the first conspiracy? To trick her? Twice she almost lost him in the throng of patrons that haunted the pubs. But his height and arrogant bearing didn't allow him to be misplaced for long. In contrast, she was able to blend into the dark shadows along the walls and very few noticed her. The ones who did quickly left her vicinity once she gave them a taste of the tip of her blade.

As they left the tenth tavern, a filthy place simply called The Draught, she decided she'd had enough of this chase, especially when the watch pinned to her bodice indicated it was four in the morning. Besides the lateness of the night, she couldn't help but see that McFearson limped from the cut she'd given him on his thigh. The several times he'd been bumped, causing him to wince and grab his side—the area where his enemies had inflicted their wounds upon him—hadn't been lost on her, either. Not that she would ever admit sympathy for the degenerate. "Cease."

The muscles bunched in his jaw. The hollows around his eyes gave him a skeletal appearance. "I have three more places to visit." He turned to continue along the almost-deserted walk. Two blocks down were three gentlemen staggering toward a carriage. When the carriage rumbled away, the street became abruptly quiet.

She stepped in front of him, forcing him to stop. "You're staggering and your wounds are most likely festering."

Startled, he stared at her. His look of puzzlement confused her, but when she stopped to think about her comment, she realized it was the first time she'd said anything remotely kind to him.

He leaned close as if trying to see her face behind the ebony netting.

"Could the Black Widow actually care for the man who slashed her friend?" The harsh tone he used startled her, warning her exactly what kind of man he was.

What was wrong with her that she had to be reminded of his perfidy? Giving him a cool appraisal, she arched her brows. "Not hardly. For all I care your whole torso can turn green with gangrene. But I'm not ready for you to die. Not until I get some answers. And I'm thinking of myself. I'm tired," she announced.

"Many thanks for clarifying your stance," he replied in a dry tone. "Well? Where do you live?" he asked when she continued to stand and glare at him.

"Near St. James Square." When a hackney rumbled near, she hailed it, not wanting to walk one more step and mindful that McFearson weaved with the effort to keep upright. Nevertheless, he surprised her by handing her into the coach. When he collapsed in the seat opposite her and his leg brushed against hers, she jumped, her whole body warming in response. His thigh was impossibly hard; the heat of him burned through her skirts.

Leaning back, he closed his eyes, seemingly unaware of the contact. Beneath the concealing netting, she studied him. A swath of sable hair waved over his broad high forehead. A thin scar marred the perfection of one bold brow. She wondered how he'd come by the mark. Another duel? Strange that when she'd first seen the scar during Selena's wedding breakfast, she'd assumed the mark was from something more innocent—perhaps a childhood injury. If she'd only kept her heart hardened against Selena's happiness and viewed him in a more cynical light, her friend might be alive today.

Then she glanced down at his hands and noticed a familiar ring on his pinky. It had been Selena's favorite ring—the one she'd bought from a circus. It was cheaply made from gun metal with a crude etching of a shape Selena always claimed looked like a faerie. Just to humor her insistence, Tessa had agreed that it was a faerie, although she thought the sketch was a blunder by the maker.

The thought caused a lump to form in her throat. And why did he wear such a useless bauble? Did he wear the band as some sort of prize? Or because of guilt? Surely he didn't wear the trinket for sentimental reasons.

"A shame that a person's evil isn't found by simply looking at him," McFearson murmured, making her realize that he clearly wasn't as oblivious to his surroundings as she had assumed.

"I don't need anything as obvious as that. In time I'll discover the facts that will reveal your black character."

The hackney slowed and she realized they had reached her home. Ignoring the sudden jitters that rippled down her spine at the thought of McFearson at her house, she jumped out of the carriage before he could alight and assist her down. She didn't want to explore her reaction to his nearness or the source of her sudden nervousness. Surely her skittishness was because she suspected him of Selena's murder and not because of her second thoughts. And certainly not because of her unexpected weakness, this infernal compassion toward his injuries.

Despite her self-deprecation, she was ever aware of him as he descended from the coach with stiff movements and followed her toward the front door. Surely he was a relative of some evil sorcerer—she couldn't seem to ignore his masculine scent wafting over her as she ascended the steps and entered the foyer. Of course old Addington was sleeping in one of the high-backed chairs he'd gotten from the drawing room as he waited for her return. The longtime butler never obeyed her orders not to wait upon her return. He was too protective of her to do otherwise. She supposed his protectiveness arose from his younger days in the king's army, but he'd always been that way throughout his years of serving the Ballards.

At the click of the door, he jumped to his feet, still half-asleep as he tried to bow. If she hadn't rushed to his side to steady him, he would have toppled over. "Dear Addington, I thought Dr. Collins advised you to get a full night's rest. You were supposed to have young Keefeover keep vigil over my return."

"Begging your pardon, my lady, but that young fool wouldn't stay awake during a full-fledged battle with Wellesley bellowing orders in his ear. I thought it best that I take the watch."

The glint of laughter in McFearson's eyes was as unexpected as her responding smile. Their shared humor startled her—she didn't want to feel the least bit of camaraderie with the man. Ignoring the sparkle in McFearson's gaze, she patted the old man's shoulder. "I don't know what I would do without you, Addington. I appreciate you every day."

His balance recovered, the servant bustled to take her wrap and McFearson's overcoat. "Do you need bandages to care for his lordship's injuries?"

Addington's awareness never ceased to amaze her. She imagined he must have been quite a soldier in his day. "Please. And could you have the Dutch Room prepared for the Earl McFearson? He will be staying with us for a few days."

From political refugees and fellow spies to charity cases and crime victims, Addington had learned to expect the unexpected, and never batted an eye. "Very good, my lady," he replied with a bow and quickly hobbled to the tasseled rope against the wall to ring for Mrs. Brown, the housekeeper. Tessa had decided long ago that the woman must sleep in her dress. It wasn't two minutes until she came. Although Mrs. Brown's attire never had a wrinkled look, her white cap was slightly askew and her hair mussed. That the servant anticipated work was evident, since two maids followed her with their arms loaded with fresh bedclothes.

Addington led them upstairs to their tasks while Tessa led McFearson to the drawing room.

"Your staff seems to anticipate surprises such as my sudden arrival. Does this happen often?"

She wasn't about to confide in him anything about her lifestyle. Instead, she concentrated on his injuries. "Pull off your shirt."

When he swallowed and his gaze found hers, she realized how improper that had sounded. Interest glittered in those gray eyes before he shuttered it so quickly she wondered if she was imagining things.

Then his lids drooped half-mast as he looked her over. "Baroness, such eagerness you show. Shouldn't we wait for our private bedchambers?"

Despite herself, heat rose to her cheeks. "I want to check your wounds, you fool."

"Ah, you have such a silver tongue. It's no wonder all the gentlemen fall to their knees with avowals of love." Instead of waiting to hear her response to his outrageous comment, he took off his waistcoat and laid it in a nearby chair. It was then that she saw how the blood from his wounds had congealed on the fabric of his shirt.

"I'll have to soak the wounds to remove your shirt."

"You humble me, my lady, with your single-mindedness to get me in the nude."

His tone was mocking, and she despised him even as forbidden images of him without a stitch of clothing entered her mind. He *was* a sorcerer, conjuring up these thoughts in her head with his wicked words. They were images that she had no business contemplating because of who he was—Selena's husband and murderer.

By then, a maid had entered the drawing room with a basin of water, a washcloth and Tessa's basket of bandages and herbal ointments. The young servant halted in her tracks and gaped at McFearson, her gaze brightening in undisguised appreciation before she recalled herself. She darted a look at Tessa, biting her lip in chagrin. Keeping her eyes down, the maid placed the items on a nearby table.

"You may go," Tessa told the girl and watched her exit. The incident reminded Tessa to beware of the earl with a sinful handsomeness that hid the rottenness of his soul. With that in mind, Tessa dipped the cloth in the warm water, wrung it out, and put the soaked cloth over the place where the shirt had stuck, pushing his arm out of the way as she did so. As she held the washcloth to the wounds, she found herself studying the side of his neck above his cravat and the manner in which a dark curl caressed his skin.

His stare burned her face. "Will you take this much care when you ravish me?"

"If you don't cease your rude comments, I shall leave you to tend to your own wounds."

"What is stopping you from doing just that?"

The seriousness in his tone made her look up into his gray eyes, despite her resolve not to meet that penetrating gaze. "Doing just what?"

"Why are you doctoring me? Why aren't you making

me take care of my own injuries? Why show kindness to the man you believe murdered your best friend?"

Why indeed? His questions made her want to do just that—drop the washcloth, march to her chambers and be rid of him. But if she did that now, she would be as much as admitting that he was affecting her.

With as much indifference as she could muster, she looked at the white fabric now stained a deep red. Through the holes, she could see the deep cuts still oozing blood. "Since I've bandaged abandoned animals, it would be remiss of me to do anything less for you, although dogs are on a much higher plane of respectability."

"Then let us proceed, shall we?" Without further warning, he stepped away from her. The washcloth dropped to the wooden floor as he pulled his shirttails from the waistband of his trousers and yanked the garment over his head. The scabs ripped away, leaving blood coursing down his side into the waistband of his breeches.

Horrified, she glowered at him. "Why did you do that? Now your wounds will be twice as difficult to bandage." Not true, but she couldn't imagine why he would want to hurt himself like that—she knew the action had caused pain.

He stalked toward her, his dark brows bunched together, his gray eyes fierce as he glared at her. "I don't deserve your kindness, or your soft touch. I'm a murderer, remember?"

The flash of vulnerability, the starkness of his look froze her in place, and for a moment she could only return his glare with a befuddled look of her own.

"Just get this infernal womanly fussing over with, please," he growled.

By then Addington was hovering at the entrance to the drawing room. "Better yet, take care of yourself," she said. "Or if you behave, Addington will assist you." She turned to the butler. "Have the bandages taken to the earl's chambers. Oh, and make sure that you lock his door. We wouldn't want a murderer free to roam the streets."

With that, she marched out of the room, determined not to dwell on the confusing man with the haunted gaze.

Chapter Five

As damp cold seeped through his overcoat, Largo raised his weary head and stared at the desolate mirage of a castle looming in the distance, the turrets seeming to drift in and out of the fog. The troll, Gergross, crouched several yards away from the oak on which Largo and Allegro had alighted. The cruel beast had just snatched a rabbit.

Despite the distance, Largo could hear the pitiful cries of the doomed creature. A sudden snap of bones, and the wails abruptly stilled. Stomach churning, he blocked out the images of the bloodthirsty troll feasting on innocent flesh. Instead he concentrated on their unwanted mission. "How many estates have we, er, visited, Allegro? I've lost count."

Although he could easily pull out his journal and answer his own question, he wanted to hear his friend's voice to get the ugly sounds of the poor rabbit out of his mind. Plus, he didn't want to reread his entries because he couldn't bear to relive his heartache over his callous words that resulted in Dulce's lost love.

"This is mansion number seven." Allegro rubbed his forehead, the gesture bringing to Largo's attention the deep hollows beneath his companion's eyes. Allegro was unusually slow these days, creaking around like a faerie beyond his years. As he gingerly lowered himself on a soft, mossy tree branch, Largo realized he favored one arm more and more.

"Does yer hand still pain ye?" Largo asked, concerned. He noticed how Allegro allowed his arm to dangle as he caught himself with his other hand.

Settling back against the moss, Allegro closed his eyes. "Naw, it's just this infernal frost that leaks into the bones. Insidious, numbing cold that drains any remaining hope and works its way deeper and deeper to freeze your very soul."

Frowning, Largo forgot his fatigue as he stared at his friend. He'd never heard Allegro talk this way, and it bothered him. No, more than that—it *scared* him. "Allegro? Allegro! What's happening to ye? Tell me!"

Starkness was mirrored in Allegro's eyes before he blinked. "Nothing's wrong . . . other than the fact you're using too much elixir—*again.*"

Now that sounded more like the fussy Allegro he knew. Largo realized his imagination was getting to him. He sighed, knowing that the world was all right as long as his dear friend was scolding him. "You know why I had to do it." Days ago they had decided to trick the trolls by projecting false images of themselves going through the motions of searching for the missing Royal Shederin.

The trolls seemed to know a lot about pixies and certain properties of faerie dust. In particular, they knew about mixing the dust with special incantations to expose any shapeshifters in a ten-mile radius. Thank the stars that they didn't know much about elixir and its ability to deceive, for that was the only way he and Allegro could protect the last Shederin if they happened to stumble upon the poor shapeshifter.

Largo glanced at the castle again . . . or rather, the image of the castle. Complete with five towers, drawbridge, postern gatehouse and outer curtain wall, the mirage looked eerily realistic, so much so that Largo had to remind himself he'd recently created it with the elixir, along with Allegro's help, of course.

Soon he and Allegro would fly high enough so that when they threw the dust, the magic would cover the area. Then they would say the chant that would reveal any lurking shapeshifter. From the studies on ancient Quelgheny, he knew that a white light would mark the Royal Shederin's whereabouts—if he was around. Largo prayed that he wasn't.

Of course, even performing the magic as far away from civilization as possible, they were still taking a chance because the Royal Shederin conceivably could be walking in the woods. But this seemed unlikely. Anyway, their plan was the best way to appease the trolls for now.

But what had become of the last Shederin? Who knew if the poor shapeshifter was even well . . . or alive. Why hadn't he made himself known? In these past twenty-seven years, why hadn't he challenged the evil Morthdones? Until they knew more about the situation, they had to protect him—not to mention sweet Dulce.

He grew antsy thinking of Dulce as a captive. "How long are we going to have to keep this up?"

"Only until the trolls relax and they think we're no trouble." Allegro closed his eyes and Largo thought he dozed. He well understood Allegro's fatigue. Not to mention the stress of constantly being watched by the fetid-smelling trolls. They traveled great distances during the day and rarely slept at night because they had begun a routine of sneaking into the trolls' camp to look for a chance to free Dulce.

Gergross sucked off the last strip of raw, bloody rabbit flesh, then tossed the bone in a pile. Giving the faeries an evil glance, he lumbered to his feet and headed toward the tree on which Largo rested with Allegro. "Get going, you lazy, fat bugs. Fly up there and throw your faerie dust. And don't tell me you're almost out, because if you are, you can say goodbye to your girlfriend," he said with a leer.

They had tried that excuse at the beginning, but it hadn't worked. That they had plenty of both faerie dust and elixir was all due to Diminish. Where was the famous pixie? Although Allegro didn't believe in his uncle—and, in fact, hadn't mentioned him since his disappearance—Largo couldn't help but think the old codger was getting a rescue team together.

Gergross kicked the tree, making it tremble. "Move!"

Groaning, Allegro opened his eyes with obvious effort, causing Largo concern again.

Jumping to his feet, Largo shook his fist at the disgusting creature. "Stay back, ye mangy troll."

"Then move your arses."

"All right, all right. Let me go and do it by meself. Me friend needs his sleep."

Gergross squinted in sudden suspicion. "The troublemaker? What's wrong with him?"

"As if ye dinnae know," Largo retorted.

"There's nothing wrong with me. I'll go," Allegro answered and struggled to his feet, weaving. Thrusting out his good hand, he caught himself and leaned against the tree bark.

Biting his lower lip, Largo watched his friend in dismay, then frustration. "And why should both of us go? That dumb troll is simply being unreasonable," he exclaimed loud enough for Gergross to hear.

"Fine, I'll be reasonable just as soon as I burn off a pretty faerie's finger."

"Dinnae ye dare to touch her!" Largo shouted. His anger so overwhelmed him that he hadn't realized he'd started down the tree to confront the evil creature until Allegro grabbed his shoulder.

"This isn't the time," Allegro whispered in Largo's ear, causing him to realize exactly what he was doing, and what he was risking—not only his own life, but that of his friends. For Gergross had already withdrawn a needle-sharp sliver of lethal-looking electricity.

Largo shuddered with the effort to harness his deep hatred. When he continued to glare back at the troll without moving, Gergross palmed the weapon, then stretched his snot-slick lips in a sneer. "Kill-a-pix, I was looking forward to making a crispy leaf out of one of you," he growled as he slowly, reluctantly, pocketed the pulsating splinter. He narrowed his gaze on Allegro. "You've been up to no good, I'll wager, you damned troublemaker. And I'll be looking at that arm when you get back."

Tired of the constant bullying, Largo snapped, "What, so you can take it off, too? Won't that displease your master, the Shade Lord, if he discovers you've murdered your only lead to the Shederin?"

That comment had Gergross backing up. "Just do as you're told and no harm will come to you or your friends."

With an effort, Largo ignored the devil-incarnate and chanted the spell to call forth his aerocar.

"What are you doing?" Allegro asked, alarmed, glancing at Gergross.

Creating a road by blowing vapors of exhaust in front of it, the vehicle drove toward them.

"Cease yer grumbling," Largo replied. "Yer in no condition to fly in yer tired state. We'll use my invention." To Largo's surprise, his friend said nothing more, but simply sank onto one of the fluffy clouds that served as a bucket seat.

Wasting no time, Largo wedged his bulk behind the wheel and took off, ever aware of the suspicious troll watching their every move. This time he studied them more carefully than in the past couple of days—no doubt because of the aerocar. Largo worried that the troll might catch on to their tricks with the castle illusion, and then vowed that the stupid creature wouldn't ever have the chance to doubt what he saw.

Before they reached the center of the mirage, he slowed the modern carriage.

"Can you manage . . . the charm this time?" Allegro whispered, his eyes already closed.

Something more than fatigue was bothering his friend, and Largo vowed to discover what it was. In the meantime, he had to get this troll off their backs by appeasing the creature. "Aye, I'll do it. Ye just rest."

"Thank you, dear friend," Allegro murmured before becoming unconscious in sleep, his sentimental words causing Largo to frown in concern again.

Shaking off his unease, he concentrated on the chant that would begin the search.

> *Circles of light no beginning and no end*
> *Find the Shederin from folklore and legend.*

Bright sparkles showered the air, floating downward as gently as falling stars. Despite the odds against the Shederin being there, Largo held his breath in anticipation. If the shapeshifter was nearby, according to studies done by pixies, the sparkles would congregate to make an arrow, marking the location where he stood. When the twinkling light continued to fall gently to Earth, Largo sighed in relief, a relief tempered by the sight of the troll as it continued to aim the bolt of lightning at them.

"Largo." Allegro's voice was thready, weak. "Don't let the troll see me . . . my arm."

"What? Why?"

"I don't want Gergross . . . to know he's losing magic . . . until . . . too late for him."

The troll was losing his magic? "What have ye done?"

"Don't. . . ." Allegro protested, feebly trying to keep Largo from lifting his sleeve.

With growing alarm, Largo gently but firmly moved Allegro's good hand away and folded back the fabric. A putrid stench struck him a second before he saw the wasted flesh of the limb. He stared at the blackened skin that had once glowed a healthy yellow. "Oh, my God. *Allegro.* You're deathly ill!"

"That's right, Largo. I'm dying."

Although he knew what was happening to Allegro, he still had to ask, because he hoped against hope that his condition wasn't as bad as it looked. "What have ye done?"

"Every night I've been siphoning off Gergross's magic."

"Ye've been using the vacuum spell! No pixie can withstand the dark magic of a troll!" All pixies knew that such an action would eat up a pixie—literally. With trepidation, Largo lifted Allegro's shirt. Black, rotten flesh covered his torso. "Why did ye do it? Why sacrifice yerself like this? We could have taken the trolls eventually." Largo's cheeks grew wet as tears trickled from his eyes.

"Because my uncle led you and Dulce into this mess. I couldn't allow you to suffer . . . or die from his duplicity."

All Largo could think of was how much pain his friend bore when he unselfishly sacrificed himself—and all in stoic silence as Largo continued to complain about inconsequential aches and pains. It shamed him, humiliated him, made him want to fall down on his knees and howl at the injustice of Allegro's anguish. "Surely there is something . . . someone who can help ye."

"Nothing to do. Largo. You . . . must live. Don't let . . . troll see me. Kill me . . . destroy my body."

"Nae!"

"Up to you . . . save Dulce."

Feverishly Largo wracked his brain. Something, surely there was something he could do. Twisting a band on his finger, he looked down at it, wondering where it had come from. Then he remembered. Diminish's ring.

"Hold a half note. We mustn't despair! Your uncle will save ye!"

If anything, Allegro withered more, even as he mustered enough strength to grasp Largo's lapel. "No, don't! Too dangerous. Do you want my . . . sacrifice to be for naught? Don't let the trolls know what I've done. Destroy me." He slumped, the effort to speak draining him.

"Do ye think I'm made of stone? There's no way I can kill ye. There must be another way." But as he turned toward Allegro, his friend had collapsed against the squabs, once more unconscious.

"Allegro, I cannae do this alone. I can't live without ye. I know ye dinnae want me to, but I'm going to use the ring anyway." He looked down at the ring again. Unusual and sinister looking, it formed a circle with a dragon's body. But instead of a tail on one end, it had a second head. He had never seen such a design before. Why hadn't he studied it? Was it really dangerous—was Diminish dangerous? What had Allegro meant?

He didn't know, but there was a reason he had remembered the ring: he could use its power at their darkest hour. Slowly he began to rub the ring. To his surprise, the metal became warm. Perplexed, he said Diminish's name—once. The gold heated more. Twice. The precious metal became so warm it began to liquefy, to change shape.

With trepidation, Largo took a deep breath and watched. The ring gyrated, writhed, then stilled. Cooling, the metal turned yellow, then blood-red . . . then black before it slowly lightened to a dull gray and . . . nothing else. Now it was a simple band, smooth, without any etchings, as if the replica of a two-headed dragon had never existed.

Frustration and stubbornness had him gripping the ring, not wanting to give up, even when the autumn air turned ever colder as dusk settled in. A bellow made him look toward the tree. Gergross was impatiently shaking his shard of lightning in the air.

Finally, irrevocably, Largo had to admit defeat. He had gambled on Diminish and had lost. Allegro was right. His uncle was a flashy showboat with nothing to keep him—or anyone else, for that matter—afloat.

As he turned the aerocar toward the troll, fear snaked through Largo again. Allegro's face was ashen. Soon he would be dead. Pounding the steering wheel, Largo cursed himself for a lazy, no-good fool.

Allegro was the one who was the expert with spells, not Largo. For the hundredth eighth note, he wished he hadn't cheated on his exams. Why hadn't he taken his lessons more seriously? But there was no use in crying over spilt faerie dust. He would have to come up with something.

With reluctance, Largo slowed the aerocar to a crawl, anything to delay his arrival and the doom that awaited Allegro. His mind still searched for some way to save his precious friend.

As soon as Largo braked the vehicle, Gergross grabbed

the aerocar. It fit in the troll's mighty palm. "You better not waste faerie dust using this thing. Did you?" Slime dripped from the troll's hand. "What do you care?" asked Largo. "All you have to do is kill us if we run out."

"Shut up," Gergross growled, spewing spit. Then he eyed Allegro. "Now for a look at the troublemaker." He reached for Allegro's sleeve.

As soon as the troll saw the blackened skin, he would know what Allegro had done to him, and Allegro's sacrifice would be for nothing. Suddenly Largo remembered another time, another place in which he had applied magic. On another mission that seemed eons ago, he'd caused the image of a troll's face to appear under his skirts. But then he'd done it in front of a bunch of harmonics, not a troll, who recognized magic with magic.

Could he hide the residue of faerie dust from Gergross? Could he make his voice a whisper of a breeze when he did his chant? Only if he was precise in his movements, quiet, and very, *very* lucky.

Warts and frogs, far and away
Deceive the troll and truth delay.

Gergross lifted up the fabric, revealing the unconscious Allegro's blackened skin, and Largo's heart sank, even as he reached inside his waistcoat for more dust to prepare for battle. But when the troll dropped the sleeve with a grunt and turned away, Largo frowned in confusion. Then he realized that although he saw the truth, the troll did not.

His incantation had worked.

Perhaps it was because an evening breeze had kicked up shortly after he'd flicked the faerie dust over Allegro, muffling his words so the troll hadn't heard.

But just as he started to pump his fist into the air in joy, he realized that although the troll had been fooled, nothing had really changed. Allegro was still wasting away, dying before Largo's very eyes. At the rate his comrade's skin was blackening, he wouldn't last another hour.

Suddenly the ground rumbled and a ball of fire came from nowhere, hitting the large oak with such force that Gergross toppled over with it. When the smoke cleared, the huge tree that Largo and Allegro had made a temporary home on was gone. In its place was a three-hundred-foot, two-headed dragon. Gergross shrieked and threw a lightning bolt that fizzled and went out. But the dragon didn't look at the troll; both heads with two sets of eyes searched, then stopped and looked at the ae-rocar where Allegro remained inside, unconscious.

With a gentleness that belied its appearance, the dragon lifted Allegro's lifeless body from the vehicle.

"Leave him alone!" Largo cried and threw a fistful of faerie dust onto the dragon.

The beast simply shook itself like a wet dog, flinging the glittering gold from its back so it fell uselessly to the ground. Then, with a shattering cry, the fire-belching creature flew into the darkening sky and disappeared.

All was lost. Allegro was gone and Dulce would die, too! If he felt as if his heart would break at losing Allegro, how much worse would it be when he watched Dulce get destroyed? For he couldn't save her, not by himself. As Largo stared into the night, he remembered the vacuum spell. Right then and there he vowed he would not be the one left to mourn.

He would use the vacuum spell and drain Bilen of his magic. He would share Allegro's fate and meet his friend at the pearly gates of heaven.

Chapter Six

Nolan awakened to the familiar sound of a strop rubbing against leather.

He lifted his head to see his valet, Murray, sitting on a stool with a boot between his knobby knees, buffing it with vigor. The other boot was next to him, gleaming in the soft morning sunlight slanting through the gap in the forest-green drapes. They were the Hessians he'd worn last night. For a moment he wondered if he were home in his own bed.

But the bedchamber was different; the walls had been decorated with pink, gold and green stripes of different widths. Intricate needlework of ribbons and flowers had been embroidered in the bed hanging. In one corner, an oblong looking glass stood elegantly on a green stand, etched in gold.

The bed creaked and Murray glanced up with a zeal he couldn't quite contain. He set the boot aside and bustled to retrieve the basin and shaving tools, setting the items on a table next to a comfortable-looking chair. "My lord. I came at Baroness Ballard's request. Several items of yer clothing I've already stashed in the wardrobe; more are on the way."

"I must have been dead to the world because I didn't hear you come in." Nolan resisted the urge to frown, not wanting to discourage the overeager servant. He wasn't sure he wanted the man there with him. For the past several weeks he had avoided stepping into his own house, where memories of Selena swamped him, threatened to overwhelm him. It was enough to make him a candidate for Bedlam. How did he feel seeing Murray now? Although the setting was different, the memories were still there.

He recalled Selena's insistence that the servants wear flame-colored silk stockings and that the female servants don satin dresses with wide ruffles. That Murray still wore the bright red stockings brought a pang to Nolan's heart. He didn't know if he could bear looking at the man every morning. He resigned himself to Murray's care this once. He pulled on the proffered shirt and obliged the servant by reclining for the shave.

Murray brushed on the cream and took a practiced stroke up Nolan's cheek with the razor. "Ye were sleeping quite soundly, my lord, so I had the servants be very quiet as they brought in the items. I must say it will be nice serving ye here for a change. I maintain the condition of all yer clothing, but nevertheless, I've felt remiss in my duties since I haven't had the opportunity ta dress you properly these days since. . . ." His voice trailed off and he glanced, horrified, at Nolan.

Since Selena's death.

Running a finger under his collar as if it were too tight, Murray cleared his throat. "Ah, I daresay we still carry on as if the countess is with us. She were such a dear, dear woman. I would like ta think she would be proud ta see me in the red stockings she so loved the servants to wear. Truth ta tell, we didn't know how ta

proceed with her death, and with yer long absences—
not that I'm criticizing you, by any means—but we decided ta carry on as if everything was normal. Even
Betsy, the chambermaid likes . . ."

Everything normal.

But nothing was normal, not since Selena's violent
murder.

With sure moves, Murray chattered on, continuing
his description of the daily chores of each servant.

Murray's rambling brought up questions he'd never
bothered to ask, not until now. He'd discovered that Selena knew of an assassin. What did it mean? He'd been
too out of his mind with grief to think clearly, but now
he wondered what had happened after the murder: Oh,
he knew what the *haute ton* said to his face: Ruffians had
tried to rob the place and had murdered Selena in her
bed. But many thought—and rightly so—that he'd done
the deed. "I never asked, but I want to ask now. What
do you think happened to the countess?"

The valet swallowed and darted an anxious glance toward Nolan. "Uh, housebreakers, my lord."

Did the servant think that if he claimed something
often enough it would become true? "Housebreakers?"

Wiping the flat of the razor against the towel draped
over his shoulder, the valet nodded so hard that Nolan
wondered if he'd give himself a headache. "Nasty, im-
moral criminals of the worst kind broke into Foxley."

Nolan waited until the valet finished shaving his chin.
"Did you see any indication of a forced entry?"

"Who, me? No, no, not me. I saw nothing, heard
nothing—but that isn't to say there wasn't evidence of a
break-in," the servant rushed on to emphasize. "Mrs.
Campbell would know. She would never say anything
remiss."

The housekeeper. A woman who seemed more like a
mother to him than a servant, who had been his mother's

midwife when he'd been born. Although his mother couldn't be saved, Mrs. Campbell had shown such skill at reviving the babe when he hadn't taken that first vital breath that the earl had placed her on his staff and had her work upward in station.

"What do you mean, remiss?"

"I mean she's very loyal to you, my lord . . . and rightly so. And I'm loyal, too. You're a good employer and I want to stay and serve you . . . for the rest of my life."

"Or mine," Nolan muttered.

"Excuse me?"

"Never mind. Tell me, Murray, why do you think I'm so deserving of loyalty? You must know that I could have been the one responsible for the countess's death."

Murray's eyes widened. "*Ye?* Never. Yer too good. Ye can be a bit bizarre and I don't understand how ye seem to disappear the way ye do, but yer too good to the common folk ta be bad."

"You think I'm good?"

Murray had set the razor aside and wiped his hands on his trousers. "Aye, ye are always lenient with working hours and allow us ta get off when we need ta, and ye pay the best wage in town. As Lady Selena always said, good always wins, given the chance. Such a fine lady she was. Did ye know that I couldn't write my own name when I first came ta Foxley? She took me in hand and taught me how, even taught me how ta believe in myself. She was a true angel."

The talk reminded him of the reason he'd stayed away from the servants who loved Selena—the reason he had resorted to bawdy houses who would shave him for a price. Listening to Murray was enough to make him want to howl at the moon. Or, since it was morning, rage at the rising sun. He did neither. Instead, he grabbed Murray's wrist and gently but firmly eased the shaving tool away. "That will be all."

"But, my lord, I need to finish the other side."

"Leave me."

"My lord, begging your pardon, but what have I done wrong?"

"Nothing, unless you consider breathing a mistake. Now, go . . . and remove those infernal stockings."

With a stricken look in his blue eyes, Murray hurried through the doorway. Feeling like the worst kind of ogre, Nolan finished shaving, then grabbed his trousers and jerked them on, stuffing his shirttails under the waistband.

By the time he was clothed and tying his cravat, he had regained his equilibrium. Seeing Murray was like revisiting his past—like being with Selena again. She had been so profuse with her love and her faith in humankind. But she'd been wrong to place her faith in him. No use wishing otherwise; he *was* the devil incarnate. He would have to live with the notion until he discovered the assassins and whether Selena had gotten mixed up in the conspiracy.

He needed to talk to Mrs. Campbell.

As he finished the last loop of the simple knot that he'd begun to wear, ever since he took over the task of tying his own cravat, he realized the baroness stood in the doorway, watching him.

Her dark eyes tilted at the corners, looking as sensuous in the day as at night. Dark locks of hair willfully escaped the pins that held the rest of her coiffure in place. She wore a frothy peach-colored day dress that showed off her high breasts and contrasted with her olive coloring. For the first time he found himself wondering about her heritage.

"Your manservant was quite upset. At my questioning, he told me he had failed you."

"Murray exaggerates."

"What did he do? Try to slice your throat for murdering his mistress?"

"If only he would have. . . . Then all your troubles would be over, as well as mine. No, you're going to have to put up with me a little longer, Baroness."

"What's wrong with his stockings?"

He swiveled and headed for the only way out of the chamber, the doorway in which she stood. "Save your barrage of questions for Mrs. Campbell."

Luckily she moved aside. Otherwise he might have been tempted to be the ogre she thought he was and sample her luscious skin.

She rushed after him as he took long strides down the hallway. "What do you mean? What have you discovered?"

"It's what I haven't discovered."

Keeping in stride as he took the stairs, she scowled at him. "You're talking in riddles, which means you're trying to thwart me. And your stride is much stronger than last night. Obviously your cuts are better."

"Ogres don't make sense and they heal quickly."

After giving him an intent look, she motioned to the butler hovering in the foyer. "Addington, please call for the barouche."

"Yes, my lady," he said with a bow and pulled on the tasseled rope.

As she led the way to the courtyard to wait for the coach, she continued to peruse him. "Why don't you like his stockings?"

"I apologize, but I simply don't want to talk about it . . . not to you, or anybody else."

"I'll find out sooner or later, so you might as well tell me. You see, I'm very good at ferreting out information."

"Save your efforts for finding clues about the assassination." Although he meant the dismissal to dishearten her, he felt as if the action had served more as a gauntlet thrown at her feet. He could almost see her digging in her heels, clamping those pearly teeth upon the mystery and worrying it until it unraveled.

"Ah, but you're my primary clue. And I'm determined to understand everything about you—how you think, how you react to situations, how you breathe. Just like I learned the mechanics of a clock, I'm going to take you apart and discover your inner workings—exactly what makes you tick."

Her intense look challenged him. The thrill of matching wits with her shimmered in the close air. He'd never experienced such a challenge from a woman before and he found the occurrence . . . sensual. She was a worthy adversary, and for a moment he had no doubt that she succeeded in every endeavor she set her will to.

Which worried him.

Suddenly, he didn't want her discovering too much about him. He didn't know that much about himself. What if she found irrefutable proof that he was as rotten as he believed himself to be? Not that it mattered, but he didn't know if he could bear to learn about much more of the damage done by his black heart.

When the coach stopped in front of them, he motioned the footman aside and assisted the baroness up, then wondered at his own actions. Surely it wasn't to feel the long, supple fingers of her strong fingers as he gripped her gloved hand in his own. Nor was it because he wanted to stand next to her, to breathe in her exotic scent, to see if she was truly as tall as he'd remembered from last night. Nor was it to feel her light spring as she stepped into the carriage, nor to see her derrière or to imagine its compact curves and contemplate how they would fit in his hands.

Yes, he was an ogre—a rakehell of the worst sort. But he discovered that he would rather concentrate on her and all her enticing attributes than think of where he was going, of stepping into the house that gave him so much grief.

"How long has it been since you've visited Foxley?"

Trying to recall, he honestly didn't know. He shrugged as if it didn't matter. "Last week. I think."

"Hmm. And why is that, I wonder?"

"Perhaps because I enjoy the debauchery of the stews too much."

She steepled her fingers as she studied him. "However, even the most dissolute rake wants servants to wait on him."

"I find the trappings of a gentleman too tedious," he responded flippantly.

That she didn't look convinced worried him. He didn't want her to soften toward him. He didn't deserve it. As soon as the barouche pulled into the drive, he reluctantly turned his attention to Foxley. Although the house looked much the same as the other houses on the street, with its dark brick walls and marble pillars, every time he looked at the place he thought only of Selena. Perhaps it was the ornamental bushes that lined the walk, plants that the gardener had arranged per Selena's instructions, or the trim that she'd had painted a pretty pink to lighten the mood of the stately-looking house. In his turmoil he realized the footman had opened the door, but that neither he nor the baroness had moved to get out. Glancing at her, he saw his sorrow mirrored in her eyes.

"It's hard to believe she's gone," he said, and then berated himself for his comment. He didn't know why he had opened himself up to her ridicule, and he stiffened for a sarcastic rebuke.

She said nothing, only stared at him with that inscrutable expression. "Yes, it is," she finally replied. The moment of camaraderie was broken when she alighted from the barouche. As they walked up the terraced paving stones toward the front door, the baroness's brows puckered as she glanced once more at him—looking as if she were trying to solve a Chinese puzzle.

Stover, the butler, admitted them. Bowing enough to show a glimpse of the bald spot at the top of his head, he greeted them, giving Nolan another glance. "My lord, may I have a word with you?"

Nolan started to follow the servant, but when a sharp object pricked his backside, he turned to see Tessa shaking her head and mouthing, *Not without me*. He realized she had pressed one of her throwing knives against him, careful to keep the weapon hidden from the butler.

Again he found himself wondering about her. She was part of the *haute ton;* why would a gently born woman learn how to handle weapons so efficiently, so readily?

He glanced at the butler. "Stover, say what you need to say in front of the baroness."

The butler's shaggy brows shot up and for a moment he seemed nonplussed. Then he shifted with uncharacteristic nervousness. "The, er, unusual cargo you had three days ago was followed by a party unknown to us. We, uh, shipped the, ah, merchandise as we deemed appropriate. So there will be a small delay."

Tessa stared at Stover, her dark brows swooping down like a raven's wings. "I daresay you are speaking about the shipment of the female persuasion? Aha! So, you're forced your whole household into the nasty business of selling souls into prostitution."

The butler looked suddenly pale.

Leaning against the wall, McFearson feigned surprise. "Does that shock you, Baroness? It shouldn't. After all, you believe me capable of all sorts of atrocities. Why not add women in bondage to your list?"

"I cannot believe that poor Stover would willingly engage himself in such a disreputable business. You must have coerced him into this."

He gave her a sardonic look. "I've done nothing of the kind . . . unless threatening to sell his children into slavery counts as coercion."

Gasping in outrage, she fiddled with a pleat under the valley of her breasts, then halted. Nolan realized that she didn't want to withdraw her weapon in front of the butler.

"None of it's true!" Stover cried, overcome with anxiety.

Nolan didn't want the butler's interference, but he maintained his droll demeanor. "Stover, are you calling me a liar?"

The flustered servant turned bright red. "Begging your pardon, my lord, but if I may say so, your, ah, humor is getting carried away and I'll not have the baroness believe you ever capable of such atrocities." The butler turned his button eyes toward Tessa. "My lady, the earl is too humble by half. He's a man capable of vast humanitarian acts, my lady—a man ahead of the times."

His normally stoic butler was showing an unusual amount of emotion. He supposed it was inevitable, with all this subterfuge and the air of danger. For now the butler's eyes gleamed as he spoke to Tessa. "In fact, his actions are so unusual that nothing is how it seems. We *save* the women kidnapped by the reprobate Mad Jack. Somehow, my lord has discovered how to thwart the criminal and is able to steal away the abducted women. He comes here and the coachman takes over and drives them to Cornwall.

"Once they are safely away, his lordship gives the sorely abused women funds to last them a few months so that they can start new lives. If we're followed, we spread the rumor that a ship is taking them to Tripoli to sell them into slavery, but the deception is only for the women's protection because we don't want Mad Jack to capture them again."

Stiffening in surprise, Tessa stared at the butler, then at Nolan. Awareness sparked in her eyes, along with interest, as if she'd just received a box that held the promise of treasure, but which could also contain hidden dangers. That look tensed his body and seared his gut.

Breaking the contact, she turned to the servant. "Truly? Are you certain about this, Stover?"

"Yes, ma'am, quite definitely."

Her dark eyes widened as she gazed at Nolan. She continued to study him as if he were a strange jungle creature recently displayed in the exotic animal zoo at the Pavilion.

He could almost see the questions form in her mind. Taking her by the elbow, he glanced at the butler. "Tell Mrs. Campbell to meet us in the study."

Stover bowed. "Very well, my lord."

Her arm felt supple and strong as he gently gripped her. She jerked her elbow from him and led the way to the study, reminding him that she was familiar with the house. At least she waited until they had walked down the hall and stepped into the study to question him about his involvement in rescuing damsels in distress. And apparently she settled for one word. "Why?"

He knew what she asked, but he feigned ignorance to gain time. "Excuse me?"

"Why the sudden interest in society's problems? Why are you saving those women?"

Under no circumstance could he tell her it was because he wanted somebody to kill him. She wouldn't believe it. He could hardly blame her. He would find that story hard to swallow if anyone else told it. The servants thought it was because he was a saint; little did they know that he was the devil. The criminals last night had taunted him with that very reason; little did they know it was the truth. "Because I'm a romantic? I enjoy being a chivalrous knight in shining armor?"

"I don't believe it for—"

A knock on the door interrupted her.

"Come in," Nolan called, unexpectedly irritated by the intrusion. He realized that he enjoyed sparring with Tessa. She got his blood to pumping, reminding him that he was alive. She challenged him in ways he never thought possible.

In walked Mrs. Campbell. When the housekeeper entered, his annoyance dissolved. The sight of her burnished hair and round, kind face sent a rush of affection through him.

She'd been in his earliest memories, and had been the one to doctor his childhood scrapes and tell him stories. She had an uncanny knack of generating loyalty among the other servants. His father had recognized her steadfastness and her leadership skills and had advanced her to housekeeper shortly before he died of consumption seven years ago. Nolan knew his extended absences troubled her, but it was something he couldn't avoid.

"My lord, you wanted to see me?"

"Yes. We're not staying long, Mrs. Campbell, but we need to talk to you about . . . the countess," Nolan said, finding it difficult to even broach the subject.

He balled his fists in determination, knowing that he must discover what had happened, if only to underscore the fact that he was guilty. "We must discuss some important questions."

"Of course, my lord," Mrs. Campbell replied, glancing with a concerned frown from Tessa to Nolan, as she sat gingerly on one of the chairs. Tessa had settled on the one next to her; Nolan lowered himself onto the high-backed leather squabs behind the mahogany desk.

He looked at Mrs. Campbell. "I've never talked to you about Selena's death and the circumstances surrounding the . . . tragedy."

"Of course you haven't, my lord. You've been grieving."

At his quelling stare, the older woman glanced away, making him feel like a bloody bastard. Perhaps this wasn't a good idea; she was loyal to a fault and had blinders on where he was concerned. But he had to start somewhere. "First of all, on the night of Selena's death, did you hear anything out of the ordinary?"

The housekeeper worried a handkerchief in her hands as she continued to glance between her employer and the baroness. "Like I told the constable, I heard a thump, but I thought it was simply the house settling and so I didn't investigate."

His heart pounded at this new information. He was aware that Tessa had turned her chair slightly so that she could watch Mrs. Campbell as well as him. "Where did you hear the thump?"

"I told the constable that I thought the sound came from the drawing room, but it might have come from the kitchen."

"Those chambers are on opposite sides of the house!" he said incredulously.

Mrs. Campbell grimaced. "That's what the constable said to me and I admonished him that he can't fault an old woman just because she was disoriented when she woke up."

Attempting to hide his disappointment, he concentrated on his queries. "Was anything missing?"

"I told the constable that only an urn was gone."

"Which one?"

"The one in the foyer. It was of little value—nothing of consequence. I suggested to the constable that the thugs must have broken inside and her ladyship must have heard and they killed her when she interrupted their robbery."

"But Selena was found murdered in her bed," Tessa said quietly.

"She could have dragged herself back up the stairs to her beloved husband." Mrs. Campbell couldn't quite meet the baroness's gaze.

Could it be true? Had someone else done the foul deed? But Nolan knew it couldn't be. The images of Selena dying would not be in his head, the blood would not have stained his hands, if someone else killed her.

"Was there blood on the floor to indicate that's what happened?"

Mrs. Campbell's gentle face crumpled. "I dinnae know what happened!" Her brogue took over her speech pattern when anxiety set in. "All I ken is that ye dinnae do it, yer lordship, and ye've got to quit punishing yerself!"

Even as he fought his own despair, the older woman's anguish tore at Nolan. He looked at Tessa, whose eyes were stark but steely with determination. Strange how he knew that about her—but he'd already experienced the jut of her chin and the compression of her mouth before she made her will known.

Tessa turned to Mrs. Campbell. "That was what you told the constable. What really happened?"

The baroness was smart—incredibly observant. Most people wouldn't question the older woman, but Tessa saw right through the tale.

"I—I don't know—other than the fact that the Earl McFearson is a good man and could never harm a butterfly. But that night . . . all I know is that it was one of those magical moments."

Nolan groaned, not wanting to hear this theory of hers once again. "Mrs. Campbell, please do not."

Quelling him with a glance, Tessa smiled at the housekeeper. "Please continue. Whatever it is, obviously the earl has heard it before. But I haven't, and I value your opinion. What do you mean?"

"My lord thinks I'm a foolish old woman, but I'm not," Mrs. Campbell replied with a sniff. "I truly believe that Nolan Monroe, the fifth Earl McFearson, is special. Now, dinnae ask me how because I cannot explain it. But I've been with him for all of his life, twenty-seven years, and I've noticed things."

"Such as?"

Mrs. Campbell's blue eyes wavered toward him and he held his breath, hoping she would lose her courage. Then she straightened her shoulders in that familiar manner, and he almost groaned.

With her brogue gone, he knew he was in trouble, because she would be much more precise. She would weave her fantasy tales and Tessa would think he'd bewitched his housekeeper into thinking he strolled on top of water. But if he stopped Mrs. Campbell from saying what she was determined to say, Tessa would think he was hiding something.

"At times he'll be standing there. I'll become sleepy and the next thing I know is that he's gone. I believe he turns into an angel so that he can save poor souls in trouble."

"Bloody hell," Nolan grumbled, wishing he could disappear right at that moment. Unable to resist a peek at Tessa, he found her examining him in utter astonishment.

In a prim manner, the baroness folded her hands in her lap. "Pray continue, Mrs. Campbell."

"When he walks by a garden, the flowers bloom brighter," Mrs. Campbell said, nodding for emphasis.

Tessa didn't blink an eye at that absurdity. "Anything else?"

"He can change the weather."

"You mean, make the rain stop?" Tessa turned to look at him then and he knew that she was thinking about the previous night's rain-slick streets, and what a hindrance they had been during the fight—although not for him.

Mrs. Campbell nodded. "Or he can make it start. I truly believe he does it without knowing it in order to reflect his mood."

"What was magical about the night Selena died?"

"The whole house was draped in deep sleep. Not a natural sleep, but a . . . a healing slumber."

Nolan resisted a bark of bitter laughter. Healing? It had been more like the sleep of death . . . at least for Selena. Where Mrs. Campbell got her notions, he didn't know.

"How old do you think I am, my lady?"

The abrupt question made Tessa frown, then tilt her head as she looked at the servant. "Ah, I would guess perhaps forty. Maybe forty-five."

"I'm seventy years of age, my lady. My looks have never changed since the day I delivered his lordship onto this earth. It's because of the magical moments that come about every once in a while—a magic that is created by his lordship, even though he doesn't know he does it."

Blinking, Tessa stared for a long time at the housekeeper. Then, slowly, ever so slowly, she turned her head to look at him.

He held up his hands. "Now I didn't do or say anything to make Mrs. Campbell think this. I've always told her that her youthful look was inherited from her father's side. Tabby Campbell never looked his age."

"Explain it away all you want, my lord. All I know is what I've observed, and if the baroness takes the time for scrutiny like I have, she'll see what I'm talking about."

"I'm certain I will," Tessa murmured, giving Mrs. Campbell a warm smile. "Thank you for being candid. You have revealed much to me about his character."

What? How devious he was? How he charmed even the poor servants? Although he knew it was better if she thought the worst of him—for he was worse than Mad Jack and all the others ten times over—he couldn't help but yearn for a better opinion.

"That will be all, Mrs. Campbell."

The housekeeper turned in the doorway. "If there is anything you need, anything at all, you know I am here for you."

He didn't deserve her loyalty. Not able to look the older woman in the eye, he nodded—albeit reluctantly, since he didn't want to add to the woman's misplaced worry and grief over him.

As he watched her disappear around the corner, darkness enveloped his heart with a numbing grip he'd begun to anticipate. He turned to see Tessa gazing with an unblinking steadiness that made him want to hide. Instead, he allowed her to look her fill, to see the blackness of his soul mirrored in his eyes.

"There's more to you than the obvious," she muttered. "How do you do it? Apparently Mrs. Campbell is of a superstitious nature. But I cannot believe you used your considerable charm to induce her to believe such nonsense."

He grabbed the other choice she gave him. Rising from his chair in a purposefully languid move, he sauntered around the desk toward her. She had also risen, giving him a wary look.

"So you think I'm charming, Tessa?" he murmured, reaching up to toy with a long, graceful lock of her midnight hair. When his fingers touched the smooth skin of her neck, she shivered. The tremor echoed up his arm and desire hit low and hard, surprising him.

Her citrus-scented breath wafted over him, mingling with his own, and suddenly he wanted to mingle with more of her, starting with her luscious lips. She stared at his mouth and the realization that she wanted the same shook him through his very being.

When they were only a scant inch from touching, her eyes flew open. She stepped backward, looking horrified. "What are you—a mesmerizer?"

He noticed that she'd withdrawn one of her knives again, so quickly that he didn't know where it came from. The sight of the weapon ignited a fury in his blood. "Is the knife to keep *me* away, or to keep *you* away? I might have some questions of my own, *Baroness*. Just who are you? How is it that you know how to wield a knife so easily? Perhaps it is *you* who is the assassin."

Pursing those lips that were still infuriatingly kissable, she sat back down and motioned for him to do the same. "Like it or not, circumstances have thrown us together. So let's try to act civilized, shall we?"

"It's difficult for an assassin like me, but I'll try." He sat in the chair Mrs. Campbell had occupied.

With her spine straight and her chin up, she managed an air haughtier than any queen's. "It is time that we lay our cards on the table, so to speak. I will share something with you about this bizarre situation that Mrs. Campbell wants to romanticize, as long as you also give a little of what you know. Agreed?"

"Agreed," he replied, intrigued. Propping his elbows on the chair's arms, he became distracted when he realized his knee was inches from the baroness's delicious thigh. He forced himself to the subject at hand.

"Selena had begun having what she called premonitions."

He frowned. "Premonitions? As in predictions?"

"Yes. The first time she came to me, she told me she had it on authority that a certain lady was about to ruin the reputation of another lady who had just had her coming out. Selena was vague about where she'd obtained her knowledge, other than that she'd dreamt it. She claimed it was a test to see if she had any talent for prediction."

"Did the prediction come to pass?"

"It did." Tessa continued to search his face as if looking for the answers there.

"There were other premonitions?"

"Indeed. In the course of a month, she predicted a kidnapping attempt of an heiress, the attack of a Luddite mob, and you can deduce what else."

"An assassination attempt."

"Checkmate," she replied, all business. "Now, all the while, she continued to claim they were premonitions, but I have known her since we were children. She has never shown any inclination toward such talents nor the desire to predict anything. Why the sudden change? Why her unexpected interest in situations potentially fraught with danger?"

"You seem to have a penchant for danger, and Selena admired you greatly. Could she have been emulating you?"

Blinking, she was silent for several moments. "I—I don't think so. She always abhorred confrontations of any kind. Where would she get her sordid information anyway?"

"From you?"

Rolling her eyes, she exclaimed, "Don't be absurd. I hadn't known about the kidnapping, or the other situations, including the conspiracy, until she told me. Now, I'll assume that you're telling the truth, that you don't have any knowledge of the assassination attempt."

"That's a huge leap and must be difficult for you to make."

"Please. For argument's sake, I'll assume you're innocent. In addition, I'll assume you've never heard of these other so-called premonitions she claimed to have. Do you have any notions as to how she could have gleaned this information?"

He'd had similar dangerous predictions after his dark spells. How would she have known about them? She never experienced the spells. Had she been able to read his mind?

"Lady Ballard, I have a confession to make."

"Yes?"

The black spells were difficult to explain, and he always struggled to put the experiences into words. Words never justified the desolate, out-of-control sensation, as if a cannonball hurtled toward him and he had no choice but to absorb the impact. "For some time now I've been afflicted with spells in which I lose all consciousness, although I have the sensation of being very active."

Intelligent, dark eyes dissected him, analyzed him. "What are you saying?"

"I'm saying that at unpredictable spans of time, I am overtaken by a sea of black tar and thrown into a mindless tunnel where I see the world around me in bits and pieces. I have no control over my actions, so beware when one of the spells takes possession. I could very well maim, slash and kill.

"In other words, Baroness, you are looking at a madman."

Chapter Seven

"Hold, my lord!" Tessa yelled at him as he walked down the hallway toward the front door. "You cannot tell me you're a madman and then expect to walk away."

Stover barely managed to open the door for him before he collided with the poor butler. She caught up with McFearson and grasped his arm.

The earl slowed enough to give her a cold look. "Are you going to stop me with another of your knives? I'm afraid the only way you'll do that is by sinking the blade in my back."

"No, but I'll stop you by reminding you that we had a bargain. I told you everything I know about Selena and her premonitions. You must tell me all that you know about your bouts of confusion."

Halting in the courtyard, he grimaced. "I never said I was confused. Bloody hell."

At least he'd ceased his ground-eating strides toward the stables. She decided to give him another incentive to stay. "Dare I hope you'll recall that we haven't done what we came here to do? That is, search the premises for evidence of a housebreak? Allow me to suggest that we sit in the gazebo while you explain just a little more about these . . . episodes, and then we'll begin our search."

He gave her a sly look. "The gazebo is in the most secluded part of the garden. Are you certain you want to go there with a man who could murder you?"

The patter of her heart had nothing to do with his threat and everything to do with her growing attraction for him. Without waiting for consent, she led the way to the garden. "You're asking a woman who is adept at protecting herself with knives."

He was now walking by her side. "How many do you have, anyway? And what compelled you to learn such skills with weapons?"

Although McFearson had told her about his bouts of so-called madness, she could never consider that a weakness, for there was nothing weak about the man. Yet she realized that he'd exposed a side of himself that bothered him; she could do no less. "I suppose since you're about to reveal more on a subject you would obviously rather avoid, it's only fair that I tell you something about myself that I don't relish discussing. I promise I won't reveal your little secret if you promise not to reveal mine."

"Keeping my secret could prove more dangerous."

"To whom? Come now, my lord, if you turn rabid on me, I'll defuse the threat." She patted the pleat under her arm where one of her knives rested in its sheath, then turned and followed the path to the gazebo. When he hesitated, she held her breath, wondering if she'd gone too far in her cavalier mention of his black spells.

His step sounded on the paving stones behind her, causing her to sigh in relief. "Are you certain you want to trust me with your secret? I would have the power to blackmail you into doing anything I want—including sharing my bed."

Images ran through her mind. *Tangling her legs with his muscular ones.* Then she berated herself. Was he trying to distract her into forgetting her questions about his black spells? Or was it something else? He never seemed to want to claim any worthy deeds, such as saving the kidnapped women. In fact, she suspected that he would have never allowed her to know the truth if it had been his decision. But the butler had blurted out the facts, while the earl had leaned against the wall and had looked . . . bored. Ha! She knew the stance was a ploy men used, and she had a feeling McFearson used that tactic a lot.

She decided to address his behavior. "Your habit of trying to make me think the worst of you is a peculiar one. I wonder why you persist in that vein."

"Mm. When you discover the reason, please let me know."

"Don't fash yourself. I will." She climbed the wooden steps to the dais, enjoying the scent of earth in the fresh autumn air. The smell mingled with McFearson's tangible aroma—bay rum mixed with a masculinity that shouted of raw power. Never before was she so aware of a man, and she wondered what was wrong with her. *My God, she'd almost kissed him in the study not too long ago. His animal vitality permeated her senses enough so that she had no control.*

What was wrong with her? She'd never been this distracted by a man. And not just any man. This was a man she suspected of murdering her best friend. Logic told her that she was a fool, but her body didn't listen.

Well, her body would start listening!

Conscious of how near McFearson was in the suddenly small alcove, she sat down on one side of the bench. When he seated himself on the other side, she was dismayed to see how he engulfed almost the entire bench. His knee brushed hers and the contact sent a flame of fire through her. Ignoring her ridiculous reaction, she pasted on her "woman of business" façade. "Now. Again we deal the cards."

"Ladies first."

The glint in his eyes told her that he considered this a challenge. All right then—she would meet it. Adrenaline rushed through her as she anticipated the confrontation. Lifting her chin, she gathered her thoughts, filtering through her past to gather what she would reveal. "I'm the bastard child of the Earl Dowley. My mother was a Gypsy and the first eleven years of my life I lived with her, which is where I learned my skill with throwing knives. When she died I was sent to my father."

His silver eyes assessed her. "Why did you learn to throw knives?"

The manner in which he looked at her made her feel as if he could see inside her head. "As you must know, Gypsies aren't appreciated by the populace."

"An understatement if ever I heard one."

She forced her lips to curve but she was certain the smile didn't hide her bitterness. "We were ridiculed. Tarred and feathered, shot at so many times I've lost count. The caravan was set on fire more than once. There were a few places in Scotland we could go to that were safe. Most of the time we avoided civilization and favored the wilderness. Twice I was almost abducted by unsavory men. After the second time, my mother thought it best I learn to protect myself."

He scowled. "How old were you when men attempted to kidnap you?"

"I was five."

His scowl turned deadly. "Bloody bastards. Why couldn't the men in your family guard you? Why would they expect a child, a young girl, to do the job of a man?"

The old defensiveness reared its head at his ridicule. "Because I've always been coordinated and have had the physical ability to take care of myself. I'm vastly relieved that they didn't take that narrow point of view. There was no way to keep me at hand at all times since I've always been curious and tended to wander off; I needed my independence and couldn't rely on others to keep up with me."

"Spoiled, yet expected to fight off all sorts of danger that many grown women couldn't face. You had a difficult childhood then."

He thought the difficulty resided in the fact she'd been a free-living Gypsy. Obviously he didn't understand the liberation that learning to defend herself gave to her.

But long ago she had learned that she couldn't change the attitude of a gagi, or a non-gypsy. She wondered why she attempted the impossible with him.

She decided to take another tactic. "Ah, not all of it was bad. The family was quite close emotionally . . . and spiritually. And when I say family, I'm referring to what Gypsies call family, that is, those who travel together. Actually there were several families in our caravan.

"I learned from Jocko how to sneak like the breeze; Cristoff taught me skill with knives; Manny instructed me on moves that make the acrobats at Vauxhall Gardens look clumsy. Analise tutored me in nature's powers through the use of herbs. My life was rich and I would not trade that experience for anything in the world." And it was true. Often she yearned to return to the family. But England needed her too much—that was what Edward Perry had told her after her mother had died and she was kicked out of the family. Dear Perry. A man who was more of a father to her than her own. If it hadn't been for his interference all those years ago at the abbey, as well as Selena's friendship and support, Tessa knew she would have never been able to endure the restrictions dictated by English society.

McFearson's eyes gleamed. "You have a refreshing manner of looking at life."

"After my mother died and the Gypsies left me at my father's doorstep, he didn't know what to do with a wild Gypsy child. That was when he sent me to Treleven Abbey and I met Selena."

McFearson whistled. "Bloody hell! After cavorting most of your life like a hooligan, how did you ever learn comportment?"

She grinned. "Who says that I have?"

Unexpectedly, he returned her smile. "Point taken."

"I've learned to emulate the dictates of society while going my own way."

This unexpected camaraderie sent sparks down her spine, sparks more powerful than her simple lust for him. The shared moment of humor gave her a window to another side of him. In these hours since she'd met up with him in the alley, she wondered what Selena saw that appealed to her so much. At this moment, Tessa knew that the dark and dangerous McFearson she'd been exposed to didn't explain the whole of the man. Selena wasn't shallow—she wouldn't have loved him merely for his brooding good looks.

Her smiled faded as sorrow welled up inside her. "But without Selena and her acceptance of me—not to mention her assistance, her wise counsel and her boundless love—I never would have made it in the *haute ton*."

"And what about your husband? Did he approve of your propensity to break rules?"

There had never been a husband or a Baron Ballard. Edward had fabricated the man in order to give her more freedom as a widow so that she could move about in society. With Edward and the other members of the Special Committee vouching for the fictitious baron, society had accepted her claim without question. In fact, she'd devised her own image of her nonexistent dead husband, and had talked of him to others of the *haute ton*. Why did she feel so uncomfortable about misleading McFearson? Because she discovered she wanted to confide in him, to tell him everything—but she couldn't jeopardize the Special Committee and their network of spies. Nevertheless, guilt wracked her. "Yes, he said I was a breath of fresh air. Now it's your turn."

He blinked as if her sudden demand unbalanced him. Then his lips thinned and a shadow drifted over his features. It was a look she'd begun to recognize.

She decided to help him. "What brings on your spells?"

"I don't know."

"Do you have any warning at all, any indication that it's about to take over?"

"Not much. Just a few moments in which I feel . . . suffocated."

"Yes? Anything else?"

"It's a strange sensation, as if syrupy black tar is being poured over me, followed by a vitality deep inside me. Then I'm hurtling through a tunnel as endless and vast as the universe." He glanced at her, his expression uneasy. "I know it sounds bizarre, but it's as if I'm entering another world."

Tessa manipulated the ideas in her mind, trying to fit the concepts into something familiar. In her young days with the Gypsies, she'd seen strange occurrences, but nothing like this. She wished she could visit her family. But they were in Ireland and wouldn't return for another three months. "Is there any sort of pattern to these episodes? For instance, do they occur at night or, more specifically, during a special time of the month, such as during a full moon?"

"You mean to imply I could be turning into some fantastical creature like a vampire or a werewolf?" he retorted sarcastically.

"Just answer the question, please."

He sighed. "No, there doesn't seem to be any pattern as far as I can discern. The episodes can happen at any time of the day or night, although the past five occurrences have happened at night."

She leaned back against the slats of the bench. "How often do they occur?"

"They fluctuate. In the past, I've gone for several months without an incident. But since Selena's death, I've had at least four."

"Has anyone seen you in this state?"

"No, and that's peculiar. Remember when Mrs. Campbell told you that she got sleepy and then I was gone? Those were the times I was able to give warning, but both she and Selena always claimed they didn't know what happened to me. One moment I would be standing there and the next moment I would be gone. And if you're as intelligent as I think you are, you won't believe that I'm headed toward sainthood."

"Where do you go?"

"Hell if I know."

"What happens upon your return? Are you disheveled? Is there evidence of where you went—grass on your shoes or dirt on your clothes, the scent of out doors?"

"Yes, there's always the scent of fresh air about my person. And my hair is somehow . . . windblown. I have found dirt on my skin, not my clothes, though."

"You mean there's dirt under your clothes?"

"Yes, as if I've been running around the streets of London naked."

Blinking at that odd yet intriguing revelation, she

couldn't resist imagining what a fine specimen he would make in the buff. Those broad shoulders, the muscular curve of his buttocks, his hard stomach leading down to an even harder, more magnificent. . . . "Surely someone would have reported seeing a naked man running about the town."

"Mm. One would think so." His eyes gleamed as his gaze dropped to her lips, and she wondered if he had read her mind. "During the day, when I'm clothed, when I come back to consciousness, my clothes are a mess. Not dirty necessarily, but mussed."

"Mussed?"

"My cravat is unbuttoned and my trousers aren't fastened. My shirt isn't tucked in, as if I had a row in the beds of several whores across the town of London."

It was her turn to say, "Mm." She hoped he was wrong. Being the by-blow of a philandering father, not to mention being all too familiar with the licentious men who infested most of England, she bloody well hoped that he wasn't of that sort. "Are you inclined to follow in the footsteps of most of the rakehells in London?" she found herself asking.

With a hike of his brows, he leaned back. "Lady Ballard, I do not follow. I lead."

Although he didn't come right out and deny it, she believed him more readily this way. Besides, she could well envision him as a leader. Oddly flushed, she said, "Well, tell me when you feel an episode coming on. I want to witness the occurrence."

Before she'd finished her sentence, he was shaking his head. "You won't be able to."

He hadn't meant to challenge her this time, she was certain. So why did she take his denial as such? "Unlike Mrs. Campbell, I'm not superstitious and therefore won't let my imagination get the best of me. And

Selena—well, she used to fall asleep the moment the carriage wheels started to spin. Or she daydreamed. I was born standing alert for anything, with a knife in one hand and my amulet in the other."

He threw her a crooked smile. "And just what is your talisman, Lady Ballard?"

She hesitated, not accustomed to sharing her discovery with anyone. She didn't know why she had the sudden urge to share it with him.

But as she had with other secrets, for some inexplicable reason she wanted to open her heart, her life.

From beneath her bodice, she withdrew her good-luck charm, a musical Tuner made of a gossamer crystal-like material that she'd never seen anywhere else. Wishbone shaped, the two-inch pair of twinklers shimmered in the afternoon sun, slivers of prisms throwing a kaleidoscope of colors.

The look of awe in his eyes caused Tessa to smile, knowing that he must feel the same wonder that she had felt and continued to feel every time she saw it. "I stumbled upon the Tuner as a child when I was a hooligan, roaming the highlands."

"Incredible. So this is actually a Tuner?"

For an answer, she gently tapped it on his leg. The crystals began to sing a single note—the pure sound of middle A. It drifted through the slats of the gazebo and wandered over the autumn bluebells, seeming to frolic in an enchanted dance with the Earth. Always, even when her childhood fantasies had departed to leave her with a more sensible adult mind, she sensed a force in the crystal that she had never felt in anything else.

He continued to study the instrument after the sound faded. "What is the nature of this strange and wonderful discovery of yours? Do you sense its. . . ." Not finishing his sentence, he looked at her.

"Its what?" The sun slipped behind a cloud and the

crystal Tuner resumed its natural silver beauty—just like Nolan's eyes. As she returned his silvery gaze, she couldn't distinguish the difference between him and the Tuner.

Shaking his head, he grimaced. "All this chatter, fueled by Mrs. Campbell's talk of fantasy, has even my imagination burning. Let us begin our search for indications of any intruders, shall we?"

She tucked the Tuner back beneath her bodice and stood when he did. "Yes, I couldn't agree more. Let's."

"I'll take the north side and you take the south side, each of us starting at the corner and working toward the middle. We'll section the area into a grid. The place was painted just a couple of months ago. Examine the paint on the sashes and see if there's any scuff marks. Let me know, as I will enlighten you."

"Yes, good plan. We also need to look for shoe prints, any irregularities in the foliage, or other items that are unusual."

He nodded and stalked to his corner. As she left for her designated location, she couldn't help but watch the way he moved, as smooth and graceful as a panther.

The gardener had propped a rake against the wall, so she retrieved it, thinking the tool would help in her search. He was a riddle. She was surprised to discover herself as fascinated with him as she was with the Crystal Tuner. As she parted some holly to peer down between the branches to the ground below, she couldn't stop thinking about McFearson.

What happened to him during his dark episodes? Was he an angel or a fiend? Did he maim or save? Why did everyone around him fail to see where he went?

Thinking of him made her look to see where he was. He'd just finished searching a clump of azaleas and was walking in what looked to be five-foot squares. When he reached the paved walk, he stooped and poked at something with a stick. Then he rose and continued his tedious search. Feeling slightly guilty for her preoccupation, she went back to work.

For a while she concentrated on stirring up the grass as she maintained her grid, searching for anything that might bear scrutiny. But her mind returned to the earl.

He'd stated that he was not a follower but a leader. What was he a leader of? The conspiracy? Last night she would have readily believed in that possibility. Now she wasn't so sure. Was it because of her ridiculous notion of connecting him with her talisman? With a sigh, she concentrated on her search, determined to put aside for now the enigma he presented.

Tessa studied the grass near the hall window close to the kitchen. Now McFearson stood several feet away, peering behind the bushes near another window.

For almost two hours they searched, keeping each other in sight as they investigated.

And although she kept her gaze on the ground cover and was careful to follow her self-made grid pattern to ensure she didn't miss anything, she still finagled and rearranged their recent conversation in her mind, hoping for a revelation.

That he claimed he had some sort of fainting episodes in which he was still able to function but without knowledge of his actions was strange, and hard to believe of a man who appeared as healthy as he did. But Mrs. Campbell had said he disappeared. What of that? What if he didn't really disappear, but emitted something in the air to make the servants fall asleep? Incense-burning opium could do that. But opium was highly addictive and if used often enough, the effects of the drug would be visible. Mrs. Campbell's eyes didn't have that particular pinched look.

To become unconscious for a while and not know what happened during that time was probably more upsetting than Tessa could imagine. She supposed he was like her—a person who liked control of body movements, speech, actions, reactions. It would be inconceivable to not have that control.

Had he killed Selena when he hadn't had been able to control his actions? Somehow that possibility was more frightening than if he had done the crime deliberately.

She had to find out more about these episodes, if for no other reason than to protect her staff and others who might be harmed by his violence. With that in mind, she started toward him. The afternoon sun glinted off something in a rosebush.

Retrieving the spade she'd borrowed from the gardener, she parted the prickly stems and saw a broken chain partly buried in dead leaves. After brushing aside the debris, she picked up the pocket watch attached to the chain and rubbed the dirt from its case.

"What have you found?"

She was so intent on her discovery, she hadn't heard McFearson's approach. "A pocket watch with an emblem of some sort. It looks like a wolf."

He leaned over her shoulder to examine her find. "A vicious-looking one. Those words above it—what language is that? I've never seen such lettering. Is it Arabic or Asian?"

Just looking at the inscription caused the fine hairs on the back of her neck to stand. The curving sweeps of the letters seemed somehow . . . sinister. Perhaps the sensation came from not knowing what it said, from the foreignness of the writing. But she had the impression that the meaning was foul, destructive in ways she could hardly imagine. "No, I don't think so. It's a language I've never seen before, and I've seen plenty."

McFearson's mouth thinned. "This is our first solid clue that someone at some time was lurking around Foxley, someone who didn't belong. Perhaps the watch will give us a hint as to the identity of the conspiracy's leader."

"Perhaps," she murmured, slipping the piece into the reticule dangling from her wrist. "Let's return to my abode. I have some unattended business I wish to focus upon."

"And, pray, what is that?" he asked as he followed her back to the coach.

She allowed him to assist her inside, then watched as he settled on the squabs. She wasn't about to tell him that she planned to contact the boys to see whether or not Milo had returned. Most likely he had. It was hard to imagine that he had been detected trailing the hearse, but Tessa had to assume that he was the one who had been caught.

Nolan must have noticed her hesitation because he shifted onto the seat next to hers. "We've been progressing marvelously this afternoon, sharing our secrets. We aren't stopping now, are we? Not when we've become so intimate in our knowledge of each other?"

By now he'd draped his arm over the back of the seat behind her head. With the other hand, he caressed her cheek. His touch electrified her, sent warm currents of desire through her. His darkly handsome face, with the high cheekbones and silvery eyes, seemed to reach into her soul.

The evening sun cast a rosy glow inside the coach. She saw the bow of his lip, the shadow of hair that had grown since his shave that morning, and she had a sudden urge to run her fingertips over that roughened skin, to feel the supple lips mixed with the masculine scrape of beard. Then he lowered his mouth to hers and she had her wish.

His lips were amazingly firm, yet smooth. Their contrast with the scrape of his rough chin made her shiver with feminine appreciation.

The musky taste of him was the most unique flavor

she'd ever experienced. And why was that? She'd kissed her share of men. That all of her intimacies had been ploys to get information for the Crown shouldn't have made those kisses different. After all, she was essentially working for the Crown now, albeit unofficially. No, this mingling of breath and lips should be no different than the others.

But for some reason it was. She'd been on a runaway coach with her emotions ever since she'd discovered Selena had been murdered. Perhaps it was the fiercely reined passion that she sensed in him. Had he been on the same reckless carriage ride that she'd been experiencing? She couldn't tell. At times she thought she glimpsed a desperate despair in him. Was it because of his black spells, the violence he suspected himself capable of wreaking, or because of Selena? Or was he a superb actor?

She didn't know—and for the moment, she didn't care. For she was caught up in the ardor, and it was too sweet, too new, too exciting for her to abandon now.

When his tongue slipped in her mouth, she had the sensation of performing one of her backward flips. When she mated her tongue with his, she began a full spin and drop, as exhilarating as any life-and-death mission.

The tip of one of her knives suddenly caressed her cheek.

"You allowed your guard to slip. Don't forget to be aware of your surroundings always, Lady Ballard, because you will only get a moment's warning before the black curse will engulf me. It could very well take your life."

Be aware of her surroundings? Damnation, but he was right, and she was furious that she'd been so caught up in a kiss that he'd been able to take her knife from her. Why, that had never happened! She had been trained by the Gypsies and had even offered her knowledge to others who were to become spies for the Crown. That he thought to lecture on the very subject that she taught irritated her to no end.

Snatching the knife from him, wishing she could slash the smirk off his arrogant face, she returned the knife to its sheath. With as much dignity as she could muster, she transferred her derrière to the opposite seat, hoping her high color mixed with the deepening blush in the evening sky. Zooterkins! The fact that he hadn't been nearly as swept away as she had chafed her already sore pride.

She looked out the window at the passing carriages, at the hawkers who were packing up their goods for the day, and said no more to the confounding earl.

As soon as the barouche turned onto her street and into the drive, she vaulted down from the vehicle before it came to a complete stop.

Looking toward the townhouse, she was relieved to see Milo loitering in the nearby garden, eating an apple. As soon as he saw her, he pitched aside the half-eaten fruit and stalked toward her. His eyes widened as McFearson stepped down from the coach.

"My lady, beware of his lordship," he shouted, withdrawing a pistol from his jacket.

So. It was as she expected. Milo had been detected in his sleuthing, which was the reason for spreading the rumors about taking the women to the corsairs. He'd heard the rumors and believed them to be true. "The earl may be an arrogant rake but that's no reason to shoot him," she replied.

"No? Then why are all of the kidnapped women on a ship headed for Tripoli?"

She didn't want to have to correct the young man because he took his information-gathering to heart, so she smiled, hoping to take the bite out of her words. "You're mistaken. It's only a rumor purposely spread to protect them in the event they were followed by Mad Jack's cohorts. The women are safely hidden in a house near the docks."

"Is that so? Then why is the house empty?"

With a frown, she turned to glance at McFearson. He returned her look, his face remote, his silver eyes cold.

"Why were the women forced into a wagon?"

An icy finger of dread touched her spine. "What are you saying?"

Milo's youthful face turned uncharacteristically hard, making him look years older. "I'm telling you that I saw about twenty weeping women being herded onto a beach just outside Cornwall and transferred by rowboat to a ship. I'm telling you that the rumors ain't just rumors."

He cocked his pistol and aimed it at McFearson. "I'm telling you that he's a murdering whoremonger."

Chapter Eight

The trolls were in a vicious mood today. Dulce shivered, not because of the cold, although the sky had a sullen look. The heavy clouds hovered so low she thought she could touch them.

No, she didn't tremble because of the weather, but because of the tension that thickened the air, that seemed to stretch her skin so tight she thought she might split in half.

After Gergross had run into camp four evenings ago, his grotesque complexion of chartreuse turned to a sickly shade of gray. Slobbering snot, he had screamed about the giant dragon that bore Allegro away. The trolls had been abnormally subdued. But that was over now, evidently, because Gergross kept knocking Largo over by flicking his finger at him.

"So, fatty, it looks as if dragons like pixie meat too. But no fire-burping creature is going to get my prizes, is it?" Gergross growled, thumping Largo by flicking his middle finger against his shoulder. With a moan, the faerie took the punch.

Dulce shivered again, not liking the fact that Largo seemed to lie like a dead slug and allow the bully to keep beating him up. For that matter, Largo had acted as if he was barely alive, ever since Allegro had disappeared. She wished she could talk to him, give him encouragement.

She forced herself to forget their recent estrangement and the searing pain his obvious lack of love for her had caused her. Her feelings were insignificant now. Taking a deep breath, she decided to give him the boost he obviously needed.

"Pookie? Sweet lumps? Are you all right? Dulce sure needs to see her bold adventurer up and running again."

Dazed and disoriented, Largo lifted his head from the cradle of his arms. "Sweet lumps? So you forgive me?"

He recognized her endearment. Perhaps he would be all right. She ignored the trolls and concentrated on her suffering fiancé, or rather, her ex-fiancé. She didn't think she would ever become accustomed to the ugly sound of "ex." Bracing herself against her emotional turmoil, she pressed her face between the bars. "After all that has happened, do you really have to ask that?" she replied gently, ignoring the burning hole of sorrow in her heart.

"Do you mean to say that it's fatty that you want for a mate? Not the other one? Damn, girl, what's wrong with you?" This came from Bilen, who was just as evil as Gergross but not given to anger and bullying—although he certainly enjoyed watching.

"He's a fine specimen of a faerie," she replied in her haughtiest tone. She wouldn't explain to the stupid troll how it was Largo's very fatness that compelled her to love him.

Towering over everyone, Scaley said nothing; he rarely did. Although he observed everything with those unblinking orange eyes, he never interfered, never reacted. In fact, she wondered if he could speak at all.

Facedown in the dirt, Largo struggled to draw his

arms to his sides. Then he slowly opened his eyes and focused on her. "I'm all washed up, Dulce, like a smelly pile of flotsam from the sea. I've failed Allegro and now I've failed ye."

Peering through the golden bars of her birdcage, she realized he did look unwell. His gray complexion worried her. And never had she heard such utter desolation in his voice. Her heart went out to him. She realized he needed her very much.

It was a novel experience. Nobody had ever actually needed her. Oh, they cosseted her, put her on a pedestal because of her beauty, but to actually *need* her? No.

"What is all this mushy talk?" Bilen growled.

"Aye, what is this nonsense?" Gergross snarled.

Dulce ignored them, instead concentrating on this most recent development. What could she do about their dismal situation?

Never in her life had she made her own decisions or depended on herself. Not that she was helpless. She had always secretly prided herself for her high marks at the University of Coda. Why, several of the professors had approached her parents about what promise she showed as an agent.

But they had refused to allow her to apply for missions to Earth. When she'd asked why, they had both said that as their only child, it was up to her to marry and carry on the Sonata surname, a prestigious name that any male faerie would be honored to assume once he said the vows of marriage. Because she'd always been a good girl and had followed her parents' dictates, she'd searched for her life mate and found him. Largo had been her choice.

But in the end, Largo hadn't wanted her. And from the looks of him, he didn't really want her now. He'd certainly given up on getting free of the trolls, even for her sake. Pushing down hard on the sharp ache in her breast, she knew she couldn't indulge in it. The emotion *was* an indulgence, she suddenly realized, especially in this life-or-death situation.

However, Largo was certainly indulging. He was heartbroken over the loss of his best friend and wallowing in grief instead of forcing a stiff upper lip and trying to figure out a way to get them free of these trolls. What was wrong with the wimp?

On the heels of that thought came a wave of guilt. It wasn't fair of her to think so unkindly about her ex-fiancé. After all, Allegro was most likely dead, which was so much worse than a simple breakup. But what about her life? About his?

That was when she saw Largo stare at her with a determination that somehow scared her. His expression changed and he pasted on a pathetic look. "If I haven't found the Shederin in four days, ye might as well kill me. Aye, in four days a good thump on the head should cave my brain in and ye won't have to look at me ever again. Then ye can let Dulce loose to look for the shapeshifter. Deal with Dulce's feistiness. She's stronger than any of us combined. In four days she can wallop you and Bilen but good."

She stared at him, amazed. *Her? Feisty? What was Largo saying?*

Gergross laughed uproariously. "That wimpy girl strong? Forget it, fatty. You're not going to get out of our deal that easily." Promptly Gergross walloped him hard enough to knock him unconscious.

Curses on the bullying troll trash! Strike a flat note, it suddenly appeared as if all her hard studying, all her secret wishes, were about to be tested—for if she and Largo were to survive, it would be up to her to pull them out of this dangerous situation.

"Yoo-hoo! Oh, *boys*," she purred in her best flirty

voice, batting her eyes and giving her wings a dainty flutter.

She never would have dreamed she would be practicing her wiles on disgusting trolls! Determined not to think with whom she was flirting, she used mind over matter and imagined herself in Jubilant on a glorious day with clouds and sky in shades of pink all around her.

She pretended she was looking at a field of male faeries, their faces as enticing as wildflowers with all the variety of personalities, shapes and sizes. But Largo's face was in the center, his appealing green countenance looking up at her with adoration, with admiration . . . with love. She could treat herself one last time to the dream of Largo actually loving her, if only to trick the trolls.

With the image of Largo in Jubilant fixed in her mind, she winked and flicked her wings, her intent to show off the beautiful pink and brilliant, awe-inspiring violet. She'd been told of her beauty by several males; she only hoped it was true, that they weren't exaggerating.

Because suddenly her life—and Largo's—depended on her ability to dazzle the trolls with her beauty.

Bilen blinked at her, then stared with protruding, bloodshot eyes, as if he had never truly seen her until this very moment. Gergross just gave her a wary look and scratched a hairy damp armpit that reeked to the heavens.

Now that she had their attention, her confidence faltered and she feared she might be in over her head. What had she been thinking, trying to catch the evil trolls' attention like this? Although she'd had the coursework, she'd never thought to actually employ her knowledge. Oh, she'd practiced some magic charms on Mezzo and Ritardando, the simpering fools, but she hadn't tried any of the really powerful ones.

But she was good at convincing others to do her will,

she reminded herself. *Girl power, girl power, go, go, go,* she silently chanted to boost her courage.

Gergross approached her, his eyes now narrow slits. "What's this all about, girlie?"

She threw them a vacant, ditzy smile, deciding that the dumber she acted, the less of a threat they would consider her. "I want to catch your attention because I want to . . . uh, to give you a position."

The trolls glanced at each other scratching their heads. "A what?" Bilen asked.

"A position—or is it a proper?" Then she made a perfect O with her lips, as if she had just figured out what word she needed. "Oh, silly me—I mean a proposition. I want to give you a proposition!" She cringed at her own high giggle, hoping that she hadn't overdone the dim-witted female faerie act.

But her act had worked. The manner in which Gergross rolled his eyes almost made her laugh in earnest.

Instead she fiddled with a curl and stood pigeon toed. "You want help in finding the Shederin, is that not so?"

"Aye, but you're just a wimpy female," Gergross replied with a disgusted twist of his ropelike lips.

"Not to mention the bats in the belfry," Bilen muttered, making Gergross guffaw.

So far so good, Dulce thought. She waited until Gergross quieted down. "Well," she said, drawing out the word slowly. She clasped her hands behind her back and gazed down sheepishly as she pretended to draw aimlessly with her foot. In fine faerie dust, she made the symbols needed to generate the switch-a-roo spell, then held her breath, hoping it would work. For a split span of time nothing did and she worried that she had remembered the spell improperly. All of a sudden the cage began to shake and shiver. The trolls froze, shocked, as the bars began to move. Even Scaley turned to watch with his strange, solemn orange eyes.

Then she felt a jerk on her belly button as she was pulled into the gray nether region between worlds before popping up where Largo had lain. Now Largo was in the gilded cage, and Dulce was out. It worked!

Gergross and Bilen stared at her in consternation.

"See here now. What do you think you're doing?" Bilen demanded.

With a vacant blink, keeping her expression innocent, she shrugged. "You said you wanted to find the shapeshifter. Largo is unwell so that leaves me to do the job. And I thought you would want my fiancé in the cage to guarantee my help."

Gergross and Bilen exchanged glances laced with incredulity. Then Bilen muttered something about her not being the brightest spot on Earth and pointed to his head for emphasis. Gergross smirked, then approached Dulce with a swagger. "That's right, girlie. That's exactly what we want you to do."

"I'm a good girl, I really am."

Gergross leered at her. "Aye, you are that, among other things." With a limp hand, he thumped his chest, the universal signal for dimwit.

Now she was doing her own smirking. Thunder and turf, but she was good at hoodwinking them. "Huh?" she asked, pretending not to know what that action meant.

After another knowing smile at Bilen, Gergross turned. "Never mind. Now, do you know the Shederin charm?"

Tilting her head, she looked up at the drab sky. "You mean the one that goes like this?

Circles of light no beginning and no end
Find the Shederin from folklore and legend.

Of course, I will toss my faerie dust into the air, but that's only if you *really* want me to." She reached into the folds of her dress as if to get out her supply.

Gergross shook his head. "No, no, not now. Fatty did it before the skinny one was stolen. We'll wait until we relocate."

"That will be nice," she said dreamily and then snapped her fingers. A mirror appeared in her hand. She primped, deciding to act the bimbo to the hilt, even as she made plans of her own to find the Shederin. She'd been thinking about it for days and had decided they had been going about the task all wrong. Instead of searching for the Shederin, why not look for his home instead?

After all, homes didn't move like the individuals who owned them. Knowing their luck, they could be going in circles and the Shederin could travel where they'd already looked. And she knew a chant that would reveal his home. If the faerie dust turned purple, that would be the indicator. Once she did that, she would chant the owner spell, and the house itself would sing a song to reveal the location of its inhabitant. Most creatures didn't realize that homes were possessive and liked to keep track of their occupants.

The stupid trolls continued to watch her as if they were enthralled, which was not what she wanted them to do.

Pretending fascination with an ant in the grass, she waited until the trolls became preoccupied with one of their useless pastimes—seeing who could sling snot the farthest. When Gergross continued to watch her half-suspiciously, half-conciliatory, she decided to take her addlepated behavior one step farther, just to hurry up the process and get the trolls off her back.

"Do you know what time it is?" she asked the ant,

feeling ridiculous doing so, but delighting in outwitting the trolls in the long run.

She pretended to listen to the insect, then nodded happily. "Oh, is it too late to join your tea party with Cricket?"

Gergross shook his head. "Kill-a-pix, I thought she might be addled before when she cried all the time and wouldn't say anything, but I never dreamed she was stupid enough to talk to a bug."

With a snort, Bilen agreed. "Aye, and the really ignorant part is that she thought it answered her and invited her to tea. Well? What do you say? I wager two rabbits that I can fling snot farther than you."

"I'll meet the dare," Gergross replied with a slap on Bilen's warty back.

"Too predictable," Dulce whispered with a satisfied grin, then admonished herself not to act too cocky. She would have to continue acting like a dizzy female. Any one of the trolls could turn and see her. Then Gergross would send that lightning bolt at them and she and Largo would be murmurs of ash.

She buzzed over to Largo, who looked very pale in his unconscious state. Worrying, because she knew he was truly sick, she chanted a spell to keep the temperature in the cage warm enough for him, then produced a fluffy bedcloud for him to sleep on. She even chanted a get-well spell, hoping that his illness wasn't so serious that the enchantment wouldn't work.

That was when she sensed someone watching her every move. So much menace thickened the air she could cut it with a knife. She could hardly breathe.

Slowly she turned to find eyes staring at her. Large eyes. Large orange eyes. Large orange knowing eyes.

Gulping, as fear tightened her throat, she knew Scaley had witnessed her smile, that he'd seen through her act.

Like a fly in a spider's web, she'd been caught.

* * *

The last rays of the sun had gone from the courtyard as Tessa stared at McFearson in the growing darkness, Milo's revelations still echoing in her mind. A fool! As she absent-mindedly stroked her talisman, which hung from a chain around her neck, she admitted she'd been a fool this afternoon, beginning to believe that McFearson could actually be innocent; the crystal amulet now pulsed a melancholy blue, seeming to echo the black grimness in her own heart.

Wily and evasive, the man was good at hoodwinking everybody around him. His poor servants believed he was a saint. She'd always believed she could measure a man's compassion by what the servants thought of their master, because that reflected on his humanity. But if he wanted to gain their trust in order to use them for a greater evil. . . .

And how in the world could she be attracted to such a devil? As a carefree Gypsy, she'd seen the ugliness of evil men; she'd thought she'd developed an instinct to sniff out the breed.

Even now that she knew him for the worst sort of human being she could imagine, why did her heart wrench when she looked at him standing there, so alone, so remote . . . so lost with those silver eyes that seemed to have seen hell . . . and doomed to revisit that soulless pit of devastation?

"Shall I send for the constable?" Milo asked.

Tessa realized the lad's arm shook as he kept the pistol pointed at McFearson's chest. The thought of a bullet lodged in McFearson's heart made her break out into a cold sweat. Nor did a chilly cell in Newgate appease her in any way. Call her a fool, but she couldn't allow it to happen.

Besides, she still had to discover what was happening with the conspiracy. Yes, that's why she didn't want him in the gaol. And she certainly couldn't discover the details if she stood and watched Milo accidentally shoot McFearson. "Put the pistol away, Milo. I'll see to the earl."

"But, my lady!" the youth exclaimed. "You don't know what you are saying. He's dangerous. Why, he'll slash you to bits when you least expect it—just like he did his wife."

"The lad has a valid argument."

Did anguish contort McFearson's features before he blinked and gave her an indolent look? Studying the earl, she didn't know.

"I'm not a lad!" Milo straightened and thrust out a chest that was just starting to mature. "I'm a man grown, and I'll meet you in a duel of honor any time. Just name your weapon."

Tessa stared at the youth in shock, appalled that the situation had gotten so out of hand. "Milo! What has gotten into you?"

McFearson bowed, his expression grave. "My mistake, sir. You are indeed a man. Call me a coward, but I would never take the chance of meeting you on any field of honor. In all honesty, you might very well kill me. The other reason I would never meet you is because of the concept of honor. I have none."

Milo stiffened, startled.

Tessa couldn't help but notice the expression of pride that crossed the youngster's face. She realized that McFearson had claimed to be cowardly in order to help Milo save face. What kind of murderer would take the time to spare a boy's feelings?

She had no time to contemplate that anomaly. She still had to deal with these two men full of male arrogance. "Cease this nonsense. There will be no duel because, Milo, I'm not finished with McFearson yet.

Unfortunately, I still need him in order to discover more about the conspiracy. And if anyone is going to do any dueling, it will be me. Now put the pistol away and go see Mr. Addington for your pay. You did well, and I'm proud of you."

Shaking his head as if someone had just conked him on the skull, Milo frowned in confusion. "But—"

"Have you ever seen her throwing knives, lad, or witnessed her fencing skills? Trust me; I would have been long gone from this house if I didn't think she could protect herself." With that, McFearson walked past the pair and entered the house, leaving her staring after him.

"Is it true, my lady? I've done jobs for you over the past year or so, and you ran awfully fast when you caught me pickpocketing you when we first met. I know you can protect yourself because I've seen you draw one of your knives on a ruffian in a tavern, but can you protect yourself from the likes of him? You changed my life, helping me with my business, and I can't bear the thought of anything happening to you."

His Adam's apple bobbed as he swallowed, and Tessa found herself patting him on the back. "There's nothing to worry about. Everything the earl said is definitely true, Milo. I am well versed in defending myself, and nothing untoward will happen to me. I promise to be on my guard with him."

Milo nodded in defeat. "Not only that, but promise, my lady, to notify me if you need me for anything. Promise."

His anguished plea surprised her. "I give you my solemn vow. My fortune improved when you came into my life, and I will value your friendship always."

Blushing, Milo scuffled his feet, kicking at a half-buried rock. "Aye. Well, I'll go see if I can find ol' Addington." Self-consciously, he bowed, then broke into a gangling lope around the garden toward the kitchen, reminding Tessa just how young he was, with newly grown limbs he didn't quite know how to use.

With a sigh, Tessa took the steps and entered the townhouse. Nobody was in sight. Wondering where McFearson had gone, she checked the drawing rooms, then climbed the stairs, deciding he must have gone to his chambers, the Dutch Rooms.

Although she knew it wasn't proper for her to seek him out in his bedchambers, she did. When was she ever bothered with propriety?

Tessa found him standing in the middle of the room, facing the window. His stillness unnerved her. He didn't turn when the door creaked open. "McFearson, damn your pride, but I don't know what to believe. Bloody hell, you confuse me. I have never been jerked by leading strings like this and I tell you, I don't like it. It's your fault, you know, and you bring it all upon yourself. Tell me once and for all, are you bad or are you good? Did you kidnap those women? Are you involved, or have you ever been involved, in a conspiracy to assassinate Prime Minister Liverpool? Did you murder Selena?"

He seemed preoccupied, his attention not on her but on something inside himself. "Lady Ballard."

"Yes?"

"You wanted me to warn you when another black spell was trying to happen."

Dread lanced her as she realized what he was about to say.

"Madam, in a few seconds, you are about to witness one."

Chapter Nine

The heartbeat in time was all the warning Tessa got before a sparkling fog wisped around her.

Nolan was obscured in shadow and mist. For a dizzying moment, he seemed to crouch, then leap, all sleek movement and power. Then the haze engulfed her.

The bedchamber spun. Still standing in the middle of McFearson's room, she felt a sensation of benevolence sweep through her as well as a power she'd never before experienced. Glittering light showered her. She willed her feet to move but she couldn't budge.

Then the light faded and she was standing in McFearson's chamber—*alone. Oh my God, McFearson!*

Unbridled fear coursed through her, so unfamiliar that she staggered. Closing her eyes, she willed herself to see him. Then, after counting to ten, she cautiously looked about her again. Nothing.

He was gone, disappeared in the glittering light.

"Damn you, McFearson! Where are you?"

Surely he hadn't vanished in thin air! Panic set in as she flung herself down on the floor to look under the bed. Nothing. Springing to her feet, she checked every place she could think of—the wardrobe, the chest that held his clothes, behind the drapes. Outside. She even lifted the sash and thrust her head out the window to look up and down the side of the brick wall, thinking he could have climbed out and was hanging from one of the trellises that supported the English ivy.

Nothing.

Fear growing, she reached for the servant's bell and tugged on the tasseled rope—one, two, three times. Addington, footmen and maids came running.

Out of breath, Addington gasped for a moment. "My lady! What is wrong?"

"The earl. I've lost McFearson."

The servant blinked. "My lady?"

"Quick, everyone. Check every floor, and do not leave any cubbyhole or crevice unobserved." When she lifted the edge of the Asian carpet to look underneath it, she realized how ridiculous she must appear. Glancing up, she saw several servants raising their brows incredulously. At her irritated glare, they scampered off to do her bidding.

After over an hour of searching, each servant returned with the same missive: There was no sign of McFearson. Even combing the gardens brought no results.

Tessa had to come to the grim conclusion that McFearson had done the impossible.

He actually *had* vanished into thin air.

Not knowing what else to do, she wearily climbed the stairs and sat down to await his return. As the night wore on, she ordered a strong cup of the Arabian drink she'd discovered during her travels with the Gypsies, a beverage few English were familiar with—coffee.

The warm drink gave her a false sense of alertness, enough to keep her awake.

She was milling about the room when an unnatural gust of air swept through the chambers. That was the only clue she received before she was once again surrounded by starry light, buoyed briefly in the atmosphere. Then the light faded and in the dusky light of the candle she saw McFearson.

And stared. He'd returned.

Her relief was so acute she had to fight a wave of dizziness.

He was a mess. His dark hair was in disarray. His cravat, looped behind his neck, dangled limply in front of him; his waistcoat was unfastened; his white shirt hung haphazardly to his thighs. The muscles in his chest and shoulders bunched when he moved, and she was reminded of a primitive beautiful animal—the panther she'd seen once as a child when her Gypsy family had gone to Spain.

What had she seen in the strange mist in that brief whisper of time? Was her imagination getting the best of her? What was it about McFearson that fascinated her so? Why did she always associate him with some sort of tropical predator? Never before had she looked at a man in such a manner. Never before had her imagination run amok. She looked at the man—who was simply that. A man.

Yet there was more to him. She saw it in his eyes.

Eyes that spellbound her.

Wild, animal-like, his silver eyes called to the uninhibited Gypsy side of her, the beacon as enticing as the wild hills of the Highlands. She wanted to run her hands over the sleek muscles of his exposed chest, to nuzzle the strong cords of his neck, to wrap her legs around his and feel the strength in that beautiful body.

She wanted to taste that mouth as she had in the barouche the previous afternoon, wanted to sample the wild, exotic flavor of him that had driven her to distraction, so much so that she hadn't realized he'd taken one of her knives.

That memory was like a cold splash of winter rain against her face. She realized that she was once again falling for the alluring Nolan Monroe, the Earl McFearson.

"My God, McFearson, where were you?" She had no more voiced that question when he took a step and swayed precariously. Catching him mid-fall by wrapping her arms around his waist, she struggled with his weight but couldn't hold him up. As she yelped, they toppled onto the bed.

One of his legs nestled between hers; his head rested on her breast.

"So . . . tired. Apologize." With a sigh, he nestled against her. Although she was fully clothed, she could feel his warm breath penetrate the cloth. Her bare fingers had somehow gotten tangled underneath his shirt and now caressed the smooth skin of his waist.

The scent of outdoors clung to his clothes, mixing with his exotic tangy scent, causing a responsiveness that she'd only begun to experience since meeting him. "Uh, McFearson? Do you think you can move? You're on top of me, you know."

He shuddered. "Can't. Sorry."

Struggling to slide sideways, she tried to get his cooperation once more. "But this isn't proper. What will the servants say?"

Her answer was a snore.

Bloody hell. For years she'd fought off lecherous men, and she'd always been proud to admit—even if only to herself—that she'd never been in bed with one of them.

Now here she was. Too bad her lecher was asleep and she was trapped beneath him.

She pushed at his shoulders to move him aside but he only growled and snuggled more securely against her. Now his mouth was slightly open, directly over her nipple, the heat from his breath causing it to tighten. In his sleep, he moved the leg wedged between hers, rubbing that unmentionable place, creating a strange alertness, a sort of awakening deep inside her gut. The hot length of him throbbed against her hip. The heaviness and warmth of his muscled thigh caused a tingling warmth to pool at the juncture of her legs. The sharp need startled her, made her edgy. With a final effort, she shoved. He rolled to his back.

As she started to sit up, he captured the back of her neck and brought her mouth to his. It was the kiss she yearned for. Intimate. Overwhelming. The roughness of his tongue lapped at the tender tissues under her lip, causing her to shiver with waves of passion so strong she feared she would be consumed.

Then he sighed and kissed the corner of her mouth. "Selena, I've missed you so, my love."

With that he rolled away from her and snored once more.

Leaving her confused.

Wide awake.

And guilty.

She desired the husband of her closest friend.

Nolan awakened fully aroused, with Tessa's taste in his mouth. He stilled, confused. After his episode he remembered coming to consciousness in the baroness's guest chambers. Had she been there waiting for him? Or had he merely dreamed of her? Or had he dreamed of Selena? Somehow the two women tangled in his mind. Why, he didn't know, because they were as different as night and day.

131

He groped for Tessa, and sucked in his breath at the soreness along his back. He felt bruised and battered. What had happened during his black spell?

A morning breeze cooled his cheeks, a wind that smelled like rain. He opened his eyes to the recently familiar pink, green and blue bed hangings. Coolness hit his stomach and he realized he was partially clothed— typical of the aftermath of a black spell. He rose to one elbow. That was when he found her.

She sat asleep in the Georgian chair a few feet away, her head cocked at an uncomfortable-looking angle. Her dark hair was deliciously rumpled. Her lips appeared slightly puffy, along with a reddened chin he would wager was from whisker burn, and he knew he hadn't imagined the flavor of her.

As if she sensed him watching her, she blinked and was instantly alert. Interesting. Few men came to awareness that quickly, and he knew virtually no women with that ability. Was it born from living with the Gypsies—always keeping one eye open for danger? Or had the necessity developed from more recent perils?

"McFearson," she said, rising to her feet to come toward him and look him over. When she glanced at his lower body, she suddenly averted her eyes. "Uh, you might want to cover yourself."

He realized his manhood was exposed as a result of his unfastened trousers. Her blush surprised him, made him curious. After all, she'd been married, and, from the rumors, she'd had several lovers, including the notorious Earl Southey. To be ornery, he said, "I thought you would want to check me over. After all, we need to look for clues as to where I went yesterday evening, and as I've told you, any dirt smudges or other indications of my carousing are under my clothes."

The worrying of her lower lip between dainty white teeth made him want to kiss that sumptuous mouth.

"It isn't as if you are unfamiliar with the male body." And suddenly he wanted her to become familiar with his.

The revelation startled him and he wondered if his intense desire was the result of his black spell. After all, how many times had he made love to Selena after awakening from the exhaustion that always swept over him after a spell?

Turning toward him, she lifted her chin. "Quite right. After all, I'm a widow and have had my share of lovers, so you don't have anything I haven't seen.

"Do you recall anything about the episode?"

"Nothing that makes any sense." He rose from the bed and began to draw his breeches down. Her fascination made him want to groan in frustration. His attraction for her was wrong. What was more, it was dangerous.

He never wanted to let his guard down near another woman because that would lead to another death on his hands. As his breeches rasped down his bare backside, he grimaced at the pain that seared him from his upper back to one side of his buttocks.

"What's wrong?" Tessa asked, watching his expression. Keeping her gaze averted from his groin, she walked behind him and reached for his shirt.

He decided to tease her, knowing that would douse any attraction she was feeling for him. She had to do the rejecting, because he wasn't so certain he could be depended upon. "You're anxious to study me. I'm flattered."

She scowled. "Don't be." She lifted his shirt and gasped. "You have a long cut. The skin looks red around it."

"What do you think caused it?"

"A knife? A sword? Who knows?" She continued to hold up his shirt.

"That explains the pain the length of my back, but not the burning on my shoulder. What else do you see?"

"Mm. Raw scrape burns with splinters. What in the world were you doing last night?"

She didn't wait for an answer but walked toward the tassel hanging on the wall and pulled. "Here, lie down and let me look at it."

"I thought you would never ask." He gave her a slow smile.

She scowled. "I'm not in the mood for your games, McFearson."

Bitterly congratulating himself for dousing any desire, he obliged her, lying upon the counterpane of the ticking, giving her enough space to sit next to him on the bed. He wondered if she would take him up on his silent offer.

To his surprise, she did. Although he challenged her and irked her with his lewd looks, he secretly admired her for being practical. Her breath wafted across the skin of his back, causing him to shiver with unwanted desire.

Bloody hell.

When she poked at a particular area of the wound in the middle of his back, he gritted his teeth against the pain.

"Hmm. Glass is embedded in your skin."

Out of the corner of his eye, he saw her straighten.

"Can't you remember anything? Even if it doesn't make sense, I still want to hear it."

A knock sounded on the door. Tessa grabbed the hem of the mantle and bunched it up—he supposed to hide his bare skin. However, she didn't allow the fabric to touch his wounds.

She pulled on the latch to reveal Addington himself.

"Ah, my lady, you found his lordship!" The old servant clapped his hands in a show of enthusiasm that was normally trained out of other butlers. That he wasn't surprised to find his mistress in her guest's bedchamber with said guest missing all of his attire indicated that the old servant was used to such oddities.

Addington smiled, showing crooked teeth that somehow matched his wiry white hair. "We're so glad you have returned, my lord. Lady Ballard had us looking everywhere for you. But all is well now, eh?"

Tessa's expression softened and Nolan got the impression that she truly felt close to the elderly retainer. "Thank you, Addington," Tessa murmured. "Will you please have someone fetch me a warm basin of water and some clean cloths? Oh, and my bag of healing salves?"

"Immediately, my lady," he said and turned to do her bidding.

After a moment, she closed the door and came back to Nolan. "So tell me what you remember."

He swiveled to the edge of the bed, dragging the bedclothes with him, careful to sit on the uninjured side. He wanted to have this conversation while sitting up.

"Fog."

For a moment she seemed distracted, as if she didn't know what he was referring to. With a shake of her head and a couple of blinks, she grimaced. "Yes, we have been having fog. What else do you recall from last night?"

"A baby crying. Voices." There were other occurrences but they whirled around like kaleidoscopes in his head, just out of reach.

"What did the voices say?"

He hated that he couldn't catch any of the words. "No matter how hard I try, I cannot discern even a hint of a conversation. The voices were muffled. I don't even know if my voice was in the mix, or what I said if I did participate in any so-called discussion. Bloody hell, for all I know, it could be a dream I'm getting glimpses of."

"That isn't very helpful. What I want to know is, how did you manage that sparkling cloud that enveloped me? It must have come from you."

He simply stared at her, weary of repeating those useless words. *I don't know.*

"Do you remember anything odd, such as having the craving to, um, climb a tree?"

"Excuse me?"

"Do you yearn to return to the wild mountains of Spain?"

"I've never been to Spain. Tessa?"

Suddenly she couldn't look him in the eye. Instead she fussed with the folds of her dress. "Never mind. Ah, here's the maid with a basin of warm water and cloths," She exclaimed at the knock on the door.

Her relief puzzled him, as did her bizarre questions. He waited until the maid had set down the basin and left the chamber before questioning her. "All right, tell me what is bothering you. Why did you ask me about climbing trees and being in Spain?"

She scowled. "Forget that I brought up such ridiculous questions. Now, lie down again so I can clean your cuts. We've got a lot to do today and I don't have time to dally."

She wasn't about to tell him anything more—at least, not now. With a sigh, he rolled over onto his stomach again, pulling the counterpane out from under him, the bedclothes becoming a knotted mess.

By the time she was finished cleaning the wounds and applying her salve, he was more than ready for some activity.

"I'll leave you to prepare for the day. Would you like Addington to assist you since you dismissed your own valet?"

"No, I'll manage fine on my own."

"Very well."

As he watched her leave, walking as if she had a flagpole for a spine, he wondered how they had managed to become formal strangers. Because since the moment she'd jumped into the middle of his fight, they had totally skipped that part of their relationship.

In record time, Nolan donned his clothes, preferring the somber shades of gray and silver. After descending the stairs, he found Tessa sitting in the drawing room.

"Tea and cookies, my lord?" she asked politely as she glanced up from the London *Times*.

"Thank you." Her polite formality bothered him. From the moment he'd come out of the black spell she had been withdrawn—different. But his musings were distracted by Addington with a tray of assorted breads. "My lady, did you hear what happened to the Kendricks?"

Tessa sat forward with a frown. "No, pray tell."

"A fire broke out in the nursery. Evidently the nursemaid fell asleep while performing her duties and knocked a candle over. When she awakened, she panicked and ran screaming down the hall, leaving the babe in his cradle."

"Good heavens," Tessa exclaimed.

Addington nodded. "Although the servants managed to beat out the fire, they feared the wee babe had succumbed to the smoke. But the babe was gone."

Tessa widened her eyes. "Gone?"

"Yes," the butler answered in a grave tone. "My good friend, Mary Crosby—she's the housekeeper—found the sweet child on the front doorstep, cooing and babbling as happy as you please."

"Nothing was wrong with the child?" McFearson asked. A flash of fire heated his memory, then was gone.

"Only some ash on his swaddling, is all. Someone

must have saved the infant, although how he did, nobody can figure out. The nursery is three floors up."

Tessa pressed her lips together. "Is there a trellis or anything?"

"There's a huge oak tree that grows almost that high. But it's too far away from the window for anyone to reach."

Setting aside her cup, Tessa rose. "Addington, we will not be needing tea and crumpets after all."

"Very well, my lady," the butler intoned and withdrew.

"Tessa, tell me what is bothering you, besides the fire. You've been looking at me with puzzlement. I want to know what happened last night."

She looked him up and down, then blinked in that haughty way of hers. "When you came to your senses last night you thought I was Selena. Damnation, you confuse me, McFearson. I don't want to discuss it because there's another problem we must face: helping a neighbor in need. We'll express our sympathy for the recent fright and offer our assistance."

"Together? My sweet, what will the neighbors think?"

"Why, simply that the Black Widow has got herself another randy buck to amuse her."

Chapter Ten

Smoke still permeated the hallway.

Tessa resisted the urge to take a deep breath as the Kendricks' butler led them to the drawing room. A fire in London could be devastating. Thank goodness the nurse had the presence of mind to yell a warning. But to forget her charge, nearly costing him his life, was shameful.

Elisabeth Kendrick was slightly high-strung. Since her marriage, though, the woman seemed to have settled down, supposedly because of her older husband. Kendrick claimed the somber colors of purple and hunter green soothed frayed nerves and high-strung personalities. Shrugging, Tessa didn't know if the man had a position or not. Just stepping into the townhouse with its dreary decorations made Tessa yearn for outdoors.

She was astonished to see Bartholomew Carmichael from the Special Committee sitting adjacent to Lady Kendrick. A cradle sat close to Lady Kendrick's chair; a maid hovered in a corner.

Carmichael rose as soon as she and McFearson entered the room. His eyes widened, showing his own surprise as he glanced from Tessa to McFearson. She recalled the link between Carmichael and Lady Kendrick. It was the now-deceased Sir Thaddeus who had adopted a young Bartholomew, a relative of their hostess.

"Tessa! I'm so glad you have come," Lady Kendrick exclaimed, holding her hands out as she remained seated on an overstuffed divan.

Two years ago, when Tessa first met Elisabeth Kendrick, their friendship had been strained, most likely because of Tessa's reputation, not to mention the rumors that floated around about her supposed liaison with Carmichael, Elisabeth's favorite cousin. But lately Tessa had sensed that Elisabeth had finally truly accepted her.

Tessa gave her friend's hands a gentle squeeze. "You couldn't keep me away when I heard the terrible news," she murmured.

Elisabeth's eyes were bright with curiosity as she looked fleetingly from Tessa to Nolan. Then she blinked and smiled faintly. She rubbed the child's back as he lay sleeping. It was as if she feared to take her hand away; otherwise the boy might disappear. "I dare not try to stand. My legs are still too wobbly and I'm afraid I will disgrace myself. You have brought a friend. Thank you for coming, my lord," she murmured to McFearson.

"I'm at your service, my lady," McFearson replied.

"Lady Ballard, McFearson," Carmichael greeted with a bow.

"Good afternoon, Carmichael," Nolan replied with a slight nod.

Carmichael glanced at his cousin, his brown eyes solemn, before turning his attention to the newcomers. "Since Elisabeth's husband is in the country visiting relatives and isn't due back until tomorrow, I felt it my duty to see to her welfare."

Relief for Elisabeth made Tessa smile. Having Carmichael to comfort her and take care of the aftermath of the catastrophe went a long ways toward soothing Elisabeth and rectifying the situation. "Of course. Elisabeth is very lucky to have you."

Elisabeth sighed. "Yes, I'm quite fortunate, I must admit, since George is away. Both of you, sit, please."

Tessa lowered herself on the sofa across from their hostess; McFearson did the same. The heat of his body seemed to seep into the few inches of fabric that separated them.

With a sniff, Lady Kendrick brought a handkerchief to her nose even as she continued to touch her child. "Everything has been in an uproar. Why, you couldn't imagine my fright when I heard the nursemaid screaming about a fire. And then the horror when I realized that poor little Phillip had been left inside the burning chamber. . . ."

Lady Kendrick glanced down at the boy sleeping in the crib. "But when several of my valiant servants braved the fire only to discover that the baby wasn't to be found . . . lo and behold, Mrs. Crosby, that dear wonderful housekeeper, found him. How could he have gotten on the front stoop? He is but four months old and has yet to crawl! The only explanation anyone can come up with is that someone, some mystery hero, rescued the dear child."

"Were there no clues?" Tessa asked. "How could anyone get into the room when it's so high? Mr. Carmichael? Do you have any theories as to who it was or how he got to the third floor?"

The Special Committee member cocked his head in thought. "It is definitely a mystery, Lady Ballard. I saw no evidence of anyone on the trellis, no marks in the ground that would indicate a ladder."

"The oak tree, perhaps?" Lady Kendrick suggested.

"It's certainly sturdy enough to bear a man's weight, but frankly, the tree is too far away. Even if our mysterious rescuer was able to tie a rope to a branch, I don't see how he could swing it in an arc great enough to reach the window without bashing himself into the trunk."

Elisabeth's lips curved in a tremulous smile. "Perhaps he was a deity, an angel, because we've been blessed. Obviously he doesn't want to be known, and I will have to be content with his wishes. But I wouldn't want to explore the mystery of his identity for any reason other than to give him my profuse thanks."

"Yes, I would feel the same way," Tessa murmured. Glancing at McFearson, she wondered what he was thinking as he sat with one leg crossed over the other, his hands clasped over his raised knee. Was any of this familiar? She couldn't wait to get him alone to ask.

Carmichael stared at McFearson's hands. "Are those blisters from a burn?"

Tessa froze, then cautiously glanced at Nolan.

Glancing down at his wrists, Nolan smiled easily. "Ah, yes, fire does damage large and small. Fortunately my accident was on the lesser side. It's from hot wax. Last night when I was writing a missive to my steward, I was clumsy and knocked over a candle."

"Ah, yes, one must be careful," Carmichael murmured, giving Nolan a narrow-eyed look.

Lady Kendrick fiddled with her handkerchief. "Yes, we must all be extremely cautious around candles! I don't know what we're going to do with the upper floor, although the damage seems to have been contained in the nursery. The fire could have been much, much worse."

Carmichael reached over to pat one of Lady Kendrick's busy hands. "Now, Elisabeth, dear, you mustn't fret. I will get someone to fix the damage. The main thing is that nobody was hurt."

"Yes, to think of poor, sweet baby Phillip succumbing to the fire. . . ."

"You mustn't dwell upon it, Elisabeth," Tessa replied in a soothing tone.

"No, no—that is what Bartholomew keeps telling me. I've got to concentrate on the little soirée that I'm giving this Friday. Oh! Do you think I'll get the smell out of the house before then? Whatever will I do? Selena had a concoction of herbs that she used to burn as incense to freshen the house."

At the mention of Selena, McFearson shifted his weight in his seat. Tessa resisted doing the same. What did Elisabeth think of her association with Selena's husband?

Elisabeth quit rubbing her nose as if she suddenly comprehended the awkward atmosphere. Her blue eyes rounded as she looked at Tessa and McFearson in dismay. Tears formed in her gentle eyes. "Oh, oh my, that was thoughtless of me. Although I'm glad to see the two of you together. I've worried about Nolan." At McFearson's raised brows, she held up her hands. "It's none of my business, I know, but I couldn't help but worry when I heard how you rarely came home, staying in the stews to mourn your loss. It's natural; after all, you both loved Selena. I think it's lovely that you've found one another and can give comfort to each other. Do you have any idea as to who could have murdered her?" she asked hastily, as if aware that talk of their supposed liaison had gone on too long.

Tessa curved her lips in a faint grimace. "Not yet. But Nolan and I are working on it. And we're not having an affair," she blurted.

"Of course not," Elisabeth intoned, blushing but obviously not believing a word of it.

Why did Tessa experience a bout of self-consciousness? It wasn't as if she hadn't pretended to have liaisons in the past. In fact, she'd taken on several roles in her life of espionage. But suddenly she felt tongue-tied, as if she wasn't pretending, and couldn't if her life depended upon it.

In her confusion, Nolan stepped up behind her and stroked her back. The action had been done before by men, and it hadn't meant anything. Then why did it feel somehow special, as if she'd been branded as his? "You're right, Lady Kendrick. Shared grief brings together the most unlikely people," Nolan said.

Face burning, Tessa decided to ignore the whole social blunder—and ignore any liaison that Nolan implied. "I am quite familiar with the recipe, since I was the one to give it to Selena. I will leave instructions with the housekeeper."

Smiling faintly, Elisabeth leaned her head back on the sofa. "Thank you, Tessa."

McFearson leaned forward in his chair. "Could Tessa and I see the remains of the fire? I consider myself an expert on architecture. It is a subject I endeavor to study upon occasion, and I would like to try to discern the extent of the damage, if I may."

Tessa blinked, amazed. To her knowledge he wasn't remotely interested in the subject.

Lady Kendrick lifted her head, her dejection gone. "Why, you and my dear husband George share a common interest. Yes, feel free to view the damage. I'll call the butler to lead you there."

Carmichael stepped forward. "Don't bother, Elisabeth. I'll be glad to escort McFearson."

Tessa arose from her chair. "I would like to participate in the adventure, if for nothing else but to guess what sort of a man would attempt to rescue the baby."

Carmichael gave his slow smile. "A delicious mystery

for the Lady Ballard. Ah, as a matter of fact, why don't you take McFearson to the study and show him George's drawings of the house? The butler can show him to the nursery afterward."

Tessa could sense Carmichael's curiosity; she should have guessed that he would think of an excuse to get her alone in order to question her.

"Marvelous idea, Cousin. This way, my lord," Lady Kendrick said to Nolan and jumped up, obviously forgetting her weakened state.

"Don't start without me," McFearson leaned over to murmur to Tessa before he rose and followed their excited hostess.

Carmichael escorted Tessa up the stairway. The somber décor continued on the second and third floors, and Tessa wondered if Kendrick had a point about using colors to change a person's mood. As they got closer to the damage, the smell of smoke became stronger.

She waited for Carmichael to start the discussion; she was certain he hesitated until he was assured of complete privacy from the servants.

When he halted at a white door that was charred and covered in soot—obviously leading to the nursery—he turned to her. "I've instructed all the servants to stay away from this floor until the damage is assessed. So, Lady Ballard, not a fortnight ago, you vowed to prove that McFearson was your dear friend's murderer. Now you're having an affair with the man?"

Her defenses went up; she gave him an arch look. "What better way to discover a man's secrets, mm?"

Suddenly he grasped her hands and said urgently, "Please, Tessa, trust me with anything, no matter how abnormal the notion sounds. Is McFearson all you think he is? Or is there something odd about him?"

Under no circumstances would she tell Carmichael

about the strange crystal fog or the way McFearson seemed to turn into . . . something inhuman before he disappeared. Damnation, she couldn't accept the notion herself, much less put the idea into words. "Nothing other than he's extremely arrogant, just like any other man," she retorted.

Carmichael stepped back and seemed to collect himself. "You are a clever woman, Tessa, with a cool head about you. What are your thoughts of him? Your inclinations?"

A fierce inclination to protect McFearson swept over her.

"I want you to understand that I value your intuitions more than anyone I've ever known."

Pleasure swept through her. Carmichael was truly a gentleman. "I've thought the very same of you, sir. You have a canny way of understanding situations that is rarely found in a person."

"So? Judging his character, is he capable of the heinous crime?"

Why did she feel as if she were betraying McFearson by discussing him? The very thought of doing so made her want to fidget. But this was her job, and Carmichael's questions were valid. She shouldn't react this way.

But she did. "He is the most confusing, complicated man I've ever encountered, and, truthfully, I'm not prepared to discuss my perceptions of him yet."

Carmichael's brown eyes pooled with sympathy. "Could it be because your emotions are involved? Allow me to caution you. You've never been on a mission close to the heart like this. After all, your suspect is the husband of a woman who was more like a sister to you, a woman whose life ended violently and much too soon."

Her heart wrenched at his words; emotion caused her throat to swell so much that she could hardly swallow.

Squeezing her hand, Carmichael gave her a look full

of sincerity. "As I've said, you are the most logical, intuitive person I've had the pleasure to know. But even the most level-headed person can lose sight of the real dangers and I would not want you to put down your guard. Although I tend to think you are invincible, you are not immune to death."

She knew he was right. "I appreciate the word of caution. Don't worry. I will keep my head about me."

"I knew you would. I simply had to state my opinion. After all, I would never be able to live with myself if something happened to you and I hadn't spoken my mind. And promise me that you will come to me if you need me, or if you find you need someone to guard your back."

Blinking back the unexpected stab of tears behind her eyes, she gave him a tremulous smile. "I give you my word."

"Good. Now, let's see if we can find any clues as to who our mystery hero could be." He pushed down the latch and revealed the chamber.

The smoky stench made her eyes water. A gentle breeze wafted through the room, most likely stronger now that they had opened the door to create a draft. The stink from burnt carpet, drapes, the stuffing from two chairs and charred oiled wood stung her nose. "My word, it's lucky the whole house didn't go up in flames."

Carmichael's lips thinned. "Damned fortunate. As it was, several servants had rather nasty burns."

She thought of the burns on McFearson's body.

"Lady Ballard? What are you thinking? Is there something you know that you're not telling me?"

She realized she was frowning and forced herself to smile. "Not at all."

Several shoe imprints were outlined in the soot and ash that covered the floor.

"The servants pretty much destroyed whatever evidence there was of the intruder," Carmichael said, noticing her speculation. He took the charred remains of a chair leg and poked at some of the ashes near the baby's crib.

Tessa inspected the floor as she slowly made her way over to the window, but there was no way to discern one footstep from another, or to tell which ones were first. When she got closer to the only other opening to the room, she had to pick her way through the shards of crushed glass.

She examined the jagged edges of glass and slivered wood still in the frame. It amazed her how the sturdy oak support that held the panes of glass had been splintered, as if a huge object had been hurled at the window. It was then that she saw blood on one of the sharp edges of broken glass. Slightly above the bloodied glass, on one of those broken strips of wood, was a clump of matted hair.

She retrieved a handkerchief from her reticule and, with the cloth, carefully picked at the hair, cleaning the entire mess away from the jagged wood. Then she studied it. The hair was coarse, some of it wiry.

Definitely not human.

Carmichael's foot crunched on glass a couple of feet behind her. "What have you found?"

The insane notions bouncing around in her head were too addlepated for her to voice aloud. She couldn't wrap her mind around what she'd found, or the significance of it.

Instinctively, she wrapped the evidence in her handkerchief, shoving it in her reticule before he reached her side. "Blood," she said, pointing to the broken glass.

Bending close to her, Carmichael studied the smear. "Well, I think we can say that our mystery hero is someone who didn't escape unscathed. Do you know of anyone who suffered a cut from broken glass last night?"

McFearson. She didn't voice his name, though, because she was having too many strange notions about him, not to mention her almost animal-like attraction for him. Ha! Animal-like? Heavens, she *was* fit for Bedlam!

"I don't know of anyone with a cut," McFearson replied, appearing at the doorway. She glanced at him, startled, wondering if her thoughts conjured him up, then telling herself she'd better get a grasp on her wayward imagination.

McFearson's fierce gaze zeroed in on her, then his silver eyes fixed on Carmichael. His expression turned almost bored as he sauntered across the chamber, forcing his way between her and Carmichael, causing the other man to take a step backward. Ignoring both of them, he gazed at the jagged glass with the dark brown stain, then turned to look at Tessa, his gaze unfathomable. "Do you, Lady Ballard?"

"Not yet," she exclaimed without missing a beat, noticing how he turned his back to Carmichael. She was irritated at his rudeness.

Carmichael studied the opening a little longer, then turned to Tessa. "I've heard that determination in your tone before, and I would wager a large sum that you're on to something. Do you have suspicions? If so, you must share them with me. Whoever he is, I would personally like to reward him."

"I have my sources. I'll let you know if I discover his identity."

"I would appreciate it, my dear. Well, McFearson, do you think the structure is damaged?" he asked, turning to Nolan.

McFearson studied the room with eyes that seemed to note everything. "No, simply cosmetics. I believe all that the room needs is a good cleaning, repairs to a few wood treads, and some fresh plaster on the wall around the window. And, of course, some of the frame replaced as well as the sash."

"Elisabeth will be glad to hear it."

McFearson grasped her elbow in a firm hold. "If Tessa finds it prudent to share information with you, she will. In the meantime, we have an appointment to meet, and so must be on our way."

"Oh?" Carmichael said, raising his brows.

"It's a personal matter. Shall we say farewell to Lady Kendrick and be on our way?" He didn't wait for her answer but guided her out of the chamber, down the hall. She barely resisted jerking her arm from his hold as they descended the stairs.

Lady Kendrick waited in the parlor for them. "Tessa, Lord McFearson, thank you so much for coming by. You will come to the soiree two days hence?"

"Of course, we wouldn't miss it for the world," Tessa replied when she was certain McFearson was about to say no. "And I will be sure to send around my recipe for purifying the air."

"I appreciate it, Tessa," their hostess said, giving Tessa's fingers a squeeze.

As they were ushered to the front door and were handed into the barouche, Tessa frowned at McFearson. "What was that rudeness all about? Why did you practically knock over poor Bartholomew?"

McFearson scowled. "Oh, now it's Bartholomew, is it? Is he one of your former lovers?"

"My God, McFearson. Could you possibly be jealous?"

He froze, then ran a hand through his dark hair. "Bloody hell, I hope not." He looked at her with such horror that she was deeply affronted.

For several minutes silence reigned. Irritated, angry and . . . hurt, she refused to acknowledge the man's presence.

He gave her a moody glance. "If nothing was going on between the two of you, then why did you give me that look?"

"What kind of a look do you mean?"

"The look that most people reserve for a three-armed man in one of your Gypsy circuses."

She didn't want to share her idiotic ideas with him. He would laugh. He would scoff.

He would look at her as if she were a Gypsy freak.

"You were sharing something with him that you didn't want me to know. If it wasn't sex, then what was it?"

Suddenly his casual reference to her supposed infidelity irritated her, made her want to shout. She knew she was being irrational, but she didn't care. "It's something that I refuse to share . . . not with you. Not with anybody. *Because it's mine.*"

"And what is that?"

"My virginity."

Chapter Eleven

An unbearable aching cold had permeated Allegro, numbing his whole side. It was an insidious cold, and it had begun to freeze his heart.

Now fire licked at the frost, thawing his wasted skin, breathing the warmth of life back into his flesh, causing another ache to flash through him so hot he thought he'd gone to purgatory . . . or Sedah. Days melted into nights, a voice came and went, a creature with scales floated into his dreams. Its leathery, clawlike fingers touched him, carried him off.

He dreamed of Largo crying out for him, of being lifted by a dragon, of the thrum of great wings beating the air as he was carried away into the night.

Then his dreams turned grim. Green grasses curled up, withered into nothing as evil seeped into the lands. Grief and hopelessness hung in the air as humans wore chains about their necks, marched to slave in mines for their troll masters, who ultimately answered to the evil Morthdones. He was too late. He had failed to find the

152

YES! <input type="checkbox" />

Sign me up for the **Historical Romance Book Club** and send my THREE FREE BOOKS! If I choose to stay in the club, I will pay only $13.50* each month, a savings of $6.47!

YES! <input type="checkbox" />

Sign me up for the **Love Spell Book Club** and send my TWO FREE BOOKS! If I choose to stay in the club, I will pay only $8.50* each month, a savings of $5.48!

NAME: _____

ADDRESS: _____

_____

TELEPHONE: _____

E-MAIL: _____

☐ **I WANT TO PAY BY CREDIT CARD.**

☐ VISA   ☐ MasterCard   ☐ DISCOVER

ACCOUNT #: _____

EXPIRATION DATE: _____

SIGNATURE: _____

Send this card along with $2.00 shipping & handling for each club you wish to join, to:

**Romance Book Clubs
20 Academy Street
Norwalk, CT 06850-4032**

Or fax (must include credit card information!) to: 610.995.9274. You can also sign up online at www.dorchesterpub.com.

*Plus $2.00 for shipping. Offer open to residents of the U.S. and Canada only. Canadian residents please call 1.800.481.9191 for pricing information.
If under 18, a parent or guardian must sign. Terms, prices and conditions subject to change. Subscription subject to acceptance. Dorchester Publishing reserves the right to reject any order or cancel any subscription.

JOIN NOW!

Shederin and now all was lost—the dark world of Sedah had taken over. He looked up at the sky toward Jubilant, but the sky was empty, only ashes and a shuddering pall. Gone was the ring of light that always outlined the rainbow city. Death was everywhere.

"Noooo," Allegro cried out, overwhelmed by the suffocating darkness and pain.

Then everything went black as he was swamped in a dreamless world of nothingness.

Time passed.

Savory scents of bacon and eggs drifted over his senses and he wondered at that. How could the dark world of Sedah have such heavenly smells? And the ground wasn't cold, lifeless. He could sense Mother Earth softly vibrating underneath him as she loved her lands and put nature into dormancy. Where was he? He opened his eyes, his curiosity getting the better of him.

His vision blurred. He blinked, and focused. In the early morning light he saw . . . Uncle Diminish.

No, surely not! The horror of that possibility had him sitting up too fast. The landscape, including Diminish, tilted and Allegro collapsed with a groan.

Diminish jumped up from the campfire and rushed over to him. "Laddie! You made it to the living! It was touch and go, I tell you, and for a while I feared you wouldn't make it. Ah, but you're a sight for sore eyes!"

Diminish's true joy at seeing him awake made Allegro feel churlish. He supposed he could be civil to his uncle, but that didn't mean he had to trust or like his relative. "So how did I escape the dragon? Did you save me from its clutches?"

Ruffling Allegro's bright yellow hair as if he were a pixie-child, Diminish reluctantly withdrew his hand and stepped over to the grill. "Save you from the dragon? No, no, laddie, you've got it all wrong. The dragon helped heal you from that horrible troll magic that you sucked into your body. For shame! Didn't you know what that black magic would do to you?"

"Of course I knew. But I had to save Largo and Dulce from the danger that you brought them."

"Nonsense! I would never put you or your friends in danger. Don't you know that by now? I had it all under control until you went and did something foolish to endanger yourself.

"That was *my* dragon what dragged you from the trolls and saved you from the troll poison, boy."

"What do you mean, your dragon? How could any dragon do something good, like saving me? Where did you get a dragon anyway?"

Diminish flipped an egg. "My dragon. I brought him with me from the Dark Ages. We weren't always friends, if that's what you're wondering. Nooo, not by a long shot. Let's just say we came to an understanding."

"What kind of an understanding?"

Sitting back on his haunches with the spatula dangling from his gnarled fingers, his uncle shook his head. "Now, now, don't give me that kind of look, like you can't trust me farther than you can throw me. Enough of that, or else all of my hard work to get you on your feet will go down the cesspool. I'm fixing a celebration breakfast for your return to good health."

Deciding he was still too weak to challenge Diminish, Allegro relaxed, concentrating on letting the energy in Mother Earth seep into his overtaxed body. But memories of the past two weeks kept a tight grip on his thoughts and he couldn't let them rest. "You led the trolls to us, then left us as bait for the evil creatures."

"Not so," his uncle retorted. "How was I to know they had followed me?"

Allegro couldn't help narrowing his eyes as suspicion kept a tenacious grip. "Why did you use the anti-troll chant before they came?"

"I'm a paranoid son of a half note, that's why. You ought to know that."

Allegro was well aware of his uncle's eccentricities. But the events just didn't make sense. And Allegro was sure his uncle was leaving out a vital part of the explanation— as always. "Why didn't the dragon save Largo and Dulce, too?"

Diminish shrugged as he used a stick to turn the bacon. "Because they are needed where they are."

"What do you mean?"

"I have complete confidence that your fat little friend will take care of those trolls and find the Shederin."

Astonishment washed over Allegro. He was already halfway off his pallet before he realized it, and settled back down. "Then you're more insane that I would have ever believed!"

"What kind of friend are you not to trust in Largo's ability?"

"A protective one who knows Largo's limits. As soon as you feed me, I've got to go back."

"Now you're talking nonsense. You'll only be in the way."

"What?"

"Largo and Dulce. Understand? *Comprende, amigo?* You're forgetting that Largo is in love with Dulce and he won't think kindly of you stealing his thunder, taking the glory of saving his beloved."

Allegro's breath whooshed out of him as he lay there, startled at Diminish's words.

His uncle dished up fried eggs and bacon, his expression calm. "Your fat friend has been lost in your shadow for too long. Let Largo prove his salt. Let the lad save his girlfriend. Besides, he and Dulce have a friend they're unaware of right now."

"What kind of friend?" Allegro asked suspiciously.

"A troll friend."

"A troll friend? Diminish! The words "troll" and "friend" do not go together!"

"Little do you know! There are lots of different kinds of trolls and they're not all evil. Now, listen to me. If, after we're finished with our urgent mission, the Shederin still needs to be found, we'll find him."

Allegro's head was already starting to hurt again. "What urgent mission? What's more urgent than finding the Shederin?"

"Well, he's important, that's to be sure. But there's another dire need that must be addressed."

"Well?" Allegro said, impatient as Diminish fiddled with dividing the bacon, taking one from one plate and putting it on the other.

"Remember the Crystal Tuners?"

"Of course I remember them. They were taken by the Morthdones."

Diminish shook his head, giving Allegro an apologetic glance. "Not exactly. After the Morthdones used the Tuners, the evil rogues discarded the instruments." His uncle handed him a plate.

Allegro stared at his relative. "So? Why are you telling me this?"

"Because we need them."

For a moment Allegro stared down at the eggs dripping in bacon grease as a wave of nausea washed over him. He didn't know if it was due to the cooking or the creeping sense of dread their conversation was giving him. "Why?" he asked warily, drawing out the word.

Diminish chomped on a piece of bacon, dipping another into the runny yolk of an egg and swishing it around on his plate. "Lad, the whole royal city of Aberdora is trapped in one of the Tuners."

Allegro stared at his uncle, trying to understand. "What do you mean by trapped? How can a whole city be ensnared in something as small as a Tuner?"

"That's how the Morthdones took over, by using the magic of the Tuners against the Shederins."

"And they're alive?"

"Yes, but only as long as the heir is alive. He's the city's link to Earth, and he's the only one who can make the Tuners work. He's got to be holding one of the Tuners—which he has access to, by the way—when they sound their notes in order to set the people free."

"Why didn't you tell me this before?" Allegro stared at his uncle, who was suddenly preoccupied with lathering a biscuit with butter and fussing with his napkin. He seemed unwilling to meet Allegro's gaze.

Then, with a shrug, Diminish set his food aside as if he wasn't hungry anymore. He got up and kicked at a rock protruding from the dirt. "And . . . well . . . where the Crystal Tuner containing Aberdora is now, it can't play its key."

Sudden suspicion made his head swim sickeningly. "Where is this Crystal Tuner?" he whispered, already dreading the answer.

Diminish looked up, regret shining in his button eyes. "The Crevice of Silence."

The Kendrick ballroom glittered with the prisms of its impressive chandelier. The results dazzled all the guests.

Nolan inhaled in frustration, even as he noted with surprise that the charred odor was gone. Impatiently, he watched as Tessa was swept away once again onto the dance floor, this time by a dandy in tight yellow breeches, purple waistcoat and a cravat that was tied high enough to choke. Idiot.

Something had changed between him and Tessa. He didn't understand the cause, but something had been different in her attitude ever since their first visit to the Kendrick house, two days ago. When he'd stepped into the nursery and had seen Carmichael bend close to her, practically slavering over her breasts to speak to her in that low, intimate tone, Nolan might have jumped to conclusions. Their relationship was clearly more than mere acquaintances. There was a sense of camaraderie between them—a secret shared.

Like lovers.

All right, that was fine. He had known she'd had lovers—even Selena had known that. And Nolan had no claim on Tessa, not by any means. So why was he so troubled by her her apparent relationship with Carmichael?

He had the distinct feeling that she'd discovered something she wasn't telling.

Tessa confused him. He had to admit that she posed more of a mystery than any other woman he'd encountered. He'd laughed over her quip about being a virgin, calling her witty. But where had her statement come from? He didn't know, but noticed that afterward she had been irritatingly silent.

What did she take him for, anyway? The damned woman had been married, after all. Now, with a scandalously low-cut bodice, dressed in a scanty yellow dress with black lace, she was flirting and wielding that fan for all she was worth. When the steps of the quartet took her closer to him, she threw him a dazzling smile with those sensuous lips and thrust out her breasts, then spun away. Instantly hard, for a few moments he was thoroughly preoccupied by that glimpse of creamy skin.

"You are one lucky man, McFearson."

Annoyed by the interruption, Nolan turned to see the

Earl Southey, a man known to throw away mistresses as often as he did his shoes.

"Pardon?"

"Talk is that you and Lady Ballard are now an item. To have snagged someone as enticing as the Baroness Ballard makes those of us left in the cold quite envious. Truth be told, I have tried to snag her for myself, but I can never catch her between lovers. You will let me know when she's no longer your high-flyer, won't you?"

Something foul and dark slipped over him and he discovered himself staring at the degenerate. "I'll do something for you even sooner that might amuse you."

"Yes?"

"How about grass before breakfast?"

"Excuse me?"

"A duel, Southey. I'll even allow you to name your choice of weapons."

"Over the baroness?"

"Who will be your seconds?"

"Uh, I meant no offense, McFearson, and I deeply apologize for any grievance I caused." In a nervous gesture, he bowed hastily and retreated into the crowd.

Bloody hell, he'd wanted that fight.

When Nolan searched for Tessa again, he found her watching Southey's hasty withdrawal, then looking at him curiously. Nearing him again, she dipped once more, displaying her enticing cleavage before skipping away. He reveled in the knowledge of that smooth skin. Then he recalled what dangled between those luscious mounds, and his thoughts turned to the problem at hand.

The pocket watch they'd discovered near the drawing room window at Foxley, the one with the vicious-looking wolf and the strange markings, dangled neatly at her bosom.

The fob was very likely the link to the conspiracy, a

connection to dangerous men with murder on their minds.

Obviously she was trying to draw out the culprits. The recklessness of her actions tightened his gut. Damnation, he didn't want her to take chances like this.

When she flitted toward him again, he grabbed her by the arm and hauled her toward the terrace. She didn't fight him; in fact she gave a low laugh and pressed her breasts into his side. The enticement caused him to catch his breath.

He was aware of other men watching them, their gazes envious. "You're playing a very dangerous game, Tessa."

"Oh, are you referring to my necklace? I figured someone might step up to claim it. One never knows. If we don't get a reaction here, I want to go to Vauxhall Gardens."

"You're a walking target waiting to be struck down."

She gave him an incredulous glance. "Do you think I would be attacked in a crowded ballroom? Not likely."

"Someone could lie in wait for you. Madam, you are quite adept at defending yourself, I must admit, but when you're with me, I expect to be warned. That way I can be prepared to assist you in the event the odds are overwhelming."

She threw him a sly glance. "As I helped you several nights ago?"

"Exactly."

"Mm. I'm thirsty. Would you be so kind as to fetch me a glass of ratafia?"

After talking to her about being accosted, he wasn't about to leave her alone in the secluded gardens. "Come with me."

"I'll sit here on this nice stone bench. There's a servant right in the doorway so you can see me from there. Go on." With a smile, she dipped her head in the direction she wanted him to go.

Puzzled by her unpredictable behavior, he reluctantly approached the servant and retrieved two drinks from her tray, all the while keeping his eye on Tessa. As he walked back toward her, he noticed how intensely she studied his hips, his legs, his whole body. He could feel the stroke of her gaze as intently as if she'd run her hands down him. His blood pounded, pooled below his waistline.

"Do you realize you move like a big cat? Perhaps a lion, or a jaguar . . . or a panther. That fluid motion of yours, the way your hips roll, is so smooth that at times it seems as if you hardly move at all. Even the roll of your shoulders when you walk is . . . animalistic." She appeared fascinated. Blatant sexuality darkened her eyes, excited and . . . afraid.

Afraid?

"Tessa? What is it, my sweet?"

She blinked as if startled by the endearment, but not objecting. "I—I found something the other day in the nursery. I've nearly gone insane trying to explain it, but my imagination keeps getting out of hand and I don't know what to do about it anymore."

"What was it? Tell me."

"You'll think I'm some half-Gypsy madwoman."

"No I won't."

"All right, let's review the facts from my point of view. You had a black spell while I was standing a few feet from you, and you told me a few seconds before that it was coming upon you."

"Yes, go on."

"As you remember it was already getting dark in the chamber and we hadn't lit any sconces. After a few heartbeats, a mist covered the room, a vapor of which I've never seen the like."

Pausing, she took a sip of her drink, her hand shaking slightly. "When the vapors started to cloud my vision even more than the dusk of twilight, for a very brief instant I saw you hunch over. . . ."

"Yes?"

After setting her glass on the bench, she jumped up. "I'm a very logical woman, Nolan."

He blinked in surprise, wondering if she knew that she called him by his Christian name. "I didn't say you weren't."

As if she didn't hear him, she continued. "I'm not prone to fantasy, and I'm not superstitious, unlike some of my Gypsy counterparts."

"Of course not."

"My mind must have been playing jests with me."

"Tessa? Just spill it out. What do you think you saw?"

"You—you seemed to change to something else."

His heart pounded, but he tried to calm himself when he said, "Into a snarling madman?"

"No."

"Then what?"

She didn't answer him directly. "That next morning, you said you only remembered snatches of what happened to you during your black spell. You mentioned a baby crying and voices, but that was about all you could tell me."

"That's all I can put words to."

She scowled at him. "I'm trying to summarize what information I have. If you have any more to include, tell me now."

"No, madam. Pray continue."

With a curt nod, she resumed her pacing. "Then we heard about the fire in the nursery. The nursemaid had left the infant in the chamber, a babe too young to walk or even crawl. It was late at night; all the servants were asleep. When the nursemaid returned with help, the baby was gone and the window was broken. Nobody was seen leaving the hall, which leads me to conclude that whoever or whatever saved the child went in and out through the window."

"Your use of the word 'whoever' I understand. But 'whatever'?"

She rounded on him, her expression fierce. "If you don't have anything constructive to include, I would appreciate if you keep silent and hear my thoughts."

"Excuse me, Lady Ballard. I'll try to contain myself."

Seeming appeased, she propped an elbow with one hand and tapped her chin with the other. "All right, where was I? Ah, yes—someone or something used the window to come into the room, lifted the infant and carried him out through the same opening, then left the boy on the stoop."

"What did you find at the window, Tessa, to get you so bedeviled?"

Sitting down close to him on the bench, she opened her reticule and withdrew a handkerchief. With slow, careful movements, she unfolded it. "This," she said, holding the white cloth toward him.

He gazed down into her cupped hands and saw a clump of black hair, some coarse, some more fine and wiry. Dried blood held it stiffly together. "A cat or a dog could have gotten caught on the wood after the window had been broken."

"I thought of that. But Nolan, how could a man leap through a window that's twenty-one yards away? Even a large house cat couldn't drag a child through the window. And how did whatever it was keep the baby from falling to his death? Perhaps a huge dog could have carried the infant, but dogs can't climb trees."

"My aunt's Yorkshire terrier can."

"But it's a small dog. I've never known a large dog to climb trees."

Something dark, unknown, roiled inside him. "Just what are you implying, Tessa?"

She wadded up the evidence in its protective cloth and thrust it into her indispensable. Then she rubbed her temples. "I don't know! I can't put my finger on what happened after your spell descended. You crouched down, then what? All I know is that I've got to stay awake the next time you have a black spell. Somehow, some way, I must find a concoction that will counter the vapors rendering those around you unconscious."

She patted her indispensable. "I've mixed together a number of ingredients that have helped me keep alert in the past. Cayenne, pennyroyal and a pinch of shepherd's purse do the trick well."

"The night is late. Shall we bid our hosts farewell?"

"But I cannot possibly retire as yet. I hear another reel beginning to play."

"I have watched you cavort all evening with an energy I've found lacking even in the king's army. Tessa, how will you know when to take the concoction when you only get a few moments of warning before one of my black spells?"

"Yes, I've thought of that."

Her eyes were incredibly dark. "Well, how do you propose to do it?"

"I'll continue dosing myself night and day until you have another spell."

"Don't you think it would be best if I don't have one of my black spells in front of the *haute ton*?"

"Oh! You're quite right, my lord. So let me suggest another activity to keep me entertained in my stimulated state. Another stimulant, so to speak, just as rambunctious as dancing."

Despite his resolve to keep her at arm's length, he felt his lower body tighten. "Such as?"

"To keep your blade sharp, and to keep my rhythm honed. I've found the greatest success is all in timing."

Damn, but she was serious. His blade lengthened, grew hard.

"But we must keep our activity private since I don't want to upset the servants."

"Tessa? Can you entertain such activity without getting emotionally involved?"

"Of course. After all, emotions only cause one to become reckless, which might cause one to make the wrong move."

Confused, he frowned. "The wrong move? How could it be wrong?"

She threw him an incredulous stare. "Why, one slip could get a person killed."

Chapter Twelve

"Psst," someone whispered from the shadows of the Kendricks' dark garden.

The look in McFearson's smoky eyes had sent sensual shivers up and down Tessa's spine. Just talking to the man, sitting close together on the secluded bench, caused a strange flutter in her stomach. It took a moment to realize someone was trying to get her attention.

But when Milo stepped out from behind the bushes, it was as if she'd been doused in an autumn rain. "My lady? Is he causing you trouble?" He glared at McFearson.

"Milo! What has gotten into you? Surely you came here for another reason, not to berate members of the *ton*."

Sticking out his lower lip, he shot another suspicious glance at the earl, then pulled out a slip of paper. "A missive for you, m'lady. I'll leave now, but I must warn you once again to watch your back." With a last warning glare, he slipped back into the shadows of the foliage.

For several moments, she looked toward the spot Milo had vacated. "What's wrong with him? Why is he so hostile toward you?" Disturbed by Milo's change in attitude, she stared after him a moment more.

"Don't you know by now? After all the men you have conquered?"

"What does that mean?"

"The lad's in love."

"Pshaw. Don't be ridiculous." As if she conquered men! Rolling her eyes to hide her embarrassment, she unfolded the paper. Skeet had sent the message.

I've got someone who wants to talk to you in exchange for protection. Come to The Cock and Bull tomorrow night at ten o'clock.

Excitement flowed through her.

"What is it? Good news or bad?"

Caution reared its wary head. This was the first lead she'd had since she started searching for clues about the conspiracy. Although she was beginning to doubt that McFearson was involved, she still couldn't completely rule him out. She slipped the missive into her reticule. "You'll discover the importance of the message in due time. Shall we leave?"

"Lady Ballard," someone said from the doorway of the ballroom.

She turned to see Edward and smiled in greeting. "Mr. Perry. It's good to see you, sir." In silent invitation, she grasped Nolan's arm and led him back inside.

"Likewise, my dear. I heard from Carmichael that you were here."

"Have you met Nolan, the Earl McFearson?"

"Yes, we served in Parliament together, as well as other business. But that was years ago. It's nice to see you again," the older man murmured, bowing his balding head.

McFearson nodded. "Likewise. Although the war is

over, I'm certain you have your hands full with matters of national security. After all, Bonaparte is still a threat."

Although it was known that Perry involved himself in the safety of England, the speculative look McFearson threw her made Tessa wonder if he suspected she was a spy.

Perry didn't miss a beat, not giving any indication that he was alarmed by the comment of public protection. "Yes, Bonaparte is a worry. I really believe the best place for him is a deserted island in the Pacific."

"I'm in agreement with Perry," Carmichael said as he joined them. "One can never be too careful with a man as wily and conniving as Boney is."

"Well, I will continue in my attempts to persuade the powers that be to relocate him," Perry murmured.

Tessa tapped Perry on the arm. "Enough talk about politics, dear sirs. What I want to know is, has Lady Benson returned from her trip abroad?" She knew full well that both Perry and Carmichael would understand her unspoken question. By mentioning the fictitious Lady Benson, the decoy to camouflage the rendezvous house on Borough High Street, she was really asking whether or not they had heard anything from Count Aigre, their primary contact in France.

"Not yet, my dear," Perry murmured. "My sister isn't due back for another week or so. I'm sure she'll want to invite you to tea when she returns. She enjoys telling you of her travels."

So Perry expected to hear something soon and when he did he would inform Tessa. She smiled. "And I do love to hear of her adventures."

"Yes, although I'm certain hers could never match yours," Nolan murmured.

The ballroom was becoming crowded. A man backed into Carmichael, causing him to jostle Perry's drink.

She saw the glass tilt but couldn't step back in time. The cold shock of brandy hit her bare skin as it spilled down the front of her gown. She gasped. Jostled, pushed this way and that, she struggled for balance. Then for a moment she was sandwiched between Perry and McFearson with Carmichael's arm jammed against her side. But she was most aware of how her derrière seemed to be cradled against McFearson's hard, masculine body.

When the crowd ebbed, giving them a little breathing room, Tessa sighed in relief.

"Oh my dear, I'm terribly sorry," Perry cried, retrieving a handkerchief from his waistcoat pocket to dab at her chest.

Immediately McFearson pushed his hand away and tucked Tessa into his side in a possessive move. The reaction surprised Tessa. A warm ribbon of pleasure coursed through her.

Perry's eyebrows shot up. Then he gave Tessa and McFearson a significant look.

"We must take our leave," Nolan said. "Please inform Lady Kendrick," he added over his shoulder as he ushered her through the throng. His ability to do that was impressive; the crowd fell back and parted as the guests saw him coming, his impressive stature too large to ignore.

When they finally reached the courtyard and had a footman retrieve McFearson's town coach, Tessa's sensation of being trapped finally subsided. "Do you think there was such a crush because of word of the fire and baby Phillip's survival? I saw several guests going upstairs."

The footman arrived with their coach. McFearson waved the man aside as he took over the duty of handing her up in the carriage. The warmth from his gloved hand cradling hers and his touch on her lower back left her skin tingling even after she sat down.

He settled on the seat across from her. "You don't think the interest in going above stairs was guests searching out little interludes?"

What would it be like to have an interlude with McFearson? No, she wouldn't think about that. "Perhaps a few; but I heard several people discuss the incident and speculate who the baby's rescuer was. I heard theories ranging from a hunchback who was ashamed of his looks to a rake who didn't want to spoil his image—all the way to angels."

"But nothing said of a dog or cat with magical abilities?"

Heat burned her cheeks as embarrassment surged through her. "That is certainly more plausible than the idea of angels. After all, if there were such things as guardian angels, don't you think Selena would be the first to benefit from one?"

His lips thinned as he simply stared at her. Then he turned his head and looked into the darkened streets. She had the feeling that he could see in the dark—like a cat.

Cease your fantastical thoughts, she admonished herself. Then he turned to glance at her. The almost languid look in his eyes made her heart pound. Sensuality oozed from him. He grasped her hand and caressed her fingers. "So you know Perry. You are beginning to make sense to me now."

"I don't know what you mean," she replied a little breathlessly.

He merely smiled and rubbed the backs of her fingers against his full lips. The motion caused her to shudder with desire.

By the time they arrived at the townhouse, she couldn't bear to sit any longer. The smell of brandy from the spill, not to mention the uncomfortable dampness, combined with the effects of the stimulating concoction she'd been drinking, made her feel like a madwoman.

"As soon as I change into another dress, I'll meet you in your bedchamber," she murmured as the wheels rolled to a halt. Not even waiting for McFearson to disembark first, as was customary, she vaulted from the carriage.

Addington sat in a chair he'd propped in the corner of the foyer. He leaned against the wall, his snore gentle. Briefly, she wondered if she should have the servants put a fainting couch there instead. He would be much more comfortable. She patted her butler's frail shoulder to wake him. "You may retire, Addington."

Not waiting for him to stand, she was already climbing the stairs. She turned in time to see McFearson supporting the old servant as he walked toward the servants' quarters. Warmth continued to curl its way through her at the sight of his gentle handling of the old man.

But energy thrummed in her veins and she began yanking down her dress. She blamed her urgency on the herbs and on her worry of possibly missing the black spell should it hit him tonight. She'd never spent this much time in a man's presence. The fact that they'd been together day and night for the past week, ever since she'd jumped to his defense in the alley, was unusual.

She'd become accustomed to his presence. That was all. It wasn't that she'd begun to crave his presence. No, certainly not that.

And of course there were the strange black spells. She mustn't forget those. If a black spell came over him, it could happen in a couple of heartbeats. That was the reason she didn't want to be separated from him for long.

Her bodice was already half off by the time she stepped

into her chambers. Tossing her reticule on the bed, she made record time kicking off the rest of her skirts. Her corset was soaked in brandy. Since her maid had long retired, Tessa had to struggle with reaching the hooks in the back, managing the top two, then twisting the thing to get it off, tearing the middle two fasteners.

Even though she now stood naked except for her stockings and garters, she could still smell the stench of alcohol on her. She didn't want to bother with disturbing the servants for warm water so she used the cold water in the basin from earlier that evening, sousing a cloth with her favorite bar of rose-scented soap. Her chilly ablutions along with the fresh scent of her perfumed soap helped calm her strained nerves. Patting herself dry, she considered what she would wear. She pulled on her favorite chemise, made of sheer linen and scalloped in intricate lace.

Not bothering with a corset or petticoats, she went straight for her day dress, one of several that she had specially made because she couldn't always depend on a maid to help her. It buttoned easily up the front and she slipped it on gratefully. The worn, soft cotton felt good against her skin.

Grasping her sword, she went back down the hall to engage McFearson in a little fencing practice. She wondered if he was up to the vigorous workout she planned to give him.

The blood zinged through Nolan as he thought of his upcoming sensual play with Tessa. He'd heard of Tessa's remarkable, abandoned lovemaking, and despite his resolve to not become involved with another woman, he knew he was going to make an exception tonight. He was glad that she was no bath miss, that she was well experienced—a woman of the world. That way, she would expect nothing from him, nothing other than physical release.

For he couldn't risk getting close to woman again, not after Selena's violent death.

Her eagerness to prepare for him was promising. He wondered if she would come after him with the same enthusiasm that she demonstrated in her swordplay.

The thought of all that feminine strength and vitality zeroed in on him made him hard, produced a fine sheen of sweat on his overheated body. He'd just stripped down to his waist and was pulling off the second boot when she walked into his chambers uninvited.

She wore a faded blue dress sprigged with pale pink primroses, fascinating because it had an intricate row of buttons down the front, something that already played havoc with his imagination. He envisioned himself using his mouth to undo each one of them, taking his time. The scent of brandy was gone. In its place was freshly scrubbed skin smelling of roses and woman. His whole gut tightened in response.

"Are you prepared for our exercise?" Blinking in surprise, she stared at him for a few seconds before a frown wrinkled her delicate brows. "I can appreciate the fact that you might not want to wear your waistcoat because it would hinder your movements. As a matter of fact, I suppose I could even understand how you would want to take off your shirt. But your boots? Won't you need them to help your balance?"

"I would rather run my bare feet up your calves and feel your silky legs wrapped around me than keep my boots on."

"What kind of fencing are you proposing?"

It was his turn to frown in confusion.

The corner of her full lips suddenly curved up. "McFearson, you like to live dangerously. What is this? Did you think I came here for an interlude?"

It was then that he noticed she carried her sword. "Ah, a little exercise in swordplay, is it? Then let's do this; instead of drawing blood, the loser must remove an article of clothing."

His proposition made the air suddenly hard to breathe. Tilting her head, she tossed him a superior look. "So you enjoy sparring in the nude, do you?"

He finished yanking off his boot.

"Ah, shouldn't you leave that on? After all, you don't have much clothing to spare. You'll be naked in five minutes' time."

He decided to rile her a little. Smiling, he gave her a conceited look of his own. "On the contrary, madam. I thought to give you a little advantage because I'll have you stripped before you can do much more than get my socks off."

"Boastful, are we?" She threw him an arrogant smile, but he could see the snap in her dark eyes.

"One more condition. Whoever wins all the clothing will abide by the victor's dictates for the rest of the night."

"I shall enjoy having you as my slave for the evening." Tessa was competitive and he discovered that he liked that trait. Never had a woman pitted herself against him in the manner that she did and he found the experience enthralling.

"*En garde!*" she said and took her stance, thrusting her left leg forward, raising her sword high behind her.

He touched his sword with hers, assuming a similar stance and noticing how her gaze traveled over his bared chest and arms, venturing to his stomach . . . and lower. The touch of that gaze heated his already stimulated body. He wanted to conquer, but she wouldn't be easy. Her cheeks were flushed and her eyes glowed. He waited for her to make the first move.

She whipped her sword around, switching from one side of his blade to the other, her slender wrist making the shift appear easy. He countered the move by using a controcavazione, flicking his blade over and reversing positions again, causing her blade to end where it had started.

He glanced into her eyes and realized she was no longer watching his sword, but was focused on him. Although she sparred with him, she seemed flustered, her attention fixed on his bared arms, on his chest.

Shamelessly he used her preoccupation to surprise her with the same tactic she'd employed, continuing the move until the tip of his sword nicked her neckline, severing off one of her buttons.

"A point for me. Do you concede?"

Blinking, she glanced down at the missing button as if she had just realized the damage done. She frowned, then lay her sword down on the bed before sitting on a nearby chair.

He raised his brows. "What are you doing?"

"I'm going to take off a shoe."

"Ah-ah. I'm entitled to name the article of clothing. Your dress."

Her jaw slackened. "Excuse me?"

"Are you going to renege on our bargain so easily?" he asked silkily.

She frowned. "But I never agreed to allow you to choose."

He threw down the gauntlet. "Are you so afraid I'll win?"

"In your dreams." She stood. "All right, since this will be the only article of clothing you'll win, I suppose you do have to rise to caution and make your only coup a good one."

He grinned, enjoying himself immensely. "The dress," he repeated and motioned toward her with his sword.

She started to turn around to unbutton the front, but he stopped her by placing the flat of his sword against her shoulder. The frown she gave him couldn't hide the budding sexual excitement in her midnight eyes.

Slowly she slipped the buttons from their holes, her fingers slightly shaking. Her ebony hair had come down on one side; the dark waterfall hid part of her face, flowing over one breast.

Why did she suddenly seem shy? Was it an act? He decided it must be . . . and her ploy was certainly raising his temperature to a level as hot as the sun.

He used the flat of his sword to gently sweep the fall of hair behind her shoulder. The action made her freeze. She glanced up. Although a flash of vulnerability softened her eyes, he realized she was anything but defenseless. He reveled in the fact that she could walk out any time she wanted, could defend herself against any foe. At the moment, she was conquered but hadn't lost the battle. Excitement thrumming through him, he leaned back on a chest of drawers to watch.

Her hands hesitated on the fourth button, the one directly in line with her cleavage. Then she glanced at him and her jawline flexed. The manner in which she tilted up her chin told him she would meet his challenge head on.

Not taking her intent gaze from him, she continued to release the dainty blue buttons from their holes, then paused slightly before spreading the material apart to expose her only undergarment—a chemise.

The linen was incredibly feminine, the sheer gossamer fabric edged with dainty lace. But what was underneath stole his breath away.

Her breasts were magnificent. Through the sheer white fabric he could see that the small mounds were high and perfectly formed. His mouth went dry and he yearned to touch her. Then she drew the dress farther down her arms and let it fall to the floor.

His breath clogged his throat. Although the chemise

was straight, it hugged her slim hips, showing the indentation of her waist and the dark curls at the juncture of her thighs. Her legs were exquisitely shaped. Beneath the knee-length chemise he could see a pink garter above each shapely knee. Her ankles were as shapely as those of any dancer at Vauxhall Gardens, beautifully displayed above her pink shoes.

Aching with the need to stroke her, he suddenly didn't know whether or not he could carry on with this little game they had begun. He started toward her.

She retrieved her sword from the bed and held it up. *"En garde,"* she said, thrusting a slender leg forward, turning her side to him so that he could see the jut of her breasts.

Bloody hell.

Determination glinting in her eyes, she feinted and twirled her wrist in a clockwise motion, making him counter the stroke by hoisting upward. Gritting his teeth, he tried to ignore his throbbing length. But the enticing jiggle of her firm breasts distracted him, and the flex of her round derriére as she leapt toward him had him panting with desire.

Then she did the down and dirty—a bastard guardant, a variation of the hanging guard that few of his acquaintances knew, and a move that he'd only employed a couple of times. The maneuver took him by surprise. She broke through his defense.

Defiant, she poked her sword tip in the waistband of his breeches, slightly below his navel. "Point for me. Do you accede?"

The sensuous stroke of her gaze contradicted the sharp prick of her sword. He gave her an enigmatic look. "Well? Do you dare?" he asked, reaching for the fastenings of his trousers.

"Cease," she commanded, the strain in her voice evident. "I have yet to claim my reward." She haughtily lifted her chin.

She stared at his navel, then lower. Wetting her lips, she gazed for a long time at the bulge he knew was clearly outlined. "Your socks," she blurted.

He laughed in her face. "Coward," he said, then laid his sword on the bed as she had earlier so that he could sit down on the chair and remove his socks.

When Nolan grasped the hilt of his weapon and once more stood ready, he had regained his senses enough to meet the challenge she gave him. He prided himself in watching her wily sword as it flashed in and out, back and forth, not allowing himself to become distracted by her saucy breasts as they jostled under the loose fabric.

A high guard brought her arm up, her body closer. He took advantage of this by reaching with his free hand to fondle her delectable breast.

"Oh!" she cried, jumping away, her eyes wide with shock. "So you want to fight dirty, is that it?" With a press of her lips, she used a molinello, a circular cut aimed at his manhood.

With the memory of the weight of her breast in his hand, the feel of her nipple poking his palm, he renewed his efforts, wanting the prize. In a surprise move, he swiveled with a half trade, ending up underneath her blade so that he could push it aside and come up flush with her. She'd already begun her lunge toward him; he intentionally thrust his knee against her female mons.

"Ooh!" she moaned, frozen in shock as he rubbed against her. Sword dangling from her grip, forgotten, she staggered backward.

He followed her, slicing the arm of her chemise so that it hung down on one side to expose her breast.

"Coral."

"Pardon me?"

"I wondered what color your nipples are. A delicious

shade of coral. They are plump and ripe and ready for me to bite."

Pink brushed her cheeks, but she didn't look down.

"And Lady Ballard?"

"Mm?"

"You're hot for me. See the mark you left on me?" He gave a significant look toward the knee that had rubbed against her.

She glanced down and moaned.

"Your chemise."

For several moments she continued to stare at the wet smudge on his knee.

"Tessa."

When she looked at him, her eyes dazed, he motioned with his head toward her last garment. "Take it off."

Taking a deep breath, she laid her sword aside and crossed her arms in front of her, squeezing her breasts together as she tugged at her chemise.

He watched as she grasped the hem and pulled the fabric up to reveal her dark curls, the erotic dip of her navel and narrow waist, her delicate rib cage and those delectable breasts. She still wore her slippers, sheer stockings and glossy garters, and he couldn't imagine a more sensuous vision.

He held up his sword, determined to win the rest of her clothes. Determined to win her body.

"On guard," he said, finally the one to assume the ready stance.

A tremor of desire swept over her body and he thought for a moment that her legs would give. He almost threw down his own weapon right then and there because he experienced the same shiver of need. But he didn't want to give in to her. She wouldn't admit to her weakness. She would claim she'd won.

He wanted to win. "No mercy."

That chin once more shot up. "None expected."

With fierce determination, he concentrated on conquering her. Her skin glistened with the activity and he yearned to taste it. Time and again he managed to touch her—a stroke along her hip, a sweeping glide down her chest to squeeze her pouting nipple, a grasp on one firm globe of her buttocks. Each time he won another item of clothing—first one shoe, then the other, one garter and stocking. Now they battled as she wore only one stocking with the garter to hold it up.

Once, twice she nearly got a point. He countered a jab, stepping close to palm that sweet, bare skin. His nostrils flared as he inhaled a jasmine scent that was all her own. She groaned and arched her back, settling down more firmly in his hand, reveling in his petting. He forgot everything but this nearly naked siren before him. Not quite realizing what he was doing, he leaned forward to nuzzle her neck, to pull her against the crux of his desire.

"Checkmate," she murmured.

The cold tip of her sword against his bare side registered just as his fingers glided along the slick petals guarding her womanhood.

"Concede, McFearson." She waited for him to loosen his hold on her.

Reluctantly, he did, then wondered why he fought so hard. Obviously she was just as caught up in the fire of lust as he was. No doubt her sexual demands would be as entertaining as his demands would be on her—perhaps even more so.

"Drop your sword, then your breeches. In that order."

He allowed his sword to clatter to the floor then brought his hands to the fastenings in front of his trousers. Pausing, he gave her a wolfish grin.

She brought up her sword.

Deliberately, he undid the hooks, intently watching her expression as he did so.

Almost reluctantly, her gaze dropped from his face to his hands and what he was doing.

When his trousers were loosened, he hooked his thumbs into the band and pushed. His manhood sprung free as if glad to be out of captivity.

For several moments she stared, transfixed, as if she'd never seen such a wonderful male specimen. He almost laughed; she was so good at her pretense. But he felt himself pulse, grow even harder, and he admitted he liked the idea that she might find him superior to all the other men in her life. He dropped the breeches, anticipation sweeping through him, already tasting the honeyed delight between her legs, her tight sheath around him.

"Lie down on the bed," she said, her tone hoarse. With her blade still pointed at him, she backed up warily, sweeping each leg behind her as if searching for something. When one foot reached the discarded dress, her face relaxed. Keeping her attention on him, her sword ready, she reached for it.

He wondered at her skittishness. "Ah-ah, Lady Ballard. That dress is one of my possessions now."

Slamming her brows together, she slowly straightened, abandoning her quest. With a sigh, she shrugged, the motion tilting her breasts toward his mouth. "You think that you've won in the losing, but you are wrong. The bed, McFearson. Now."

He suppressed a grin over her demanding tone. Didn't she know that she didn't have to demand anything? He would gladly give . . . and take. He lay upon the bed, watching as she retrieved his breeches and put one slender foot in the opening.

"You can't wear anything, Tessa. I earned the right to see you in all your glory."

181

She drew them up; the waistband reached to just below her breasts. "You're getting confused. These breeches are now mine, McFearson, to do with however I want."

In his opinion, they didn't cover much. They looked ridiculous.

She reached for his shirt.

"You didn't win that, so it's still mine," he informed her.

She pouted, then looked around and reached down to grab his socks. Briefly he wondered if she would try to cover her breasts with them. It could prove interesting.

When she stooped over to grasp her sword, the breeches fell precariously to her hips. With the blade, she cut his socks into four strips, then advanced toward him.

He held his breath, wondering what she planned.

"Put your hands over your head and spread your legs."

He liked it when she wrestled one arm above his head, especially when she had to crawl upon the bed to do so. Laying the other strips of sock at the edge of the bed, she reached again for his arm.

"Bondage, hmm?"

"You'll discover what's in store for you soon enough," she replied, her tone breathless as she tied one end of the strip to his wrist. But when she tried to reach the post, the strip of sock was too short. Frustrated, she put one hand on a slim bare hip and considered, glancing from his wrists and ankles to the four bedposts.

He couldn't help but note how after her initial fit of self-consciousness when they were dueling, she seemed at ease with her nudity. Her hair was completely down by now. The silky mass hung to the middle of her back with part of the dark mass covering her breasts.

However, the sulky tips insisted on peeping out their coral heads to tease him. Even though she'd made a weak stab at propriety by donning his trousers, down the gaping material he could see her curly dark mound beckoning to him, causing him to throb with desire. He knew her insistence upon wearing his trousers was a defiant act because he'd refused to allow her to wear her dress.

With a sigh and a nod, she shucked the breeches, the waistline not needing much encouragement to drop from her hips. As she lifted one leg to grasp the clothing, he got a glimpse of her pink mons and groaned.

"Lecher," she said without heat.

"I cannot wait much longer for the activity you have planned for me." He allowed her to see the desire in his eyes as he ran his gaze hungrily over her.

"Don't worry. You don't have much longer." She turned her back to grasp her sword.

Heedless of his own nakedness, he rolled onto his side and propped himself up on one elbow to see what she was going to do.

She headed for the dresser and laid the material on top. First, she laid one trouser leg on top of the blade and sawed it off two inches below the crotch, then did the same to the other leg. Holding up the shortened breeches by the waist, she donned the butchered remains.

He couldn't help it—he fell back on the bed and laughed. "You're outrageous. Are you always this stubborn?"

"Always," she said with a smile, then laid the pant legs on the dresser's surface to systematically shred them.

She was every bit as enticing. To think of his breeches touching her as intimately as the fabric had touched him made his head swim. The waistband caught on the swell of her buttock, showing off the enticing curve of her lower back. And her limbs. His mouth watered at the sight of the backs of her legs—he'd never seen a woman's legs so shapely, so sleek. Again he wondered what sort of woman would know how to battle. Ah, he knew of her past as a half-Gypsy, but why did she keep up those fighting skills?

When she began to walk toward him with that long-legged stride and his low-riding, cropped-off breeches, he wondered if he would ever survive the sensuality she presented. As of this moment, he realized that his reaction was as undisciplined as that of a young unlicked cub.

Again she climbed upon the bed. He was hard-pressed not to reach for her. But she had won and it was her call. She tied the strip of his ruined trouser leg to his wrist and then to the bedpost. He tried to relax as she did the same to his ankle then walked around the bed to his other side, but his heart pounded so hard he thought it would leap out of his chest. When she grasped his other wrist to tie it to the bedpost, he had a moment's uncertainty. "Not my other leg," he blurted, then wondered why he had sudden reservations.

"All right," she said in a calm tone. She sat and stared at him.

"Now what?"

"We're going to wait."

"For what? My blood to boil? Don't worry; it's already scorching."

That she actually blushed amazed him. "No. We're waiting for another black spell. If you're bound to the bed, perhaps you won't disappear."

Aching, waiting for her to kiss him, to rub her body over his, he didn't understand exactly what she was saying. "You fettered me to take advantage of me?"

"If the tables were turned and you had won, isn't that what you had planned for me? To take advantage?"

He laughed, the bark leaving a bitter taste in his mouth. "Darling, I would have made it pleasurable. And under no circumstances would I have done anything that you wouldn't have wanted me to do. Although I now understand that you don't want any part of me—madman that I am."

Her face crumpled. "I'm sorry," she whispered before curling against his side, her head under his armpit, her knees against his hip.

Long periods passed by; he didn't know how long because he lost the sense of time. During the excruciating hour when the night was at its darkest point, he was aware of Tessa's shivers. He couldn't bear her suffering; he twisted to wrap his leg around her. It was damn awkward; his bicep stretched and his left shoulder felt as if it would be torn from the socket.

She responded by curling her arm about his neck and burrowing her face into his nape. Despite all his discomfort, not to mention his deep hurt at being rejected, his damnable body responded to the firmness of her breast against his chest.

He sighed, acknowledging the fact that he deserved any discomfort, for he wasn't worthy of pleasure or happiness. His life was damned.

The black spells were proof.

Chapter Thirteen

It was right before dawn, the darkest part of the night when even the most evil man goes to sleep, that the black spell hit.

Tessa fought with guilt and desire as she lay next to Nolan, for she burned for him as she had for no other man. But her desire was paltry next to the need to discover what happened during his black spells. Morality called for truth—she had to ignore her silly need for love.

After he'd settled in the bed, stunned by her deception, he'd run his bare foot down her leg, then wrapped his leg around hers, in an attempt to comfort her. My God, why was it that she needed solace when he was the one who was vulnerable, bound like an animal for slaughter?

Unbidden tears burned the backs of her eyes when she thought of his kindness. When did she ever cry?

All her tears had died with Jocko, a Gypsy who'd shown her more kindness than her own father had. He'd been murdered by the Butcher for his six-foot, ten-inch frame, his body donated to the medical school of Edinburgh. The fact that she'd avenged his death was no comfort to her. Although she refused to cry, she was on the warpath again, this time to avenge her dear friend, Selena.

Then why did she feel so guilty about thwarting McFearson? About tricking him into being tied up? After all, it was for his own good. And hers. She didn't know what happened when the black spells came upon him, but the restraints would keep him from disappearing, from running away. For he didn't realize what he was doing—she was convinced of that.

Even if he was subconsciously doing something to render others around him comatose, it wouldn't matter.

She had bound him tightly. He was incapacitated. It was necessary. Damnation, then why did guilt wrench her throat so that she thought she might suffocate?

An unnatural alertness suffused the air.

The atmosphere began to shiver with awareness, prickling Tessa's skin, lifting the fine hairs on the back of her neck. Glitter suffused the air. Immediately she knew the cause—the black spell. Throwing herself upon him, she held him tight, calling his name.

"Tessa?" he whispered.

"Nolan, I'm here—don't leave me. Fight it!"

But it was too late. The fog swirled and thickened in the room. She felt him shift beneath her, his bones changing, as if he was altering in size, then the haze took over and she knew no more.

Nolan heard Tessa's frantic call. His arms hurt; the left arm ached worse, twisted as it was back behind him. He couldn't seem to move his leg. But he could feel Tessa's hold around his chest, the plump fullness of her breasts against him, her strong limbs wrapped around his.

Then a rush of power that wasn't his own swept over

him. The force broke through Tessa's restraints, despite his fierce attempt to stay within her earthly bonds. His shout of denial went unheeded and he was swept away from the chamber, from Tessa.

A heat enveloped him as the darkness spiraled him into the tunnel he'd long ago named hell, even before Selena's death.

In his mind's eye he zoomed through the pitch-black passageway. Then a light appeared, so white that it nearly blinded him. He struggled to understand what was happening to him.

Images wavered in and out, so much so that he couldn't grasp them.

He heard threats, cries, shouts.

And yet he could do nothing.

He hovered in the air of nothingness, helpless to respond.

What was happening?

Chest hurt—hiding—fear lanced him immobile, fear that wasn't his but someone else's. Someone's harsh breathing. Air thick with tension, panic. Killers searching.

Then the soulless night swallowed him as the nightmare spiraled into the passageway and winked out, smothered by the consuming black.

"Cock . . . warn him. Death . . . hurry."

Tessa awakened to Nolan's mumbled words in her ear. For a moment she was disoriented. Blinking the sleepiness away, she recognized the pink and green bed hangings, and realized she was in the guest room with Nolan.

That was when she realized she was half-sprawled on him, bare skin upon bare skin, and she recalled their sensual game. Heat suffused her—partly from embarrassment—but she admitted that a fair amount of her reaction was caused by excitement.

Then she remembered it all: winning the game, binding him to the bed, the glittering haze, trying to hold onto Nolan. . . . Him slipping from her grasp, from his bonds, despite her efforts.

Damnation! Another black spell had occurred and she'd been rendered senseless again.

Lifting her cheek from where it rested on his chest, she glanced up to see that his hands were once more tied to the bedposts.

Nolan shifted beneath her, his eyes closed, obviously still asleep. ". . . danger. Hurry. Hurry. Help. Hide."

Scowling, Tessa listened to his ramblings. Was this how Selena had discovered her so-called premonitions?

"Hurry, make haste, no time . . . too late."

"McFearson," Tessa called, giving him a shake. "Wake up. You're dreaming."

His eyes rolled under his lids before he slowly opened them. The stark fear she saw in those silvery depths squeezed her heart.

"McFearson?"

He closed his eyes, his face contorting. "It happened again."

"Yes."

He flexed one elbow as far as it would go with his wrist bound. "So tying me up didn't help."

"No."

"Oh, my God. I don't know if I can take much more of this feeling of helplessness."

His thigh muscle tensed against her femininity at the same time his manhood throbbed against the inside of her leg. He froze.

So did she. She realized her core was open to his side and that he was pushing against that most intimate part of her.

"Don't tell me that I missed something wonderful," he said.

Belatedly, she withdrew the leg that was wrapped around his torso, embarrassment heating her face. Feeling vulnerable, she got off the bed and headed for her discarded dress, aware of his gaze stroking every part of her.

"Mine," he said.

For a moment, she thought he referred to her.

"As a memento. You see, I've had several interludes but never one this interesting. Next time I'll win and I won't hesitate to claim the prize," he murmured.

Her fingers trembled with what—desire?—as she retrieved the dress. "Don't worry. I'll bring it back if you insist, but I have to have something on to get back to my chambers."

Without another word, she drew the gown over her head.

"Tessa, would you mind terribly releasing me now?"

She blinked. "Oh! Of course," she said, realizing how numb his arms must be. Retrieving her sword, she cut away his bonds.

As she worked on his last restraint, he reached up and stilled the hand with the sword. "You were cheated in your win. You can fetter me again and claim your prize if you ever get the nerve."

The tingling of desire hit her all over again. If she had the nerve? She wanted to just because she never let a challenge go. But she wasn't willing to go that far, not with him. Not with someone who confused her so much. Flustered, she avoided his heated gaze and severed the last strip of cloth.

He grimaced as he brought his arms down, sitting up at the same time. Then he began flexing his fingers, rotating his shoulders, obviously trying to get the blood flowing again.

She tried not to look at those magnificent muscles as

he flexed them. They were too distracting. "So do you remember anything about the spell?"

"Not much. Just voices, fear, mainly from others. Nothing really tangible."

He stood, magnificent in his nudity, and walked around the bed.

For a moment she forgot what she was about to say. She sat down and pulled on her stockings, securing the tops with garters. "You talked in your sleep."

"I did?" He'd just pulled breeches from the wardrobe. His brows raised in surprise at her statement. "What did I say?"

Slipping on her second shoe, she rose, concentrating on their conversation. "You seemed very disturbed, almost frantic with worry. You kept saying something about a cock, mumbling about danger. And you kept repeating to hurry."

"A cock as in a rooster or this cock?" He glanced down at himself, fully extended.

She rolled her eyes to hide her shameless reaction and the fact that she wanted to continue their sensual games. "No more of that. I think we've got a problem. During your black spell, I think you stumbled into a dangerous situation."

His mouth thinned, and the haunted look returned. "I know—you're right." Frowning, he rubbed his bare chest, ruffling the dark hair, making her want to do the same. "I . . . don't know, but I'm getting that urgency and I don't like it because it has happened in the past with my black spells. Somebody's about to die."

Alarm swept through her. "Do you think you could have meant The Cock and Bull? Good God, hurry!" Tessa rushed out of McFearson's chambers. By the time she reached her rooms, her maid had already laid out a fresh dress.

Pulling the cotton day dress off, she turned to her abigail with her arms up. "Hurry, Bernice. I must be dressed and ready to leave quickly."

Bernice showed no surprise that Tessa wore nothing beneath her dress, or that she hadn't slept in her own bed. Wryly Tessa supposed it was because she'd become used to her eccentric employer.

"Yes, my lady," Bernice replied and drew the corset around Tessa, hooking it up the back.

The Cock and Bull. A feeling of dread slithered down her spine. Last night she'd gotten the best promise of information from Milo. Why did she have a terrible feeling that McFearson's mindless mutterings had to do with Skeet and the information he was about to give her?

In record time, she pulled on a violet gown with a pale yellow overtunic and had swept her hair up into a simple chignon.

When she reached for her reticule, she didn't hear the crackle of folded paper. Loosening the drawstrings, she peeked inside.

The note from Skeet was gone.

Tessa looked out the window as the hackney rumbled down Cannon Street toward the Cock and Bull. She fought her growing dread, the nagging sense of betrayal.

"What is wrong, Tessa?" asked McFearson.

She was going to wait until she talked to Skeet and made sure he was all right. But doubt gnawed at her, and the creeping dread wouldn't go away. She decided to confront McFearson before they reached their destination. "Remember last night at the Kendrick ball when I received that missive from Milo?" She waited for him to nod. "Well, the note is gone from my reticule."

"When did you notice it was missing?"

"This morning."

"Could it have fallen out of your reticule? Was there loose stitching?"

"Not loose stitching." Calmly, quietly, she handed the purse to him. But he noticed her fingers shook slightly as they released the fabric.

Inspecting the bag, he discovered the hole almost immediately. "This is a clean cut from a knife. You danced several times last night. Do you remember anyone who was close enough to you to slice your reticule and slip out the paper without your knowing?"

"It couldn't have been anyone who danced with me because I didn't engage in any such activity after receiving the note."

"The crush was at its peak right before we left. Who would have had the opportunity? Perry and Carmichael talked to you for quite a while. Lord Tinsington stood quite close to you before we left."

That he noticed these things amazed her. "Tinsington's little flirtation was before I received the missive."

"What about Perry or Carmichael?"

They were the lowest on her list since both men were from the Special Committee. But she couldn't very well tell McFearson about the committee.

"Under no circumstances would I ever believe either one of them could take my missive."

"Why? Because you work for Perry? Don't look so surprised. A woman with your skills who knows about a conspiracy, who travels a lot, and who has a sordid reputation but blushes when she's naked . . . I could kill Perry for ruining your reputation like that."

"He did it so that I could move freely about society."

His expression turned stormy. "I'll just wager he did. Were you even married? No, don't answer because you'll only tell a falsehood to keep your cover. Why didn't you share the missive with Perry? Because if I didn't kill Selena, then someone from Perry's network of spies did, isn't that so?"

She tried to swallow a lump in her throat. "You saw me receive the missive from Milo," she replied in a hoarse tone.

"Yes, but I imagine other guests did, too. As a matter of fact, I precisely recall that Mr. Perry even commented upon the note and asked you if everything was all right. Mr. Carmichael approached moments afterward." He stared at her. "What was in the note, Tessa?"

She decided to tell him, since the situation had changed and she didn't know what they would discover when they reached the tavern. "You were going to discover what the missive was all about when you accompanied me to The Cock and Bull tonight. Skeet wanted us to meet him at ten this evening."

His eyes darkened. "Is there a possibility that the missive simply fell out of your reticule?"

"This is a knife cut, McFearson, not a seam that became unstitched."

He gave her a long, searching look. "You seem accusatory, Tessa. Are you implying that I took the note?"

Her heart said no, that he didn't do it. But logic told her otherwise. As she reached for her talisman and comfort, she realized she was just hanging on by a thread. The talisman pulsed a warning red, as if scolding her. Strange. Why did she sense the talisman believed in Nolan? As if the crystal *belonged* to him. . . . "I can't help but think how coincidental your black spell was, coming last night of all nights, then your mumbling about The Cock and Bull and danger this morning. It's all quite suspicious."

"And when was I supposed to do this dastardly deed?"

"Perhaps at the Kendrick ball. If you'll remember, you were crushed quite close to me in the crowd."

"However, I distinctly recall my cock being quite flush with that delicious little derrière of yours. I would have had to reach around to slice your reticule and get the note. Too awkward for a spy like you not to notice."

She jutted out her chin, angry that he belittled her observation skills—although he was justified, because she hadn't known her purse had been pilfered. "You did have your arms around me for a while."

Curving his mouth downward in a sneer, he turned to gaze out the window.

She shouldn't feel guilty for her accusations—she was justified in her doubts. Then why was her throat closing in remorse?

"Wasn't Carmichael in front of you during that crush, as well as Perry?"

"Actually, I believe it was Perry who got pushed into me; Carmichael got pressed into my side. So conceivably yes, either one of them could have taken the missive."

"So Carmichael is part of the committee, too. I saw how close you stood to Carmichael when you two were in the nursery. I saw the whispered words you exchanged with him. Perhaps you should recommend me to work for national security, also."

She was appalled at all he knew. Since when had she gotten so careless? Since she'd become distracted by him.

"But heed me, Tessa. The next time I see Perry, I'm going to see that he make amends for your reputation. Otherwise I'm going to find myself on the field of honor every week for the next several months."

"What do you mean?" she asked, startled. "Are you telling me you issued a duel in *my* honor?"

"Don't be so surprised, my dear. Don't worry; Tinsington didn't accept, but I think he'll hesitate to smear your character from now on."

"McFearson, you don't need to go to battle for me," she murmured, shocked at the gesture. Nobody had ever risked so much for her. The very notion flustered her. "Oh, never mind all this nonsense. Are you swearing to me that you didn't slip that note out of my reticule?" She needed to get back to a safer topic, for she didn't want to analyze too deeply how she felt about McFearson's jealousy or protectiveness. She didn't want to explore the melting walls of her heart.

He stared at her for a moment and she had a feeling he knew just how much he affected her. "Yes, Tessa, that is exactly what I'm saying. I did not slash your purse and take the note."

She contemplated him for a long while, the silver eyes, the proud line of his nose and jaw, the length of his dark hair arrogantly flipped over his collar, signifying to one and all that he was above propriety. That was a trait she valued in herself and couldn't help admiring in him. Not to mention the fact that he came to her rescue when nobody else would. Perhaps she was a fool, but she believed him.

The coach slowed, then pulled to a stop in front of The Cock and Bull. Allowing McFearson to descend and assist her, she noted the street was eerily empty. Two sailors, one with a wooden leg, walked into a coffeehouse several yards away, but after the door banged shut the street was silent once more. The atmosphere had a sullen attitude, wisps of fog making the air heavy. The Thames was only a block away, also contributing to the damp, sour scents of garbage and human refuse.

A black crow cawed. Its muscular body landed on The Cock and Bull's tired-looking wooden sign. The large bird emitted another raucous call as it stared down at them with menacing yellow eyes. A shiver rippled along her spine as she met its gaze and she had the strangest feeling that the beast wanted to attack her.

McFearson grasped her elbow, then withdrew his

sword to tap its tip against the sign. "Get out of here," he growled at the bird. After one more scream, the crow flew off.

"I didn't like it," he muttered as she stared at him in amazement.

"Neither did I. I'm glad I wasn't the only one who was unnerved by a ridiculous bird."

Lifting his hand to knock, McFearson froze. "The door is ajar."

The flicker of worry that rippled across his features mirrored her worry. "Mr. Egbert?" Tessa called out, stepping inside.

"Tessa, get behind me," Nolan commanded with sudden urgency. "It might not be safe."

"Don't be ridiculous," she said, walking across wood treads stained with ale. I can take care—my God!" she cried as she saw Skeet lying face up, his blue eyes glazed, lifeless. Although the rest of his body was hidden behind the bar, she didn't have to see anymore. She knew he was dead. Nevertheless, she rushed toward him, sensing McFearson close on her heels.

Blood was everywhere. "Oh my God, look how many times he was stabbed. The poor man was shredded to ribbons. What kind of vicious fiend did this?"

McFearson was ominously quiet. When she glanced up at him, he was as white as the bedclothes on her ticking.

He stared at the massacre, his throat working, his gray eyes anguished, hopeless.

"McFearson?"

"It has happened again, and it happened during the black spell."

"What are you saying?"

His face contorted in pure anguish. "I killed Skeet, just like I murdered Selena."

* * *

The black raven blinked in surprise, then cawed in pleasure. So McFearson thought he'd killed his wife . . . and now this traitor, Skeet? This was delicious! The fool was anguished over the fact. Guilt could make for a wonderful way to coerce a person to bend to his will.

But what did McFearson mean by a black spell? There was something about McFearson that made the raven suspicious. A subtle power in the manner in which he walked, the way he'd stared at him in his raven shape, as if he *knew*.

The Shade Lord flew after the hackney, deciding he must watch more carefully because he had the sensation he was very close to discovering his nemesis.

Chapter Fourteen

"Explain why you believe you killed both Selena and Skeet," Tessa said to Nolan as the hackney rolled down the street. She'd sent a messenger for the constable to take care of poor Skeet, then insisted on returning to the townhouse. The tortured remoteness in Nolan's expression worried her and she hadn't wanted to stay in the tavern any longer than needed.

When he narrowed his eyes at her, she continued, "Well, surely you'd realize I would need details after you just announced that you're the murderer."

For several moments he stared out of the window. The emptiness in his eyes made her shiver. "What's there to explain? Other than the fact I didn't wake up beside Skeet with blood on my hands, as I did with Selena, the slashes are the same."

"You're referring to the black spells? You didn't tell me you'd had one the night of Selena's death."

"What difference does it make?"

"I don't know. And I've decided not to jump to any

conclusions about you, so why are you surmising that you committed such a heinous crime?"

His eyes were bleak. "Because I lose total control over myself. For hours I don't know where I am or what's happening. I only get glimpses of streets, of people . . . of scenes. The night Selena died I saw a brief vision of her terror, of her holding her hands up to defend herself, then of blood . . . everywhere blood . . . of gashes in her body. The next things I awaken to are her ashen face and her blood all over me, on my hands. What is happening to me? I'm not only a murderer but apparently part of a conspiracy to overtake the Crown. If you don't stop me, Tessa, you could become my next victim, and so could Liverpool and the prince regent!"

She studied him and realized she simply did not believe he could be part of it. "If what you say it true—that your devilish self takes over your good character when you have a black spell—you aren't the only one involved in the conspiracy. I would like you to see someone."

He frowned. "Who?"

"McFearson, do you really want to know what happens when you become unconscious?"

"Yes."

"I can't guarantee anything, but we might as well visit Madam Chiartano."

"And just who is she?"

Tessa took a deep breath against the ridicule she was sure to get from him. "She's a psychic."

His brows raised and his eyes widened incredulously.

"Now don't look at me like that. Even the Gypsies think she's good at her profession, albeit they are disdainful that she's only half-Gypsy. Do you have any better options?"

His head dropped wearily to the hand he'd propped against the door. "Just shoot me."

"That's not a choice—at least not yet." Tapping on

the roof, she advised the driver of their new destination and leaned back.

"Why aren't you trying to carve out my heart anymore? Is it because of our sexual play? If so, then you are a fool for allowing desire to cloud your judgment."

Never would she admit that she feared she might be just that—a fool. Instead, she turned the tables on him. "What makes you such a pessimist, McFearson? You see only snatches of things and you jump to the conclusion that they are entirely your fault. Well, I'm very meticulous in my research—always—and I have never relied on such sketchy information as what you've given me."

He looked at her, his hair slightly rumpled from running his fingers through it. "It wasn't long ago, a mere handful of days as a matter of fact, that you were ready to lay the blame for both your best friend's death and the conspiracy upon me. Why have you changed your mind?"

Because I couldn't bear the thought of desiring a man capable of such atrocities.

But she wasn't prepared to admit her desire—not yet, not when it made her too vulnerable. What if her growing certainty of his innocence was wrong? She threw him a cool look. "I haven't decided one way or another about you yet, McFearson. I'm simply playing the devil's advocate by wondering if you have any other memories of your violence that you aren't telling me. You are the key, I believe, to a lot of the obscurity."

"You enjoy your subterfuge," he stated.

The coach bounced over a rut in the road, unsettling her, but not nearly as much as Nolan disturbed her. Then why did she feel compelled to reveal more of herself to him?

Because he understood her better than anyone ever had.

"I suppose it's that Gypsy wildness inside me that isn't

content with a life attending balls and gossiping. I've developed a fascination for politics and mystery. It's my life. Ah, here we are," she said, trying to hide her relief that she didn't have to dwell more on what fascinated her the most—him.

After handing her down from the hackney, he glanced around. "Damnation, this is a waste of time."

Madam Chiartano was eccentric to the extreme, even in the manner she'd refurbished her townhouse. The place looked like a miniature palace in Russia, with three onion-shaped towers topped with needle-sharp spires. Colorful tiles outlined the stoop.

Tessa ignored the disapproval radiating from Nolan. She led the way up the walk to the ornate door and knocked. She heard a cackle and turned to see a black bird flying away from the awning. Her skin crawled at the sight. Why was she so jumpy?

When a servant in a flowing white gown admitted them and had them wait in the foyer, she could see Nolan scrutinizing the exotic silk draperies covering part of the the drawing room entryway.

"Madam will see you now," the servant announced in a dramatic tone as she curtseyed low and made a sweeping gesture toward the darkened entry.

Cloying smells from incense assaulted her as she walked inside. Today Madam was swathed in brilliant blue and red silks. Although Madam's skin was flawless, Tessa guessed the woman to be close to sixty years in age. A few strands of gray appeared in the masses of dark tresses that curled becomingly over the jewel-encrusted gold band about her forehead. Her pale green eyes never failed to make Tessa shiver in apprehension.

"Ah, Lady Ballard, it is so nice to see you again. My lord, I have not had the pleasure of meeting you until now." Madam Chiartano dipped her head in acknowledgment, then stilled, her expression distracted . . . disturbed.

"The pleasure is mine, I'm sure."

The older woman raised her brows at his dry tone. "So you don't believe in my abilities. No matter to me. I'm accustomed to the cynical *haute ton* and am quite aware that they come to me for entertainment, which I willingly provide because it's much easier. Not as draining as when I have to delve into the emotions and turmoil of others' lives. I get paid the same amount regardless. But a word to the wise—you would be foolish if you do not heed my counsel."

"Then by all means, tell us—are we a love match?" He caressed Tessa's cheek.

Although she knew he stroked her to mock the seer, she couldn't hold back the tremor his touch produced.

The mystic raised her brows. "You would not accept the truth about that. Besides, first you need to know about the black spells."

The stiffening in Nolan's posture indicated he felt the same surprise she did at the psychic's words.

"Please sit down with me," Madam Chiartano intoned, waving her arm toward the comfortable-looking Tudor chairs across from her. The movement caused her many bracelets to tinkle and wink in the candlelight.

"You know that you don't need the frills with me," Tessa murmured, motioning to the crystal ball cradled in the ornate golden stand on the table between them.

"Perhaps it will make your companion more comfortable if I do use the medium. Most of my guests from the *ton* prefer the dramatic flair. It might make his lordship better able to accept what I have to tell him. It's harder to believe that I can discern the supernatural by merely scenting the atmosphere that surrounds him."

"I beg your pardon? You wish to smell me?"

"Shhh!" Tessa admonished him and smiled apologetically at the mystic. "Do not heed him. He'll do what he has to do. There are too many questions that he would like to have answered."

"Very well." Taking a deep breath, the seer closed her eyes and relaxed.

Tessa watched as Madam Chiartano turned up her palms and lifted her face, her eyes fluttering back into her head, her expression open as she took herself into her familiar trance. Twice Tessa had seen the madam do this—once when Tessa was a young girl with the caravan, and then again two years ago. The last time was when Tessa's life had changed—when she'd decided to work for the Crown.

The mystic sniffed the air and Nolan scowled, having the nerve to look offended. But when she began to mumble in Romany, he blinked in confusion.

The seer's green eyes popped open, unseeing—filled with horror as she began chanting in a language Tessa had never heard before. Her voice was low and monotone, then gradually became louder, more frenzied.

The fine hairs on the back of Tessa's neck quivered as sudden fear snaked down her spine. She'd never seen the psychic react this way.

"Should we try to snap her out of it?" Nolan asked as he turned toward Tessa, his brows knitted in concern.

"I don't know."

Suddenly Madam Chiartano screamed, her head lobbing back and forth, her grimace one of pain. "Oh my God, oh my God! He's the one, the one I've been waiting for! The time has come!" The psychic suddenly collapsed against the sofa, her head lolling. She was unconscious.

"Good heavens," Tessa exclaimed as she jumped up and began gently tapping Madam's cheek.

Nolan leaned over the woman with a frown of concern. "I assume you don't carry smelling salts in your reticule?"

"I've never had any need for them," she replied, watching the older woman as her lids finally quivered.

The seer blinked her eyes open, then struggled to sit upright.

"I'll call your servant for some water," Nolan said.

"Dear Lord have mercy on me," Madam whispered as tears from her pale eyes streaked her flat cheeks. Clutching her chest, she took several deep breaths.

"My lady?" the maid squeaked in fear as she appeared in the doorway.

"Queen of the meadow, Iris. Get the tea with my relaxing herbal treatment, not that I think anything will help. I'll never be calm again." Her expression stark, her cheeks wet with tears, she buried her face in her hands.

Tessa patted the woman on the shoulder. "Wait until you get your restorative drink before you try to say anything about it."

Rising from his chair, Nolan prowled like a restless tiger. When the servant rushed into the room with the tea, he turned to watch as the maid poured her mistress a cup and handed it to her.

Hands shaking, Madam managed to take a few sips. Even though Tessa's attention was still on the woman, she was also aware of Nolan as he paced, for he seemed as agitated as the seer.

A little color returned to the mystic's cheeks. She glanced up at Tessa, the starkness still stamped in her eyes. "Oh, my dear Baroness, so much danger, so much darkness awaits all of us and I'm so very afraid. But we must make him believe!"

"Tell us what you saw." Tessa said, dread squeezing her as she studied the distraught woman.

Shoulders quaking, the older woman looked down at

the teacup clenched between both hands in her lap. "It's so out of my realm that I don't know if I can. But I must."

"Please try."

Madam Chiartano seemed oddly reluctant to meet their gazes. "Well?" Tessa prompted after several minutes had slipped by.

"I will begin with something a little less . . . intimidating. I've seen his lordship's memories of the night when his wife was killed."

Selena's throat tightened. "Did he do it?"

Squinting, Madam considered. "*He* thinks so," she replied evasively.

Nolan narrowed his eyes. "If you're trying to convince me of your psychic talents with that piece of information, you're wasting your time."

The mystic fixed her eerie pale eyes on Nolan. "McFearson is . . . not what he seems to be."

Nolan leaned against a nearby wall and fingered a tassel from one of the exotic wall hangings. "What does that mean? If you're saying I seem sane, but I'm not really, then that's no news to me."

His nonchalant, almost bored attitude didn't fool Tessa. She knew he ached with the belief that he was a violent monster. Her heart had somehow taken on that same pain—how and when she didn't know—but she stopped her hand from rubbing the dull throb in her chest.

"No," Madam answered, staring at Nolan as she seemed to search for the right words, "that is not what I'm saying. Powers such as I've never seen before exude from you, powers not of this world. Dark forces surround you and the world is in terrible danger. Deaths have followed in your path and more are to come, terrible deaths that will destroy both England and Europe. Only you as the Royal Shederin heir can conquer this dark evil, an evil that has cast its shadow over me as well as the lands."

"What evil, Madam?" Tessa asked.

"Black evil, which has enlisted my help but I'm defying him even now."

"Who?"

"The Shade Lord! I don't know his true identity, but he's here and he'll conquer England soon, and Europe as well. Earl McFearson, who is really a Royal Shederin from the lost city of Aberdora, is the only one who can challenge the Shade Lord. Nolan must master the energy that flows through him, his own powerful magic, or else all is lost."

Nolan straightened from his position leaning against the wall. The indifference had disappeared from his expression. In its place was cold anger. He strode toward Tessa and urged her to her feet by grasping her arm and pressing a warm palm to her back. "I won't stay to listen to this rubbish. Good day, madam."

The seer gasped, then clasped her jeweled hands together. "No! You mustn't go, not until I can convince you to remove the shackles from your eyes. You don't see what you become during the black spells because your mind refuses to believe. But you must! It will be your downfall and the rest of the world's if you do not! The next time you shapeshift, open your mind, visualize denizens the way you imagined them as a child. I know your mind hasn't always been so closed."

"Excuse us, Madam Chiartano, but we have other more urgent business. We must bid you good day." He grasped Tessa's arm and started pulling her out of the drawing room.

The seer jumped to her feet and for a moment Tessa thought she would say more to McFearson. But instead she gave Tessa a panicked look, grabbing onto Tessa's other arm. For a moment, Tessa felt as if she were a bone between two dogs.

The seer sobbed. "Tessa! *Chavaia!* Stop! We are

didikai, Gypsies of mixed blood outside the Romany tribe and we must support each other when we can. This *gagi* doesn't understand us or the importance of my warning, and you are our only hope in opening his eyes to the truth." She barely paused before more words spilled forth. "A glittering fog protects him from our eyes when he uses this force to change into something lethal. Once he masters his power, the fog will no longer protect him from others' eyes. But Tessa, the fog is keeping you from the truth and you're the only one who can help him see it. Therefore we must open your eyes so you can teach him to control his power. Only you can aid him with your strength."

Madam knew about the fog. Numbed shock froze her whole body. Nolan's grip had slackened as he stared at the seer. Tessa grasped the seer's hand. "Do you know what happens to him when the fog renders others unconscious? Where he goes?"

"He uses his power to change into another form. He can change into virtually anything. But his most dominant form is a panther."

What? For several moments she blinked, unwilling to believe what she heard. "A panther?" she whispered.

"My dear, as in the Gypsy fables, he has the magical power—the power of a shapeshifter. Not just any shapeshifter, but the only surviving Royal Shederin. He will save the world if only he will believe."

Although Tessa had suspected Nolan might be a shapeshifter, a shiver of unreality rippled through her. In the back of her mind, she'd considered the possibility, but common sense had told her that shapeshifters were only fables. Now that she heard the Madam declare the phenomenon as fact, Tessa knew in her heart the fables were reality. That explained what she'd experienced when she laid half on top of his shackled length before she became unconscious, the feel of sleek fur and the body of a wild animal under her in those few seconds before she became comatose.

McFearson's harsh bark of laughter grated on Tessa's nerves. "What the hell is this? Do you think we're imbeciles? That we're so gullible we would believe such idiocy?"

The mystic clasped her hands together. "Think! Remember the images in your memory! Do you not see yourself when you shapeshift?"

For a moment he blinked, his expression confused as he appeared to take the seer's advice and recall the images. Then he rubbed his face and glared. "No, I won't listen to your nonsense. If you'll excuse me, ladies, I believe I'll wait for Lady Ballard outside."

"Please, for the sake of your country, the next time you have a so-called black spell, open your mind," the mystic called out to him. "Relax. Let loose of all doubts. No cynicism. Remember the denizens you fancied in your childhood. You must believe!"

The mystic watched him leave the drawing room. "He even moves like a panther. Can he not sense the sleekness of the animal lurking in his body?"

Tessa couldn't help but blink in awe. "A shapeshifter. I *know* a shapeshifter."

"Not just a shapeshifter, but a very special one," the mystic whispered and sat down hard, as if the shock of her vision had suddenly sapped her strength. "I have been waiting for years for him to come. Although I don't understand this unearthly power that controls him, what I've seen throughout the years is the truth. It's so upsetting that he's resistant to my divination. He doesn't want to hear my words and it will be the death of the world as we know it," she said, her eyes hollow and desperate.

Too many questions swirled in Tessa's mind, but the reality of McFearson being a mythical creature dominated. A weightlessness buoyed her, and she felt as if she were walking in a faerie world. "What can I do? I've tried to stay awake by taking a mixture of cayenne, pennyroyal and a pinch of shepherd's purse, but it didn't help."

"Yes, because of the glittering fog that renders you senseless," Madam muttered, her expression anxious. "Let me explore this problem. There must be something I'm missing."

Tessa paced, restless energy surging through her. "Why doesn't he know what he is? Can't he see what happens to his body?"

"He's in denial. I've seen in my visions that this would be a problem, but I always thought I could impart the truth. My time is limited and I cannot make him believe, so you must help him see the truth," Madam replied as her lips thinned. "And when he does realize what he is, he needs someone nearby to help him cope with it—someone who cares. His lover," she stated and stared at Tessa.

"We're not lovers," Tessa responded even as heat rose to her cheeks.

"Aren't you? You have been in very erotic situations with him; desire is thick between you. You are lovers in every sense but the true act, which will come soon."

"I don't know about that. Both of us are opposed to having such intimacy. We seem to be fighting more than anything," Tessa replied.

"Mm. Telling, very telling. I don't have to go into a trance to see what is happening between the two of you."

The seer looked for several minutes toward the doorway and Tessa had the strange notion that she still watched McFearson, even through walls. The notion sent a shiver down her spine.

Madam turned toward her. "You are the closest to him and you must convince him to take a concoction. We must help remove the scales from his eyes so that he will believe. He must understand what is happening to him. And you are our only hope."

"I agree. But what can we do?"

"Does he have any warning when the black spell is to occur?"

"Only briefly—perhaps a minute, perhaps even less."

"Then you must keep a concoction on hand for him. Wood betony, coltsfoot and a pinch of peppermint will open his eyes and help him see. Mix the ingredients in cold water and have him drink it as soon as he gives you warning of the spell. This will help him to remember, to accept what he is. You must follow him, Tessa. Stay awake and aware. But be careful because I fear he's dangerous, extremely dangerous."

"Did he kill Selena?"

"I don't know. But I know he has killed when he was in his panther state."

"How will I stay awake to follow him?"

"Use herbs that stimulate."

"But I have."

The mystic dropped her gaze. "Not herbs to stimulate awareness."

"Then what?"

Madam worried her bottom lip between her teeth. "Herbs to stimulate in other ways, ways that could be dangerous to you because you will be tempting unknown forces, forces that could destroy. But you must not let them."

"Just what are these herbs?"

The Gypsy seer gave her a piercing look with those

pale green eyes. "Fenugreek. Jasmine. Saffron. Saw palmetto."

Shocked, Tessa could only stare.

"Aphrodisiacs." Madam suddenly paused. "But beware of this attraction you have for each other, because it could blind you." The mystic pinned her with a stare. "Your affection for him could cause your death."

The Shade Lord appeared from the shadows. Madam Chiartano had known he would come; after all, she'd seen her demise when she'd been a child and she knew the end would be near once she'd met the Royal Shederin. She'd already been using her mind to call for the other denizens' help with the Shederin. Tessa would open his eyes to the truth; now if only her summons would be answered. But with the Shade Lord's arrival her pleas would end. Now her death was inevitable and she could only hope that what she'd done was enough. Life was so short, especially for her. Oh, how she hadn't wanted it to end like this!

"You betrayed me. You told him who he was."

Her hesitation was her downfall. The Shade Lord struck, a bolt of lightning burning from off a finger. The words involuntarily escaped her lips—what, she didn't know. With effort she used a meditation technique to control the pain and calm herself. Next time he asked a question, she would be ready. She would play on the Shade Lord's arrogance and temper. If she could anger him into killing her quickly, he wouldn't know what she'd done.

"Does he believe?"

Lifting her head, she smirked. "Yes, he believes, and he's stronger than any of you put together. I've called for help, so your days are numbered, you bastard. Very soon now you'll be going to hell."

The Shade Lord's roar warned her of the blast of unbearable pain before he threw the bolt of electricity at her. For several seconds she was introduced to a fiery agony she'd never known. Then she saw the gray world of death.

But not before she had the last laugh.

Chapter Fifteen

"Milo is waiting for us in the courtyard," Tessa said as the hackney turned into the drive.

"It's getting to be a habit with the lad, one that I'll have to break," Nolan muttered, his mood black.

He hadn't said a word since they'd walked out of Madam Chiartano's drawing room. He hadn't commented even when she'd asked the coachman to stop by the apothecary so she could purchase the necessary herbs for the next black spell. Not deigning to accompany her into the place of business, he'd remained in the carriage, his expression closed and withdrawn.

Impulsively she squeezed his hand. "Don't worry, McFearson. Whatever happens, I'll be there to help."

"Just as Selena promised me? Forgive me if I'm not comforted by the idea."

A tremor swept through her at the memory of Madam Chiartano's last warning. Still she gave him a determined look. "The tactic of throwing Selena in my face will no longer work, so you might as well cease."

The coach pulled to a stop as Nolan frowned at her. "What are you talking about?"

"You cannot scare me away with your reminders of our beloved Selena, so you might as well cease trying. Let's see what Milo has to say." She didn't wait this time for McFearson to assist her but alighted on her own.

Milo stood with his legs slightly apart, aggression radiating from his small frame. His gray breeches had a hole in the knee and his coat had a tear in the sleeve. When she neared, she noticed a scattering of fine facial hair on his upper lip. Although he'd been thrown into the world having to take on a man's responsibilities, it startled her to see evidence that he was fast becoming one. In fact, the buttons on his shirt strained and she realized his chest was wider.

He approached her, glaring at McFearson as he did so. "Prepare yourself, Lady Ballard, for some bad news about the earl." Milo pulled out a pistol.

Eyeing the weapon, Nolan threw the boy a droll look. "Not again. Even more bad news? Nothing can be worse than what Madam had to say about me."

Drawing himself to his full height, Milo gave his attention to Tessa. "Well, let's see if she topped this. I've discovered what McFearson did with the kidnapped women. He imprisoned them in his own townhouse!"

"Surely that's not what you think," Tessa exclaimed.

"I saw them there with my own two eyes. Hope you don't mind I took the liberty of speaking for you by ordering the town coach drawn around. I'll keep close watch on the cove for you, my lady."

Glaring at the boy she couldn't quite consider a man, she waved a hand toward the weapon. "You may ride in the cab with us only if you put away that infernal pistol."

"I trust him, Lady Ballard. He has a steady hand and

handles his pistol well. Let him keep it trained on me. After all, one never knows when I'll become dangerous."

"Dangerous? What does he mean, my lady?"

Oh, only that he's a shapeshifter. No, she didn't want to tell Milo anything that she didn't fully understand—or accept—herself. "Nothing, Milo. The earl just likes to be dramatic." She turned and walked toward the carriage, aware of Nolan's sardonic look as she passed him.

The fact that he continued to shoo away the footman in order to assist her into the coach touched her heart in a way she knew was unwise. But his actions spoke of a possessiveness on his part. She discovered that she wanted to belong to him, and that realization bothered her. Where had her independence gone?

The last to get into the cab, Milo sat beside Tessa, diagonally across from Nolan, careful to keep his pistol trained on him. "Milo, put that blasted—"

Shifting, Nolan wrapped his leg around hers, the action hidden under her skirts. Startled, she glanced at him and saw the warning look in his eyes. He gave an indiscernible shake of his head.

"Pardon me, my lady? You were about to tell me something?"

The flash of vulnerability in Milo's expression surprised her.

Nolan intercepted. "The Baroness has a fine protector and I know she appreciates you. Is that not so, Lady Ballard?"

Ha! As if she needed a protector! But as she looked at the lad's hopeful expression, she paused. "Uh, yes, that is, you're doing a fine job."

Beaming, Milo straightened his shoulders, his posture proud.

Since when did he want to be her protector? How would she react if she took out her handkerchief and rubbed the smudge of dirt off his cheek? Or straightened his cravat in the motherly gesture she was used to giving him?

As the carriage rumbled down the streets toward Foxley, Tessa's attention was drawn to the boy. What the devil was that smell on his clothing? Bay rum? Since when had he started wearing men's cologne? Was his hair actually combed, slicked back?

Tessa continued to mull over the lad. The changes in his appearance and scent, in addition to the manner in which he thrust out his chest, made her realize he would be deeply offended if she treated him like the boy of yesterday. This new Milo confused her and she suddenly didn't know how to handle him.

But Nolan had recognized the signs. He'd identified Milo's sensitivity about being treated as a boy.

Nolan knew what was important to this new Milo just learning to fly.

The carriage drew to a halt and Tessa realized they'd arrived. As they exited the convenience and walked up the steps, Tessa wondered what they would find. Evidence pointed to Nolan, but time and time again the evidence was disputed.

Stover, the butler, answered the door. "My lord! I'm so glad to see you. I sent word that you were needed at Foxley."

"Mr. Milo was good enough to fetch me," Nolan answered in a dry tone.

"Oh! I see. Very good, my lord." Stover eyed Milo's pistol with trepidation, then put on a nonchalant expression that was ruined when he glanced once more at the weapon.

Suddenly a woman's scream rent the air. "It's one of the captured women being tortured!" Milo cried. "Keep an eye on the earl while I go save her!"

So much for her protector, Tessa thought as she watched the young man rush up the stairs two at a time.

Confused, she wondered what was happening. She refused to believe that the woman was being tortured because the scream sounded more indignant than afraid.

Hadn't it?

Stoves rubbed a hand over the bald spot on the top of his head. "I wouldn't worry, my lord. This hasn't been the first scream. Some of the women don't adjust well to the training."

"And what does that mean? What kind of training?" Tessa demanded, appalled that she could be duped again by the earl.

Nolan leaned close to her ear. "Why, the women are being trained to perform all sorts of debauched activities for my pleasures, dear Lady Ballard. Would you like to partake? I would be delighted to show you."

The look he gave made her heart race, even as she scowled at him.

Another screech, this one higher and more fearful sounding, tore through the atmosphere before a barefoot young woman with an unkempt faded dress and wet hair sprinted down the stairs. Following her was Milo, holding a trembling Mrs. Campbell by the arm, pointing his pistol at the housekeeper.

"Help, my lordship," the young woman screamed, "that madman is going to shoot our dear Mrs. Campbell!"

"Your dear Mrs. Campbell? She was torturing you! I was going to save you!"

"Save me? From what?" The girl, close to Milo's age, stared at him, her blond brows puckered.

"From the dragon lady. That's what you called her, ain't it?"

"She's no dragon lady," the girl muttered with a blush.

"Then why did you scream?"

"Because you burst into the chamber with the intent to murder us!"

"Not then," Milo muttered, his expression exasperated. "Why did you scream bloody murder the first time?"

"I didn't want to wash my hair."

"Hunh?"

"I didn't want to take no bath, either. And I didn't want to wear one of those torture devices."

"Torture devices?"

"A corset."

Mrs. Campbell shook Milo's grip from her arm and took her charge in hand. "Now see here, missy, it isn't proper for a woman to mention her unmentionables—ever. You're going to learn how to be a servant in a fine house so you can make your way in this world. Unless you want to live on the streets again?"

"No, no, never," the young woman responded, ducking her head. "Will I ever learn?" Her lower lip quivered.

"Now, now, none of that. Of course you will, dearie. You'll be just fine." The housekeeper turned toward Nolan. "If you'll excuse us? I'm terribly sorry about the interruption."

"Carry on, Mrs. Campbell. You're doing well."

"Thank you, my lord." With a plump arm around the girl's fragile shoulders, Mrs. Campbell led her up the stairs, continuing in her instruction. "And getting wet won't be the death of you."

"I won't catch the ague?"

Mrs. Campbell chuckled. "Nooo, sweet cakes, you'll see."

Their voices faded as they topped the stairs and walked toward the servants' quarters. Tessa turned to look around her. All three men continued to look up the stairs.

"All of that screaming because she didn't want a bath?" Milo asked incredulously.

"Women and their theatrics." McFearson shook his head.

"Who can understand them?" Stoves commented in agreement. "You'll learn about them soon enough, Mr. Milo."

Nolan chuckled. "That he will."

The camaraderie between the men, despite their differences in stations, amazed Tessa. Incredible.

With a grimace, Milo stuck his pistol in his waistband, his action stilted. "I need to apologize, my lord. I was wrong about you."

"You weren't completely wrong about me. You have good instincts, Milo. Don't forget that."

Milo reddened, though his smile was pleased. "Thank you, my lord. And I believe I was definitely amiss with you—I see that now."

The look on Milo's face was abashed but admiring. Another fan following in McFearson's wake. Tessa shook her head, amazed. "I believe we have business to attend to my lord. Do you need a ride somewhere, Milo?"

"No thank you, my lady. I'll have a few words with Mr. Stoves."

"All right," Tessa replied and headed for the front door.

"Mr. Stoves, that girl was quite pretty, wasn't she?" Milo asked. "Do you perchance know her name, and do you think it would be all right for me to call on her?"

Tessa didn't hear the butler's answer since she'd already stepped outside and Nolan had closed the door behind him. Besides, she had too many other things on her mind.

As they settled in the town coach once more, Tessa tapped her chin, looking thoughtfully at Nolan. "Why did you heckle Mad Jack and save the kidnapped women?"

"Because I'm a valiant knight in shining armor, rescuing damsels in distress."

Running, that's what he was doing. Interesting and telling. Very telling. "No, there's another reason."

"You don't believe me? Tessa, I'm crushed."

Narrowing her eyes, she continued to contemplate him. "I don't know why you insist on living so dangerously. Why heckle Mad Jack and those other vicious characters? You didn't steal the women to sell for your own profit, which is what you tried to make me believe initially. Why?"

"Perhaps because I really am in cahoots with them. They're part of my criminal gang and needed a lesson."

"No, that's not it. Nor did you do it simply because you wanted to save the women, although you did go above and beyond in your efforts to rescue them. You're providing a means for the women to support themselves to keep them off the streets. But you could have done all that without the heckling, without taunting Mad Jack with your success in thwarting him. It was as if you wanted those thugs to challenge you in that alley, all of them at once. It was suicide."

"If you don't believe I'm a knight, then it's because I want to right the world of all its wrongs. I'm a saint above all saints."

"No, you aren't a saint. I can vouch for that," she said, thinking of his behavior the previous night.

"Oh? Because I love to caress your breasts? To stroke your moist femininity? Because I crave a taste of you?"

His heavy-lidded gaze made her nipples tighten. Her attention was drawn to his groin.

"When you look at me," he said, "it's as if I can feel you stroke me. Right now you touched me with those eyes and I throb for you. Did you know that?"

Heaven help her, she knew what he was doing. She knew he was trying to divert her, and she wasn't a mindless female to be easily distracted and manipulated. So why was she melting like an icicle in the sun? Why did she allow him to slip her sleeves off her shoulders to expose her breasts?

"I can't seem to get these beauties out of my mind," he murmured, running calloused fingers over their tender tips. Leaning over, he nibbled then laved, the contrasting sensations making her whole body tremble and her back arch.

Her mind was in a whirlwind of feeling. He surrounded her, his power, his scent, the charismatic force of his character. As he suckled first one breast, then the other, guided her hand to stroke the length of his manhood, then lifted her skirts to put a warm palm on the tender inside of her thigh, all of her memories crashed over her. She recalled his sensitivity toward Milo, his kindness toward the kidnapped women, his anguish over Selena. Combined with the swirling tide of desire that eddied around her like the tides off the islands of Hebrides, it was no wonder he affected her more strongly than any aphrodisiac. There was no denying her feelings any longer. She wanted him.

Nothing else would do.

The coach came to a stop. "Damnation. We have arrived." His breath wafted over her breast, cooling the tip now wet from his mouth. Reluctantly he pulled up her bodice, his fingers shaking, then smoothed down her skirts. "Shall we continue our amorous activities in my chambers? As I've told you before, everyone believes you are my light o' love. We might as well enjoy each other until we have solved the conspiracy or until we are bored with each other, whichever comes first. What do you say?"

She had turned him down before, not realizing his true nature, allowing him to prevail at throwing up smokescreens. He clearly felt confident in his challenge, especially after she'd gotten cold feet the last time they'd played. But this time would be different. This time he was in for a surprise.

"McFearson?"

"Yes?"

"Remember when you told me that I could claim my prize any time—once I got the nerve?"

His eyes widened.

"I have the nerve."

Purple stars pulsated in the evening twilight around the castle, indicating that the structure belonged to the last Shederin. For several moments Dulce simply stared, the beauty of the place stealing her breath.

For the last several nights she'd crept away, leaving a magical duplicate of her own sleeping body to fool the trolls. She didn't want them to know that she was looking for signs of the Shederin on her own.

The trolls were so easy to dupe and her dumb chit act was working wonderfully to that effect. Now Gergross and Bilen rarely watched what she did, other than to make sure she performed her five-mile radius check, which she didn't really do. She just pretended to, tossing fake faerie dust in the air for effect.

The only troll that made her nervous was Scaley. Although he hadn't said anything to her since that first night she switched places with Largo and took over the search, she had an uneasy feeling he knew exactly what she was doing.

And Largo—something was different about him. He was . . . withering away. He had certainly lost weight and that worried her. She'd thought her magical tonic would have healed him by now, but the gray pallor to his usually vibrant green glow was getting worse.

At the moment, though, all of those doubts slipped

her mind. Her heart hammered as she sat looking at the beautiful Castle of Lorne, which sat on a lofty hill in the highlands of Scotland overlooking Loch Leave.

She'd recognized it, had felt it in her bones the moment she'd first set eyes on the place. The turrets, made of yellow limestone, were inlaid with glittering granite, causing the whole castle to look like it was made of butter and stars. The castle was spectacular beneath the glorious pink and orange sky in those beautiful moments after the sun had set. The merlons were capped with three spikes made of the dazzling stone, the whole effect magical. It was amazing that the humans, or harmonics—the word Dulce preferred to use for the Earthlings—didn't sense the life in their dwellings. In fact, she thought it was rather sad. For if they only took the time and really concentrated, she was certain a harmonic could communicate with his primary home, the one he belonged to as surely as it belonged to him.

Come to think of it, she didn't think many faeries remembered the power of slumbering homes, either. Her professor at the University of Coda had told her that communicating with them was a dying art. She'd been so fascinated with the concept that she'd studied it well. Could she awaken the castle? Or had it been so long since anyone had tried that the castle would fail to respond?

Concentrating, she began the chant that would reveal the Shederin's whereabouts.

Home sweet home
Wherever my dweller shall roam
Far from the sweet smelling heather
All the wonders you shall see
In foul or fair weather
Don't forget me
Your home sweet home.

She waited with bated breath.

Nothing.

Suddenly the windows at the highest point of the turrets blinked and the whole castle gave a stone-grinding yawn. *Who called me?*

The sound of the castle's voice boomed like thunder. Gulping in sudden apprehension, Dulce cleared her throat and gathered her wits. "I'm Dulce Sonata, a faerie who has come to warn your dweller of a great danger to him and to both Earthlings and Quelgheny. Can you tell me where he is?"

The castle throbbed, sending feelers out toward Dulce. Forcing herself to relax, she allowed the ribbons of life from the castle to wrap around her, to probe. The prickling coolness that stung her like a thousand minuscule needles wasn't exactly painful but it wasn't exactly pleasant either. But from her studies she knew the castle tested her for honesty and goodwill, which made her realize what a good protective home the Shederin had.

> *Since you exude honesty and goodwill*
> *Your request I will fulfill.*
> *The man you seek is the Earl McFearson*
> *Who is at his dwelling in London.*

"Many thanks. To meet you has been thrilling. I owe you way more than a mere shilling." Cringing, she realized she was talking in rhyme. "Well, it's not a crime." She giggled.

With a wave, she fluttered away. Blast a flat note, she was a dope without hope. Talking to a castle that rhymed made her want to keep the same time. Ugh.

Perhaps she'd been a trifle more nervous talking to an ancient home like that than she'd realized. Taking a deep breath to calm her nerves, she took her time flying back to camp, reveling in her success. There was nothing to keep her with the stinking trolls now that she had what they needed. All she had to do was say the chant to get Largo out of the gilded cage and they could disappear. The trolls would be none the wiser.

Sure enough, everything looked just as it had when she'd left. Gergross lay on his lump of precious garbage and Bilen lay at the other end of camp, both snoring in their usual slurpy manner. Scaley was leaning against the only tree for miles around, his hood pulled over his face. Nervous, she watched him for several moments, trying to see if she could detect any movements. He sat as still as a tomb.

As satisfied as she could ever get, she crept over to where Largo laid on his fluffy bedcloud in the cage. "Largo?" she whispered, stroking his face with the tip of her wing in a butterfly kiss.

"Mm?"

"Shhh. Come on, sweet lumps. We're leaving."

He blinked several times, then groaned as he struggled to sit up, his eyes wide. "We are?"

"The Shederin is at a place called Foxley in London, so we don't need to stay here anymore."

The sleepiness disappeared. Now his green eyes narrowed and she saw a little spunk in him, the first in days. "You mean to tell me that you could have gotten us away from here before now? That you simply stayed around to find the royal shapeshifter?"

"Of course. It was our duty to find him."

"Not anymore. Not since Allegro was killed and it became too dangerous. A flat note on duty! All my sacrifice for nothing," he muttered and clutched his shoulder, his face twisting in pain.

"Largo, you're sick! But I can't take care of you here. We must leave before it's too late."

226

The stench of troll wafted across her nose a split second before warm snot dripped on her shoulder. "What's your hurry, girlie?"

Something sharp bit into her neck and she was twirled around to face Gergross's rotten, chartreuse face. She realized he had dug a dirty fingernail into her flesh.

His protruding eyes held a meanness that made her shiver. "You ain't leaving to warn the Shederin we're on our way to Foxley, are you? Girlie, you tricked us, played us for fools, and you're going to pay for that." He leered at her with his fetid teeth.

She decided to try her dimwit act once more. After all, it had worked so far. She gave him a worried look. "Tricked you? Do you mean I should have invited you to Mr. Ant's soiree?"

The whack he punched her with came out of nowhere. Pain exploded in her rump from her fall, causing heated anger to course through her. As she rolled to her feet she had already drawn the symbol to daze the bully. Just as her bolt of pink lightning struck him, a ray of green hit Bilen. Tar-smelling smoke poured out of Gergross before he disintegrated into a pile of garbage. Bilen was nothing but a smoking pile of clothes and bones.

Staring, amazement washed through her. "What in the world? Our strikes shouldn't have destroyed powerful trolls like Gergross and Bilen." She glanced over to see Largo's prone body, his eyes closed. The neck of his shirt had fallen open; she saw the blackened rotted skin that oozed over his wasted shoulder.

"Largo!" she shouted, heart hammering in dread as she ran toward him. He was deathly pale and for a moment she couldn't see the life ring around him. She suddenly knew the symptoms and realized he'd been draining the trolls' strength. That was why they'd been able to finally kill the beasts. "My dear sweet lumps, why did you sacrifice your life?" Did it mean he truly loved her?

The earth shook and suddenly she remembered Scaley. The huge troll approached her, his footsteps causing the earth to rumble. Orange eyes burning bright, he pried the bars of Largo's cage apart and picked up her beloved. "No!" she screamed, fear rushing though her.

Before she could reach him, he blew black smoke at Largo. The faerie yelled, and for an agonizing few seconds, he disappeared from sight. Then the smoke cleared and Largo opened his eyes.

He stood on the ground, looking around in amazement. His color had returned in all its energetic green glory. He'd gained back his weight and looked healthier than she'd ever remembered seeing him. He fingered his shoulder, his arm, amazement glowing in his face.

"Largo, you're all right!" She brushed her wings against him in an affectionate caress. "And you took such a horrible chance by using the vacuum spell to drain the black magic from the trolls. How could you risk your life for me?"

"I had to save ye, Dulce. Allegro died saving us. I could do no less."

So his actions were prompted by honor, not by love for her. It was in his natural character; he could do no less than be the hero that he was. That he would do the same for any pixie was obvious. Her heart broke all over again as she gave him a wistful smile. The look was lost on him because he couldn't take his eyes off Scaley.

"Ye cured me, ye made me whole. Who are ye?" Largo asked as he stared at his benefactor.

"Yes, who are you?" she echoed at the towering figure. The silent troll had acted as easily as if he'd snapped his fingers.

Scaley dropped to his knees. "You have discovered

the Royal Shederin's whereabouts and I'm forever in your debt, my lady," he said in a rumbling tone, bowing his head and bringing his arm across his broad chest.

Dulce stared at the troll. "What? Don't you want to kill the Shederin and obliterate all pixies?"

Scaley stretched his arms over his head and prostrated himself before her. "Nay, lady. I knew you were wise beyond all creatures when I saw how you wove your magic around the other trolls. I'm here to serve."

"Please arise, dear sir," Dulce said, feeling ridiculous to have such a huge creature bowing before her. One of his fingers could squish her like a fly. Besides, she didn't totally believe a troll's claim to be on their side.

When he cautiously sat up on his folded legs, she said, "Now tell us why you aren't trying to jolt us with fire bolts like your comrades did."

"Aye, and why you would heal me," Largo added, coming to stand by Dulce.

Scaley raised his head from between his arms. "I was recruited by Diminish. He knew about the injustice done to my clan and sought me out. I'm here to follow your dictates, to bring law and order back to the lands, to help you in ridding the world of the evil trolls and Morthdones and to place the Royal Shederin back on his throne."

Her surprise was so great that her legs gave out and she found herself sitting on a blade of grass.

Largo's eyes widened. "What? You know Diminish?"

The troll rolled and sat more comfortably against a huge boulder. "Aye, he's been a friend to the Runefyk clan since medieval times, and has been helping me survive these past years."

Out of habit, Dulce turned to Largo to exchange a puzzled look with him. When she realized what she'd naturally done, and reminded herself that he was no longer her fiancé to share worries with, she had to step away from him.

Obviously noting her wary look, Largo opened his mouth to say something, but Dulce forced herself to ignore him and instead question the unusual troll. "Scaley, please start from the beginning, and tell us why you are different from Gergross and Bilen."

Orange eyes solemn, he nodded. "I'm not from their clan, the Dingwols," he said in his deep voice, motioning toward the remains with his head. "My clan is farther north in the lands called the Runefyks. The Dingwols always coveted our lands that are rich in podzol."

Largo scratched his head. "What is that?"

"Podzol is a precious mineral found deep in the Earth's soil. Its specialty is that it prolongs life and enhances magical powers already possessed. That's what I used on Largo to revive his magic and vitality. But if podzol is misused, nature's precarious balance is threatened and Earth begins to deteriorate.

"Twenty-seven years ago, the Dingwols made a secret alliance with the Morthdones."

Dulce frowned. "How could that be? Weren't the Dingwols in Sedah, trapped by the enchanted harp?"

"Yes, they were, as were we. But the Morthdones managed to use an ancient magic to communicate with the Dingwols, which made the harp weaken."

"Which was why Maestro has been so strict with the laws because of the weakened state of the harp," Largo interrupted. "Any misstep would cause the harp to break, which was what happened when Allegro brought a harmonic back to life."

Scaley adjusted his weight to lean back more snugly against a craggy boulder. "The evil shapeshifters gave the Dingwols the magic stolen from the Shederins to capture us. We were chained to the very power that made us. My whole clan was made slaves. The adults were easy to shackle because they had already used the podzol; it was in their blood. The children were chased down and forced to eat the mineral. Once the stolen Shederin enchantment was released, the young ones were also enslaved. My mother managed to hide me in a podzol not yet cultivated. Chained together in columns, forced to dig day and night to mine the podzol, my people have been beaten and undernourished. There are only a handful of us left."

"Good heavens, how dreadful, Scaley. I'm so, so sorry," Dulce whispered, knowing how inadequate the words were.

The orange eyes were bleak in his large face. "I could only watch from a distance. From a very young age, I was forced to rely on my wits to survive. Then three years ago Diminish found me and helped me get into a position where I could spy on the Morthdones and work with the Dingwols."

"Diminish helped you?"

"He understands a lot more than he lets on. It was his idea to have me claim I was a distant Dingwol from the south. They never recognized me as being a Runefyk, which they should have because no other tribe has trolls as big as the Runefyk. But after twenty-seven years, the rest of my clan was so stooped from abuse, the Dingwols forgot that trait. They were only too happy to have me, a giant of a troll, on their side."

Dulce shook her head. "It must have been very difficult to hide your feelings all this time."

"It was, but not any more so than what I've had to do all of my life. I was forced to learn patience, although it nearly killed me. Seeing my relative and friends die was the true test of that endurance. Even when I starved in the hills, the fire of revenge always burned in my heart. I want to see the last Royal Shederin destroy the Morthdones. And I reserve the right to destroy the Dingwols, especially the senior of that despicable clan."

Watching him as he spoke, Dulce was amazed that

she hadn't seen the difference in him. His nose didn't drip as did the other trolls' noses. On his expansive back he had hair, but only a few small warts. In addition, he didn't smell offensive like his counterparts. "Why was I so blind to the differences between you and the others? I knew you were much larger, and of course I knew nothing at all about the Runefyk clan. But I'm ashamed that I assumed you were evil like them."

"I led you to believe that. It's all part of my disguise. We aren't like the other clans. But we are very reclusive and large, which leads people to be wary of what they don't know. And if riled, we can be very vicious warriors."

Largo finished a banana and threw the peel away from their camp. "Well, Dulce, don't feel bad that you didn't notice the absence of his stink. Gergross and Bilen's stench was so overwhelming that it took over all other fragrances. Where is Diminish now? Why did he abandon us and allow Allegro to die?"

"Diminish didn't abandon us. He saved Allegro right before your very eyes."

"What do you mean? He was taken by a dragon!" Largo's face flushed with anger.

Scaley shook his head and threw him a slight smile. "That was no dragon. That was Diminish, Mr. Largo."

"It was?" Largo asked, his eyes widening in wonder.

"Aye. He borrowed a dragon's magic to trick the trolls, although I worry that the dragon might be furious to be used like that."

"Where are they now?" Dulce asked even as joy swept through her at the knowledge that their friends were alive.

"They're looking for the Crystal Tuners. The Shederin will need them to restore the city of Aberdora."

The sky was getting lighter. This amazed her because energy flowed through her veins—in fact, she was more rested and alive than she'd felt in a long time. And a sense of urgency warned her that time was getting short. "I'm worried about the Shederin. He thinks his name is Earl McFearson and he has no idea he's a shapeshifter. If the Morthdones are in London, like you say, Scaley, then they are looking for him."

Scaley's rubbery lips flattened. "And if they find him before he knows of his powers or what to do with them, the Morthdones will have easy prey."

Dulce exchanged glances with Scaley and Largo.

Largo gave them both grim looks. "In other words, he'll be as helpless as a newborn babe facing a deadly tiger."

Chapter Sixteen

"Bloody hell. Another black spell is coming," Nolan exploded viciously just as he'd unfastened his shirt.

"The tea!" Tessa cried. "McFearson, you must drink the concoction Madam Chiartano recommended." She rushed to grab the cup from the dresser.

Standing in the guest chambers, she was suddenly glad that she'd insisted on postponing their interlude until after dinner. During that time Addington had retrieved a pot of hot water to dissolve the herbs.

She thrust the cup into Nolan's hands, then picked up her own brew. The water was scalding, but she forced down the brew, determined to stay awake this time.

Nolan, too, seemed determined, although his hand shook slightly, making her wonder if he was attempting to stave off the attack.

The glittering fog had already begun to form around him. "For God's sake, Tessa, arm yourself. Swear to me that you'll take no risks. Swear it!" he yelled, grasping her arms.

"I vow that I will take special care, Nolan," she whispered. She lifted her leg to withdraw one of her knives, hoping that the sight of the weapon would reassure him. He nodded and thrust himself away from her. The stark look in those silver eyes made her heart bleed for him. He was so tortured.

Then his neck corded as he threw back his head, his face twisting in agony.

"Nolan!" she cried and moved toward him.

"Stay away!" He took another step toward the door, away from the bed.

In the past she would have been unconscious by now. The aphrodisiac seemed to be working, her senses remained alert. Then the crystal light thickened so that for a brief instant she lost sight of him. From the shimmer emerged . . . a panther.

Breath clogging her throat, she stared at the creature as he returned her look, the silver eyes as familiar to her as her own face. Then the panther leaped toward the doorway and went into the hall.

Maintaining her distance, she followed. The panther moved amazingly fast. It was away from the stairs before she was even a third of the way down. Then the cat jumped up on the front door and pushed down on the handle. Before she had run through the doorway, the sleek animal was halfway down the block, becoming one with the night.

She ran after Nolan, determined to keep him in her sights. She considered sending for a mount or her carriage, but there was no time. Gritting her teeth, she ran after the loping beast that Nolan had become.

The panther suddenly slowed. Its lazy, almost nonchalant walk as it flexed its muscles reminded her so much of Nolan in his human form that she marveled.

It seemed to know where it was going. It continued down the street, disappearing into the shadows and causing Tessa to break into a run as she anxiously attempted to keep the cat in view. Then it came back onto the street and sauntered onward, turning onto another street.

Eventually, she realized they were headed toward Cheapside. She passed several pedestrians, but they seemed unable to see the panther. Was it because the beast was so dark and blended in with the shadows? A man tried to stop her for a flirtation but she didn't slow, just flashed her knife and gave him a ferocious look.

When the panther turned toward Cripplepot and the docks, it slowed and looked around, switching its tail in an impatient, angry manner. Then it trotted ahead and disappeared into a warehouse.

Frowning, she, too, looked both ways. She could discern nobody in the street by now, only a sailor who disappeared into a coffeehouse. With determination, she trotted across the street, though not nearly as gracefully as the big cat, and slipped inside the cavernous room.

Moonlight shone through the windows from high above. Several crates were stacked in the middle of the warehouse. She couldn't see the panther.

She crept along, her soft-soled shoes quiet on the dirt floor. She was careful to stay in the shadows. A murmur of voices and the smell of gunpowder stopped her.

"The whole plan has gotten out of hand. Too many innocents have died. I won't do this any . . . oh, my God! No!" the man cried in panic, the voice strangely familiar.

Tessa ran down the long row of crates, urgency rushing through her veins.

"Don't—" The man's voice was suddenly cut off with a gurgling sound.

The cat screamed.

The attacker shouted, then there was a vicious low-sounding growl. Fear and dread crammed in her chest, she rounded the corner, not knowing what she would find.

The hugest wolf she'd ever seen bared its teeth at the panther.

"Nolan, remember what Madam Chiartano told you to do!" she cried.

The wolf stepped back and glanced from her to the panther. Then, without warning, the monstrous canine lunged. Nolan did likewise and the two beasts met midair, the huge cat's scream mixing with the wolf's snarl. The wolf latched onto the panther's neck and the cat howled in pain and fury.

A strike of claws across the wolf's face loosened the canine's hold for a moment before it attacked with unnatural ferocity.

The wolf would kill the panther . . . would kill Nolan. Not if she intervened. She charged, aiming her sword down toward the wolf's back. The wolf suddenly twisted, releasing its locked-jaw hold on the panther's neck.

The gray wolf crouched, looking for another opportunity to attack. By now the panther stood beside her, its stance ready. With strangely familiar eyes, the wolf looked from her to the panther. Then the large canine stared past them, seeming somehow . . . pleased. After a last baring of teeth, the wolf bolted.

Stunned, weak-kneed over the encounter, Tessa whirled toward the prone man. She was startled to see the panther hovering over him, then giving him a gentle nudge. When she approached, the cat backed away and sat to watch.

She looked down at the ashen face. "Chumley!" The gurgle in his lungs scared her. She took off her wrap and wadded it into a ball.

Stooping down, she carefully lifted his head and

placed the makeshift pillow beneath him, hoping she could ease his labored breathing. "Dear God in heaven, what is happening? No, don't try to talk. I'll get assistance."

He grabbed her hand, his grip surprisingly firm. "Please."

"What is it?"

"Save . . . my family. Shade Lord . . . one of us."

"Who is he?"

He gurgled something unintelligible.

Something cold and hard pressed against her palm. Looking at it, she was startled to see Chumley had given her a medallion with a figure of a wolf, similar to the pocket watch they'd discovered outside the drawing-room window at Foxley.

"Chumley, what does this mean?" She looked at him to find his eyes staring sightlessly at the ceiling. He was dead. "Oh, Chumley," she whispered. He'd been jovial, kind. What would compel him to get involved in such a nasty business? To betray his country? Then his words hit her.

Someone within the Special Committee was the mysterious, lethal Shade Lord.

She shouldn't be surprised; after all, she'd begun to suspect that someone who knew that Selena was the informant had betrayed Tessa. But to know it for a fact, that there was someone evil in the network of men she'd considered close friends, caused a deep and foreboding chill to penetrate her bones. Obviously Chumley had been coerced into cooperating because of a threat to his family. Still, she wished he had confided in her. She could have done something and he most likely would not be dead. Sadness washing over her, she silently promised Chumley she would protect his family.

The panther stood and swished its tail before leaping

onto a crate and disappearing on the other side. Tessa could tarry no longer. Jumping to her feet, she charged after the feline. The cat had already gained the street and was almost to the corner when Tessa exited the warehouse. Pacing herself, she steadily kept up with the panther.

When the animal climbed the sturdy tresses that served for ivy, Tessa decided she couldn't take the chance of losing it by using the luxury of the front door. Nevertheless, sweat broke out on her forehead when her skirts snagged on the wood, stalling her. Ripping the dress as impatience overtook her, she struggled to the already open window. She needn't have worried—the panther was there to grasp the back of her bodice between its teeth and help her the rest of the way through the opening.

The feline was incredibly gentle, loosening its hold to sit and watch her with patience as she wrestled with her skirts in order to get to her feet. Was Nolan aware of his panther state of existence? Her instincts told her no, that Madam's concoction hadn't worked.

"Nolan? Are you there?" Raising her hands to cup the panther's face, she peered deep into those familiar silver eyes. "McFearson, do you recognize me? It's Tessa."

The panther's eyes flared wide and for a moment, Tessa could vow that she saw recognition in those depths. Suddenly the cat pushed through Tessa's cupped hands, rubbing its sleek hard face along her cheek and down her neck. She froze as the panther continued to shove against her in caressing strokes along her shoulder, her arm . . . her breasts. Shocked by her own arousal at the sensual touch, she allowed the cat to rub her stomach, her hips.

"Oh, Nolan. You are as sensuous in your panther form as you are as a man."

The panther suddenly stopped and looked at her. For an instant she would have wagered that she could see his strong aquiline nose, those high cheekbones, that firm jawline beneath the panther's exterior. Then the cat shook its head and blinked at her.

"Look down at your limbs and see for yourself if you don't believe me. You are a panther."

Plopping down, the panther shook its head again.

"Yes, you are. Look! See that beautiful body of yours, how you have transformed into a sleek jungle cat? You can shapeshift into a panther. See the power of your true self. Accept this gift that has been given to you. Look, Nolan."

Tessa would have never believed that a panther could demonstrate emotion, but at that moment bewilderment flickered in the beast's eyes. Slowly it lowered its head and stared, picking up one paw to look at it, then swinging its head back to look at the rest of its body, including its twitching black tail. Closing its eyes, the panther threw back its head and screamed, the remorse of the cry echoing through Tessa. It sounded half human, half animal. Then the crystal fog glittered around it. One moment the panther screamed; the next moment there stood Nolan.

His dark hair was tousled and his clothes hung on him, the open shirt showing his bare chest and angry raw welts on his neck. But he seemed oblivious to his physical wounds because the horror of his self-discovery still shone in his eyes. "My God, I'm a monster, an abomination of nature!"

So much anguish and pain laced his voice that Tessa's heart constricted. "No, you're not!" she cried. "Heed me, McFearson. You are *not* an abomination. You've been put on Earth with these precise gifts for a reason, a divine reason, just as I have been put on Earth—me, the Gypsy freak with her unnatural skills with weapons."

He scowled in amazement. "You're not a freak."

"The hell I'm not," she retorted angrily. "Do you think life has been easy for me? I'm a woman who can't fit in with the caravan and can't fit in with the *haute ton*. When my mother died and the caravan dumped me on my natural father's doorstep, he couldn't abide the sight of me. No, I was a scourge, a shame to the wonderful earl of Dowley's good name. So he had me carted to Treleven Abbey, where the nuns hid me under the carpet. The other girls thought I was an abomination, a wild child that had no business being in their exalted presence. The nuns were beside themselves because nothing could tame me—not whippings, starvation or humiliation. After being free to do whatever I wanted to do, to suddenly be forced to live under the strict social rules of the *gagi* was a living death for me."

She might as well tell him the rest. "One of my father's best friends was Edward Perry. If it hadn't been for Mr. Perry and his offer to help me by using my skills in society's favor, I would have been lost."

Jaw flexing, he stared at her, saying nothing.

"I truly believe that espionage is my calling. Fighting evil is what I was born to do. Our love for Selena and our love for goodness is what brought us together. You were thrown in my path for a reason. I'm talking about fate, McFearson."

"How can you be so sure that I'm not one of the evil ones you seek?" he asked. "How can you be so nonchalant, so accepting of my shapeshifting abilities, when I cannot?"

"Because I can't deny what I've seen, what my heart sees. You've tried to hide your inherent good nature because of your deep guilt over what happened to Selena, a guilt you wouldn't even be feeling if you were as evil as you claim to be."

"How do you know I didn't kill Selena? Bloody hell, I

change into a panther, a dangerous predator. How do you know that the animal instincts to hunt, to kill, didn't take over?"

"Because I know. In your panther form, you didn't attack me or Chumley. In fact you saved us just as you saved that baby from the fire. It's no use, McFearson. Man or beast, you're hopelessly heroic—you simply can't help it. Just as I can't help wanting you in a very intimate manner."

"What?" he asked, his voice hoarse.

The words came out of nowhere, but once she said them she realized they were the truth. She began undoing the tapes to her dress. "I've never said this to anyone, nor have I craved anyone as much as I have you. You've become a part of my blood, McFearson, and I refuse to deny myself any longer."

He stared at her, shocked, even as his body hardened. How could she want him after she knew what a strange creature he was? That he harbored a beast within? She pulled down her dress, exposing the chemise underneath. Her lilting, upturned breasts with those delicious coral nipples pouted for his attention as they pressed against the fine fabric.

He'd lengthened—his greedy cock already poked out of his unfastened breeches. Now heat rushed to his groin, making him throb with urgent passion.

The dress fell to the floor followed by a single petticoat and shift.

Naked except for her stockings and garters, she walked to the bed, her rounded small buttocks flexing long legs as sleek as any jungle cat's.

Keeping her dark gaze on him, she lay down and held out her hand. "I want you inside me."

"God forgive me, I cannot refuse your siren's call," he growled thickly.

"There you go again! Do not be the hero with me, because in this instance, I don't want one. *I want you.* There's nothing to forgive. Do not even try to refuse our desire for each other," she replied in a fierce tone, reaching up to stroke him, then helping guide him to her.

"I'll be gentle," he promised. There was a touch of vulnerability in her expression.

"I don't want gentleness," she growled in that valiant warrior tone that endeared her so much to him. Then, without warning, she thrust her hips upward. He met with the brief resistance of her maidenhead, causing her to gasp.

Holding as still as he could, although his body ached to do otherwise, he scowled down at her. "Damnation, Tessa, I didn't want to hurt you."

"I'm all right," she replied in a small voice. After a few moments she gave an experimental wiggle of her hips and groaned in pleasure.

That was his cue. All sense of reason dissolved as he almost lost himself right then and there. He plunged deeper, reveling in her tight, slick sheath, in the scent of her arousal mixed with his own.

The sense of spiraling out of control, of sinking into an abyss of dark pleasure, of sating an insatiable thirst washed over him. Drunk with the feel of her sleek body as her legs wrapped around his waist, he felt himself spinning in a dizzy whirlpool of need. The urge to conquer her, to become as essential to her as air, was overwhelming.

A sensation not unlike the desire that came over him when he shapeshifted washed over him. The muscles in her tight sheath rippled over him as she found her release. Helpless, he gave into the dangerous pleasures of becoming lost in her siren's song and let go, giving her the full power of his lethal sword as he poured into her, lost in an exotic realm between heaven and earth.

Slowly his mind returned to his surroundings. He realized he lay on top of Tessa. One hand was covering a breast and the other cupping her derrière. Her legs clung to him. He was still buried deep within her. And to his horror, he was once more becoming aroused. He started to lift away from her.

"Not so fast, McFearson. I want to fulfill our desire again, but this time, I want to be on top."

"How do you know about that?" he asked, unable to hide the desperation in his tone. "Bloody hell, it wasn't long ago that you were a virgin."

Wrapping her legs tighter around him, she rolled them both across the bed ticking so that she ended up above him, all the while keeping him trapped inside her.

"Even though my body was innocent, my mind wasn't. During my life as a woman of the world, as I've chased after criminals, some places I've had to visit have been the brothels. I've learned of several shocking positions that I haven't wanted to try until I met you. One of the whores told me how strange and different positions can bring pleasure so intense that you feel as if you've died and gone to heaven." She gave him a wicked smile, then bent her dark head to lave his nipple with her tongue.

Heaven help him.

As his body clenched with desire once more, he knew he was doomed. His only hope was to sate his hunger for her, then walk away, not only for her safety but for his own protection as well.

Because his conscience would be damned to a fiery torturous hell if he ever was the cause of Tessa's death.

The mystic was in danger.

Tessa woke up shivering, an icy dread crawling down her spine. "McFearson?" she whispered close to his ear.

He stretched, his movements so much like a panther's

244

she marveled at the similarities. Then he blinked and stilled.

Probably remembering that he was a shapeshifter.

"Do you recall how you led me to that warehouse in the night? How we surprised one of the conspirators but were too late to save Chumley? How you got those scratches on your neck?" She stared at the skin that had been so raw and bruised. In the moonlight she could detect no injury. Gently she touched the area.

"I was attacked by a large dog," he murmured.

"You do remember! But the beast was a wolf." She fingered his flesh. "Once again you've healed in mere hours. Is it because you're a shapeshifter?"

"Hell if I know. I'm still adjusting to the whole bizarre notion."

Chills still raced down her body. Unnerved, she jumped out of bed and grabbed her chemise on the floor. "McFearson, get dressed."

"You have become amazingly demanding. First you want to tear off my clothes and now you want them on. You are incredibly indecisive."

Frustrated, she continued to search for the items of clothing she needed. "There's no time to tease. Damnation, I'm worried and I can't get it out of my mind that Madam Chiartano is in trouble."

He didn't argue anymore, but quietly slipped off the ticking and began donning his breeches. Despite her urgency to leave, she couldn't help regretting that their interlude had ended for now. She still yearned for the feel of that sleek, muscular body beneath hers.

"Why are you worried about the mystic?"

"Because of what she said. I don't know if you were there when she said it. She mentioned other powers, evil powers that weren't of this world. And she seemed frightened. I didn't know what she meant at the time.

And while we were in the warehouse and that wolf was getting ready to attack, I mentioned the psychic when I was trying to get you to see your panther form. After seeing the manner in which the beast behaved, as if it knew what we were talking about, I can't shake the apprehension that I put the mystic in danger."

He'd just pulled his shirt on and was scowling at her.

She took a deep breath. "I think we have another shapeshifter on our hands—one that plans to murder Madam Chiartano."

Chapter Seventeen

"Foxley? Are ye certain this is it?" Largo asked, irritated, hovering over Scaley's bulky form as he spoke to Dulce.

She fluttered her wings, still not trusting his love for her even after he'd almost died from draining the evil magic from Bilen. Oh, she'd panicked and he could see the love in her eyes for him as he lay there dying, but once Scaley had saved him with the podzol, she'd told him that he would have gone to those extremes to save anyone—he was that heroic. His cavalier treatment of her love just might be the end of their relationship. Heart thudding, sweat broke out along his forehead as a panicky sensation swept over him.

"Are you questioning the Goddess's word?" Scaley demanded in a soft tone that didn't hide the threat behind the words. Although night cloaked the orange eyes, Largo could imagine his expression. The large troll was very discreet from years of hiding his animosity, but Largo had learned to discern the emotion—a slight squinting of the eyes, a minuscule tightening of his rubbery lips—since this wasn't the first time they'd clashed.

It was just the outlet Largo needed for his frustration. "Goddess this, Goddess that. I'm getting mighty tired of yer condescending attitude toward me."

Scaley took a step toward him. "I'm getting extremely tired of your arrogance."

"And I'm getting heartily tired of this male antagonism!" Dulce retorted. "Scaley, I'm not infallible, and for the thousandth time, I'm not a goddess."

"So you say," he murmured in his gravelly tone. "I'm sorry to offend you, God—"

"Don't say it," she responded through gritted teeth.

Those huge eyes blinked, undeterred, but he said nothing.

She whirled to face the other antagonist. "And Largo, even if I'm not a goddess, I'm not the dimwit you believe me to be."

He blinked, appalled at her accusation. "I never said ye were a dimwit."

"You didn't have to. I understood just how you felt about me loud and clear that day near the harp when I was captured."

He opened his mouth to say something, but closed it when he saw her fierce expression. What could he say to convince her that she was the very essence of his life?

She lifted her chin. "The addled girl who doted on every word you uttered is gone. I've got a mind and good wits . . . and I'm not afraid to use them."

Largo smiled encouragingly. "Ye've always had a quick mind, lass, and that's why I've always loved ye. Would ye please come back to me? I miss my sweet songbird."

Yearning flitted across her face before it was replaced with wariness, a caution for which he had nobody to blame but himself. "Too bad, because I'm not here to please your every whim. Never again. I've discovered there are more important things in life than trying to recover lost love—not really lost since the love was always one-sided."

"Oh, Dulce. . . ." Largo whispered, his soul stricken with remorse. The pride that she held onto so desperately would be the death of their love. If only he could regain her trust!

Lifting her slightly trembling chin, she ignored him. "Even though this isn't the Shederin's principal dwelling, I suppose I can try to talk to the townhouse just as I did to the castle of—"

"No time for that, Goddess," Scaley exclaimed, his tone urgent. "I smell wolf stench mixed with the Dingwols and I fear the Shederin is in deadly peril."

The pall that surrounded Madam's townhouse caused Nolan's hackles to rise.

"The door is open," Tessa whispered, her slim brows wrinkled in dismay.

"Stay back," Nolan warned. With the fine hairs lifting on his neck, he cautiously walked inside. The maid lay prone with a black hole in her chest. Madam was sprawled in the drawing room, just beyond the gaudy curtains, her body charred, her lips pale and bloodless, her pale green eyes were open, still mirroring the horror of her death.

Tessa sniffled. "Poor Charlotte. Those talented eyes will see no more." Leaning down, she gently lowered the seer's lids. "Farewell, my fellow Didikai, my Gypsy friend. We'll miss you."

The back of Nolan's neck continued to tingle, more urgently than ever. He grasped Tessa's arm. "Let's go. We're not safe here."

As he stepped into the foyer, he heard a menacing growl. Drawing his sword, he saw three wolves crouched on the landing above them. "Watch out!"

The wolves hurled toward them. Pushing Tessa through the door, Nolan slashed the one that had landed closest to him, causing it to yelp and fall away. Then he was out the door, running toward the hackney. The driver sprawled half on his seat, half off, blood dripping onto the cobblestones. Nolan didn't hesitate. He pulled the dead man off his perch and vaulted into the driver's seat. Tessa had already climbed up next to him.

Three more wolves growled, causing the already restless horses to panic; the team bolted down the street and Nolan barely had time to snatch up the reins.

The heavy coach careened down the cobblestones, chased by the wolves. The coach swayed when something hit it.

"We've got passengers," Tessa shouted, her eyes widening in fear.

The moon's rays caught an object glittering in her hand before she swiveled and drew back her arm. A yelp sounded. There was a growl very close to the coach. Tessa flung another knife. And another.

My God, how many were there? Desperation clawed at him, but he couldn't think of the numbers. He had to keep fighting, if not for his own sake then for Tessa's. Several growls rumbled in furry throats; a wolf hurled itself toward him. With the reins in one hand, Nolan turned and buried his sword in the beast's chest. Another leaped farther; it bit into a horse's neck, causing the gelding to scream in pain.

"There's too many!" Tessa shouted.

"Jump!" he cried, praying that they wouldn't break any bones. The ground rushed up to meet him and he rolled with the impact, ignoring the pain jarring his shoulder. On his feet, he looked around for Tessa, fear clogging his throat. Relief crashed over him when he realized that she was already by his side, grasping his hand.

But relief was premature; the remaining wolves had jumped off the hackney and were loping back toward them with alarming speed.

Heart thundering, Nolan yanked on her hand. "This way!"

"Dear God, I hope you have a plan."

"I do." He thought of the most dangerous tavern in the stews of London—simply known as The Cutthroat—the place that hosted the worst criminals in town. It wasn't far, but too far for them to get to without being overtaken by the four-legged beasts.

"Can't you shapeshift?" Tessa gasped.

Frustration clawed at him. "I don't know how!"

The canines were closing in. "Too many anyway," she muttered, and apparently got another spurt of energy because she suddenly urged him onward.

A door opened, the diversion they needed to gain distance between them and their pursuers. Holding onto Tessa's hand, Nolan pushed a sailor aside and bolted into a tavern, pushing them through the crowd and out a back door that dumped them into the alley. A man screamed in terror and several curses followed, but neither he nor Tessa stopped in their flight. Tessa's stamina amazed him as she kept pace with him. Glancing back, he wondered for a few moments if they had lost the wolves, but five emerged from the alley far behind them. He urged Tessa onward. By now he had a stitch in his side and his breath came in pants.

"Not far now," he said to encourage himself as well as her. The Cutthroat's dilapidated sign loomed ahead. He reached for the door handle.

"But isn't this where Mad Jack—"

He didn't allow her to finish, but pulled her inside.

The low murmur of voices ceased. A sullen atmosphere permeated the room. Mad Jack, Rat Chaser and Deadwood Dials suddenly stood. Torch stood in a corner. All four wore nasty grins.

"Ah, we were wondering how ta get ya to our neck of the woods so we could kill ya," Mad Jack sneered. "We haven't forgotten how ya poached on our territories."

Torch grinned, showing gaps in his teeth. He moved to Nolan's right. "Thanks for obliging us."

Giving Tessa's hand a warning squeeze, Nolan lifted his brows and pretended a nonchalance he didn't feel. "You might not get the privilege. Others want us dead, too."

"Nobody will rob us of the right to kill ye."

"Then you'll have to kill the beasts that are behind us first."

"Gladly," Rat Chaser said with a smile. "And we won't take no chances." He pulled out a hefty pistol. The rest of the patrons, about thirty in all, also withdrew their weapons.

"Uh, McFearson?" Tessa uttered, nervousness making her voice quiver.

He admitted it was unsettling to see all those muzzles trained on them. Then snarling growls and barks split the air as the door burst open.

Chaos erupted. A dozen wolves entered followed by large men with extremely long arms. Men? He wasn't certain. Something seemed strange about the creatures as they swung their clubs. One tavern client's throat was ripped out. Nolan managed to grab the dead man's pistol and shoot a snarling canine in the mouth. Then he threw down the spent weapon and grabbed Tessa's hand.

"This way!" He led her toward the back door again. But this time the wolves were ready for them.

"Watch out!" Tessa cried just as a snarling dog charged Nolan. He took the impact, hand wrapped around the wolf's neck to keep the snapping teeth at bay as he fell backward. Using his feet, he pushed the beast as hard as he could, propelling the wolf away from him.

Before he could get his bearings, Tessa had grabbed his hand. They charged into the night with five of the snapping wolves on their heels.

"My God, they won't give up!" Tessa cried.

Despair began to ride him and he wondered if they would get out of this alive. He turned the corner and ran a few steps when he realized his mistake.

He'd turned into an alley with no escape. Grimly, he withdrew his sword. "Get behind me, Tessa. I'll fight them off while you see if you can scale the wall."

The scrape of sword against sheath told him that she hadn't listened to his command. Typical.

She stood next to him in her ready stance. "I'm not leaving you to fight alone, McFearson."

Desperation made him grit his teeth. "Damnation, Tessa. I'll not have your death on my conscience."

"And I'll not have yours on mine," she retorted. "Now can't you do something like communicate with these vile monsters using your shapeshifting magic?"

He caught a glimpse of a shadow—humanlike, but definitely not of this world. Its long, powerful arms grabbed one of the snarling wolves and, with a single twist, broke its neck. The five remaining wolves closed in.

"I wish," Nolan replied, palms damp with perspiration, heart thudding in dread as he prepared for the onslaught.

Just as all five beasts charged, his coat tightened beneath his armpits and he was lifted off the ground. Tessa shrieked.

He glanced to see her floating next to him. The

wolves were far below them, snapping and howling as they looked up into the predawn sky.

A pink light twinkled before his face. Fluttering inches in front of his nose was a dainty creature with purple skin and deep pink cheeks. "I saved you and Largo saved your girlfriend. You see, Largo and I are faeries and we've come to help you save the Earth."

Time was running short, and still there was no evidence of the Crevice of Silence.

The Crevice was Allegro's worst nightmare. When he'd been trapped inside the place fifteen years ago, he'd almost died. He'd wished he was dead because the absence of sound was worse than being dead. He still woke up at night bathed in a cold sweat from the nightmarish darkness that supped on one's soul.

How could he feel relief mixed with deep anxiety over not being able to find the place? He knew a whole city lay trapped in one of the Crystal Tuners, which couldn't play as long as they were trapped in the Crevice. Once the Tuners were safely carried out of the Crevice, the Tuners would be able to sing again, which would free the royal city of Aberdora. He must save the city—but at what cost? His sanity?

The rocky climb's desolation tore at Allegro's resolve to do what was right. Even Diminish had ceased his incessant storytelling.

They'd been traveling for several hours and had finally decided to land and rest their tired wings. Diminish had fallen asleep immediately, but as weary as Allegro was, sleep eluded him.

Something was strange about the land, but he couldn't put his finger on it.

Abruptly Diminish sat up. "Damnation, lad, it's blasted uncomfortable up here on this peak."

"Well, I don't like the way the ground softens between the crests. It's strange." After stepping on one of the low parts in an attempt to find water, he had noticed that the ground felt warm, flexible, almost . . . alive.

Diminish simply scowled, then muttered another troll incantation.

"There's something that isn't right about this land, and you must feel it too or else you wouldn't be repeating those troll chants."

"It won't only protect me from trolls, but from evil shapeshifters, gargoyles, dragons, gremlins, what have you. Here, I'll protect you, too, so you won't fash yourself anymore." He mumbled the charm and threw dust on Allegro.

"Thank you for your sudden interest in my welfare, Uncle," Allegro retorted with a grimace.

"I've always been interested in your welfare, my boy, just as I'm interested in saving the world." His pocket watch buzzed and he grunted in satisfaction. "There's the signal that I've been waiting for. Scaley, Dulce and Largo have made contact with the Shederin. Now it's up to us to find the lost Tuner where the city is."

Allegro resisted retorting something negative but decided to concentrate on the fact that they seemed lost. "When we were here fifteen years ago, I don't remember the terrain being this barren," he said as he looked about him, his uneasiness growing.

"Me neither," Diminish concurred, his beady eyes roaming over the rough terrain that was covered in a layer of fog.

The craggy rock peaked out here and there, but who knew what lay in the pockets of fog between the crests? "We've been circling this place for days and I haven't seen one landmark that I recognize from the last time. Obviously you haven't either or we would have found the Crevice of Silence by now. Are we lost?"

For a moment, Diminish rubbed his barklike face as

if he were at a loss for words. "Me, your Uncle Diminish, lost? Under no circumstances have I ever been lost. Perhaps a little off track but never out-and-out lost. Ah, well, nothing's going to deter us, is it, Allegro my boy? After all, we're brave adventurers out to right the wrongs in the world." His uncle's laughter rang out falsely, its echo seeming to mock them, seeming to awaken the whole earth and whatever dwelled in the murky depths below.

"Quiet!" Allegro whispered, not liking the way the back of his neck was prickling or the manner in which the ground seemed to shift, redistributing the fog.

"Damnation, my boy, you're making me jumpy and downright paranoid. I'm tired, I'm cranky and I'm going to go down where it's softer so I can sleep better."

With that, Diminish tromped down the hill. "Hunh, this goes down quite a ways. I'm going to check it out," he called to Allegro and disappeared into the valley.

"Diminish, don't do anything foolish!" There was no answer. Silence prevailed. In fact, Allegro noticed that he hadn't heard the chirp of a bird in hours. The spookiness was growing by leaps and bounds—and he had a strange feeling that he wasn't going to see the old faerie again.

"Uncle Diminish?" he called tentatively, acknowledging their relationship for the first time since he'd been captured by the trolls.

The wind suddenly picked up in galelike proportions, sucking him toward the deep valley, deeper than any of the valleys he'd ventured into. Beating his wings in a desperate attempt to escape, he kept getting pulled farther down. He was just about to slip into that black hole when someone latched onto his coat.

"Grab my arm!" Uncle Diminish cried over the howling wind.

Desperately Allegro latched on and wondered if they

would both fall into the pit. As abruptly as the wind sucked them in, it pushed them out with a blast of air, as if someone had expelled a breath. The earth's crust moved, and folded back. Horrified, Allegro realized he was looking at a humongous eye with a diamond-shaped pupil.

"Damnation. It's that infernal dragon! Quick. Hide." Diminish pulled Allegro down into a shallow crevice that appeared to be part of the huge beast's neck.

That infernal dragon. The way Diminish said it, as if he was personally acquainted with the beast, alerted Allegro that Diminish was once again up to his old tricks. "What dragon?"

The beast was already feeling around for them, lifting a long claw to scratch between the knobby protrusions on its body, working its way up to its neck where Allegro crouched with his degenerate of a relative.

Diminish peered up at the dragon. "The dragon that I borrowed a wee bit of magic from."

Appalled, Allegro could only stare. "You stole magic from a dragon?"

Diminish shrugged, not meeting his nephew's incredulous glare. "I wouldn't exactly call it stealing."

"Well, he obviously didn't give you permission! Where is this magic? Give it back."

"Can't. All used up. It was in the ring I gave to Largo, the ring that produced the illusionary dragon that got you away from the trolls."

"And now he's out for revenge."

"Yep, that about sums it up." Suddenly Diminish pointed. "There's the Crevice! Why, the old bastard was lying atop the opening, which was why we couldn't find it. Quick! You get the Tuners. I'll deal with the dragon."

Before he could object, Diminish had booted Allegro off the dragon's knobby skin. Allegro tumbled a ways before he managed to bat his wings to right himself. A blast of fire singed one of his wings, the searing heat making him cry out in pain.

"It's me you want, you mangy dog," Diminish cried out and threw a javelin at the dragon's eye. The resulting roar and blast of fire from the dragon's mouth caused Allegro to lose sight of his uncle. He found Diminish again, this time on the dragon's head.

"Get going!" Diminish yelled at Allegro. A clawed hand nearly caught the old codger. Diminish dodged just in time, bouncing down the dragon's back.

Wondering how long Diminish could keep up his dodges, Allegro cursed his uncle for the umpteenth time for his reckless ways. Then, resigned, he steeled himself to walk into the place where he'd almost lost his life, his soul, his sanity. The place he dreaded most.

The Crevice of Silence.

Chapter Eighteen

Nolan stood in the privacy of Tessa's garden as he tried to control his shapeshifting, the high walls hiding their magical visitors from view. Tessa sat a few feet away in the gazebo, covertly watching while pretending to peruse a newspaper.

"Can all humans see you?" he asked on impulse.

"Only if we want them to," the faerie named Largo replied from where he sat on a leaf of English Ivy close to the dazzling female. He took a swig of something from a flask.

Nolan thought they could pass for very colorful insects.

Scaley, the strange troll with his hulking, eleven-foot frame and greenish-brown skin, watched with those unblinking orange eyes. "Your highness, you must keep trying to wield your magic," he instructed.

For the third time, Nolan leaned back his head and closed his eyes, attempting to release his mind, to allow the urge to shapeshift to take over. "As I asked you before, how do I *prevent* the shifting when the urge overcomes me?"

The troll gave him an indecipherable look. "And as the Goddess answered you, first you must open your mind to the world around you."

"Goddess?"

Sheepishly, the brilliantly colored pixie with the violet skin and bright pink cheeks raised her hand. Dulce was her name, Nolan recalled. "He means me. But I'm not a goddess; I'm just an ordinary faerie."

Frowning, Nolan returned to the problem at hand. "Open my mind to the world. What in bloody hell does that mean?"

Largo, the fat one, looked up from his task of peeling some sort of exotic fruit. "Shapeshifters are known to be one with nature. Why is he having such trouble communicating?"

Scaley flapped his lips, showing his pointed, pearly white teeth. "He was raised as a human. Even you know that faeries need to be trained from their cradles to fly and use their faerie instincts to their full potential. Nolan was never taught."

Dulce launched off her ivy leaf and glided to sit on a nearby rosebush. "Your instincts are there, Nolan. You just need to learn how to read them, be aware of them. When a black spell came over you, didn't you sense a heaviness in the air, a pall that you couldn't quite explain?"

As he paced along the narrow garden path behind Tessa's townhouse, Nolan thought back to the dark spells. "Perhaps. But I always thought it had to do with the changes that were happening in my body."

Dulce flew between him and the troll. "When you shapeshifted, you were reacting to danger."

Setting her paper aside, Tessa stood and walked down the gazebo steps, apparently deciding to abandon her casual interest. Instead, she sat on a nearby wrought-iron bench and leaned in toward them. "But if that were true, why didn't he shapeshift when he was challenged by five of London's most dangerous criminals?"

The troll lounged back against a tree, his solemn face showing a keen intelligence. "Because they weren't magic. Nolan reacts to dangers in the magical world."

Rubbing the back of his neck, Nolan considered this, still trying to take it all in, to understand this facet of his life. "Then why—in my panther form—did I rescue a human child during a fire?"

Largo swallowed a bite of his fruit. "You shapeshifted as a reaction to a threat in the magical world. But you answered the cry of a wee harmonic in peril."

The troll's lips thinned. "Because you were unaware of these tendencies, you were like a thistle in the wind, blowing this way and that—sidetracked to the many dangers in life, not focusing on the magical threats unless nothing else waylaid you."

"I don't want to shapeshift."

Dulce brought her delicate purple brows together. "Why not?"

"Because I don't want to lose control, damnit."

Throwing the fruit's long yellow peeling into a nearby bush, Largo padded toward them and sat on the back of the bench, close to Tessa. "But if you learn to shapeshift when you want to do so, you'll learn control. Since we can't make a magical threat, you must take control by shifting at your own will."

"Why can't we?" the troll asked suddenly.

Largo drew his shaggy brows into question marks. "Why can't we what?"

Dulce jumped to her feet. "Of course, Scaley. You're so smart! Why *can't* we generate a magical threat for Nolan to react to—or in this case, for Nolan not to react to?"

Largo stiffened his posture, causing his belly to stick

out farther. The fat faerie's normally cherubic face had a belligerent cast to it, and Nolan noted, not for the first time, that this little pixie seemed to hold great animosity for the troll. "Excuse me, but it's nature's course that's driving him to shift into a panther—a protective instinct. If we teach him not to shift, he might not be able to defend himself. He might die!"

Scaley sat up straighter against the tree. "However, I think Goddess is right—he needs to learn control even during a magical threat. Just like the human warrior learns to use his or her head during battle, to not strike out blindly, so must Nolan learn to control his shape-shifting."

"Spare me from interfering do-gooder trolls—I'm going to sleep," Largo muttered, plopping down on a nearby tuft of grass and pulling the blade around him like a blanket.

Dulce had reproduced a hand-held reflecting glass and was fluffing her bright pink hair, but Nolan wondered if she really saw her reflection because she appeared so pensive. "However, Scaley, don't you think we should first teach Nolan to use nature and his magical instincts to shift? Once he gets in tune with his shapeshifting abilities, he'll understand his reaction to nature a little better. Then he'll be more successful at warding off the tendency to shift when he gets the call to magical danger."

"Aye, you're right again, Goddess." Scaley turned his huge, plain face toward Nolan. "All right, Your Highness, try again. Open your mind. Relax. Listen to the foliage around you. Search out the critters. Reach deep down inside you to find those repressed skills."

Nolan lifted his face and closed his eyes, trying to open up, to listen to sounds around him. To feel.

Damn. He felt like a fool.

The troll rubbed against the tree to scratch his hairy back, then considered Nolan with a thoughtful expression. "Your dread is interfering."

Gritting his teeth, Nolan refused to acknowledge that the troll was right. "How does all this tie in with the conspiracy? Do you know who is leading the uprising?"

Dulce and the troll exchanged glances before the faerie answered. "We're certain the Shade Lord is your traitorous leader."

"A shapeshifter?" Tessa exclaimed with a gasp.

Scaley nodded. "Yes, one who is impersonating a human. He could be someone you know. Your leader of the conspiracy is more dangerous than you ever imagined. That's why the Shederin *must* learn to master his powers. That is the only way we can conquer this evil magic. Otherwise the Shade Lord will take over all life, including the human race. All of us will be no better than slaves."

"Can't you find this evil shapeshifter with your magic?" Tessa asked as she lowered her paper.

The troll shook his large head. "None of us can, because he uses a cloaking power to hide. The only way we can destroy him is to be prepared by honing the Royal Shederin's skills. Now—what do you fear, Your Highness? Tell me so that we can progress," he demanded, turning to Nolan.

Nolan repressed the urge to admonish the troll for referring to him as royalty. After all, Dulce couldn't get him to stop calling her a goddess, despite repeated requests. So he doubted he could get the troll to cooperate either and decided he might as well save his breath. "Lack of control. I might begin killing indiscriminately."

"I have said you will not. A Royal Shederin heir could never be arbitrary in any action, especially one of a violent nature."

Scaley had told him the extraordinary story about the evil Morthdones: how they'd destroyed his family and captured a whole city by the name of Aberdora. The faerie, Largo, told him how another pixie by the name of Diminish managed to save him as a babe and exchange him for a human infant that had recently died in childbirth.

"Where is this Diminish, anyway?" Nolan asked.

The troll and two faeries glanced at each other, their expressions worried, almost anguished. It was Dulce who answered. "Diminish and our other friend, Allegro, will come as soon as they escape a dragon and find Aberdora."

Yes, Nolan had heard the whole story about how he'd been rescued from the evil Morthdones but the royal city had been captured in a dark nether region. Frowning, Nolan wondered exactly what he'd gotten himself into. Only a few hours ago he would have thought these creatures were mythical.

"And they will come," Dulce added for emphasis.

"You seem worried," Tessa interrupted.

Largo bit his lip. "It's just because we haven't heard from them for a while now. But they are both going to succeed in finding Aberdora, which is locked in the Crystal Tuner for the note of A."

"Will we have to fight a dragon, too?" Tessa asked.

"No, only the Morthdones," Scaley answered. "The Dingwols are mine to destroy." The troll crossed his long arms, making the folded forearms come way below his knees. "No more talk because we waste time. Back to your shapeshifting and your reservations. Do you accept that you are a Shederin who could never hurt anyone, unless they are evil and need to be conquered?"

"No. How do you know that to be true in my case? I wasn't raised with the shapeshifters. I know nothing of their code of honor or ethics. And how do you know I have powers enough to destroy these evil Morthdones? I bloody hell didn't demonstrate any last night as I ran for my life."

"If he doesn't get rid of his doubts, his fears, he won't be prepared for the upcoming battle," Scaley said to Dulce.

"McFearson, you need a talisman for an anchor." Tessa had stood and was walking toward him. She reached for the chain about her neck. "As I've told you before, I feel a power surge through me when I hold this crystal. I think it's an amulet against evil." She pulled the slender tuner from underneath her bodice and lifted the chain over her head.

The troll suddenly dropped to his knees, his abrupt motion sinking the paving stone into the earth. "Holy podzol! Mistress! Do you realize what that is?"

She frowned and held it up, the facets twinkling in the afternoon sun. "Merely a little trinket I found, but it has always been precious to me."

Orange eyes blinking, Scaley whistled. "Mistress, what you hold is one of the great Crystal Tuners that the Morthdones stole from the Shederins. It's the Tuner for the note of C. It is the other half of the power that belongs to the royal heir, the Tuner that will help free the city once Diminish and Allegro remove the other Tuner from the Crevice of Silence."

Largo sat up so quickly that Nolan doubted he'd ever been asleep. Dulce fluttered toward Tessa and examined the crystal before emitting a trill of music that indicated her excitement. "Where did you get it?"

Tessa continued to look at the faeries, a puzzled look on her face. "I discovered it in the Highlands."

After tapping her bright violet chin, Dulce buzzed in a circle around Tessa's face, peering intently. "She must have a little magic, herself. Are you a shapeshifter, too?"

Raising her brows, Tessa shook her head. "Nothing has ever happened to me to indicate as such."

"Or she hears the call of magic," Largo murmured.

Tessa shrugged, but the nonchalant action belied the excitement in her dark eyes. "Perhaps you're right, Largo. I've always felt a strange energy coming from this trinket. I found it when I was a young girl. It was as if the trinket called out to me to look for it in that hold between the rocks. Anyway, I found it, and I'm giving the talisman to McFearson."

"Are you certain?" Nolan asked. He knew how much she treasured the charm, for he'd seen her grasp the trinket almost subconsciously whenever a confrontation arose. He was moved that she would offer him something so significant to her.

Tessa gave him an intent look. "You heard Scaley. You are the royal heir of Shederin and it's yours. Besides, it's strange, but ever since I've known you, I've sensed that my talisman belongs to you." She extended her hand a little farther, encouraging him to take the necklace.

Humbled, awed by her special gift, he slowly grasped the chain and slipped it over his head. The tuner felt warm against his shirt. The warmth grew . . . spread throughout his body, his limbs. A glow haloed around him as an unearthly power surged inside him.

Suddenly he was aware of Earth, of Mother Nature and the power of the living things that made her flourish. The nearby oak told him of the worms that had burrowed into its trunk last spring. Lifting his hand, he felt warmth shoot from his fingers to wrap around the tree. The sick limb healed. Green leaves shot fresh and new from the branches. Amazement washed through him. "Mrs. Campbell had spoken of this but I never believed her," he whispered.

He became aware of a housecat on the wall. Using an innate understanding, a communication he was hard-pressed to explain, he listened to the scruffy, malnourished calico. She related to him that her kittens had died, eaten by strange beasts that had arms too long for their bodies, like the creature kneeling in the garden. He soothed the bereaved mother, assuring her that this troll would never eat her babies. He didn't know how he knew this about Scaley . . . but he *knew*.

Pointing a finger toward the animal, he healed her, giving her fragile bones strength, her coat luster, her belly fullness. The housecat purred her thanks and told him that he had a good soul. Amazing how animals seemed to know when humans—or shapeshifters—suffered.

"Nolan?" Tessa placed her hand on his arm.

He realized he'd moved closer to the small beast as she sat on the brick wall. Then he looked at Tessa.

It was the first time she'd called him by his given name, other than in the bedchamber. A surge of tenderness flowed through him and he wondered if his magic was derived from the talisman or from this special woman who'd careened into his life, sword in hand.

Now Tessa's beautiful face filled with awe and . . . love? "It's true. Just like Scaley said, you are the Royal Shederin, the only one who can bring the healing touch to the lands. Perhaps you can free the lost city of Aberdora."

Nolan shrugged. "I don't know about that, but I do know that cat lost her kittens to trolls."

"The Dingwols," Scaley corrected. "My clan would never kill helpless animals. We find our sustenance in the minerals of the earth. The Dingwols could do the same, but they enjoy the act of destroying too much."

"I'm ready to shapeshift."

He allowed his mind to relax, to remember the feeling of power that engulfed him when the black spell came over him. Delving deep within himself, he scooped up the power necessary to shift and willed the energy to do the work.

"The fog didn't come this time," he heard Tessa say in awe.

"What fog?"

"The glittering fog that always appeared before. It rendered me unconscious."

The pixies frowned at each other. Dulce puckered her miniature lips, lush for all her wee size. "A glittering fog? It sounds suspiciously like a pixie enchantment."

Largo tilted his head. "Do you think Diminish could have used the spell to protect the Shederin before he hid him in the McFearson family?"

Dulce nodded vigorously, her excitement palpable. "Could be exactly what he did. And now that the Shederin knows how to control his shapeshifting, the spell is no longer needed."

"Can spells just go away when they're not necessary?" Tessa asked.

"Of course, lass," Largo replied. "Diminish was a legend in his own day. He lived for centuries and understood such nuances in spells."

"Cease now. You talk as if he's dead," Dulce scolded.

Nolan allowed the voices to fade, indifferent to the conversation. He was more interested in this new awareness that charged through his panther form.

Smells of which he'd never been aware wafted over him.

The click of small feet against stone had him turning to see a mouse scamper along the stone path in the garden. It communicated with him, then scurried away.

A disturbance filled the air, strong and alarming.

Listening, Nolan realized it was a thrumming rolling across the lands—like a drum pounding out a warning of doom. Suddenly he knew the danger was all encompassing and he knew exactly where the menace lay. Return—he must return to his human state to warn the others of the imminent peril.

Concentrating on the warmth that radiated from the crystal tuner dangling from around his neck, he relaxed his mind, willing himself to change.

Nothing happened. He tried again.

Still nothing.

Panic set in.

Then he looked at Tessa. A surge of lust swept through him, so strong that it dazed him. Primal desire to conquer made him crouch, circle her. His mind registered her wide-open eyes and slack jaw as vulnerability flitted over her features. Groping near her ankle, she felt for one of her knives. But she wasn't fast enough. Before she could withdraw the weapon halfway, he pounced.

No! he screamed in his mind, trying desperately to control the animalistic urges that raged through his panther form, even as he knocked her down. He rolled her backward onto the grass and pinned down her shoulders with his large paws.

What was he doing? Alarm fluttered over his conscience, trying to make him back away from her.

But memories of another time that he'd shapeshifted crowded into his head. In his mind's eye he saw himself in his panther persona leaning over another woman, the metallic scent of blood in his nostrils and on his tongue, slick on his paws, fatal gashes in her chest, another woman who'd been dear to him.

He struggled to back off, but he couldn't take his attention off Tessa, off the delicious scent that caused his blood to pound. Although he managed to force himself to straddle her instead of stand on her shoulders, he couldn't halt his urge to taste her neck.

"Lie still!"

The shouted instruction from Scaley came as if from a distance. The words made no sense to him as he bent down close to his prey, inhaling that heady scent. Baring his teeth in a rumbling growl, he licked the delicious skin, slightly salty and all the erotic sweetness that was Tessa.

She lay so motionless that he wondered if she was dead. Panicked, he rubbed his face against hers. Her eyes fluttered open and he purred in relief. That was when he saw the flash of steel at his neck for a moment before she tossed the knife away.

"Nolan, come back," she whispered, her voice quavering. Slowly she reached for his chest and stroked the panther that was now his body.

"Nolan, return to your human form. I need you." Cupping her hand, she pressed the tuner next to his heart.

He needed her, too.

Burning . . . then a nauseating sensation roiled through him as his bones shifted. He realized he was standing in the garden in his human form, wrapped in Tessa's hold, the crystal tuner pulsating gently against his chest as she continued to hold the trinket against him.

"Thank the trumpets you didn't eat her!" Dulce cried, plopping down on her leaf with a sigh.

"Aye, ye withheld those animal instincts to rip out her throat. And ye shapeshifted on your own!" Largo said excitedly. "Yer in fine condition now. Ye can shapeshift back and forth whenever you want to."

Scaley simply stared, his face impassive, his luminous orange eyes solemn.

Relief made Nolan limp, but he couldn't indulge in the emotion. "Bloody hell, I attacked Tessa!" Remorse flooded him so much that he wanted to shout to the heavens.

"Nolan," she said, stroking first his hands, then his arms and shoulders, and finally cupping his jawline.

He realized that he stood with his hands fisted, his head thrown back with his eyes closed as he raged at the fates that made him such a monster.

"My God, I couldn't bear it if I caused another person's death."

"You didn't. And I don't believe you ever will. Not unless the person is evil and needs killing."

Tessa mattered to him too much. Like a fever in his blood, his yearning for her would be her death. He'd seen what happened to Mad Jack and the other vicious criminals at the tavern last night, how their throats had been ripped out, their bodies mangled. No human could withstand a shapeshifter's power and he refused to put Tessa in danger.

His soul couldn't bear another loved one's death. "Well, I'm not taking any more chances."

"Good grief. Nolan, you *licked* me, for heaven's sake!"

He barely heard her. With his newfound instincts, he suddenly recalled what happened on the night that changed his life—and the horror of that memory reinforced his decision. The blood. The slash marks. It all made sense.

No more intimacies with Tessa. No more falling asleep with her. Everything must end. Grief threatened to overwhelm him, even as he knew what he must do.

Gritting his teeth with determination, he looked first at Scaley, then at Dulce. "Surround me with dangerous magic so we may begin my training. Scaley, if I change into a panther, kill me."

"We need you to survive in order for Quelgheny and the world to survive!" Dulce protested.

"If I survive it will be as a human."

Scaley stood, straightening to his full height. "Your chance of surviving as a human is minimal. *You must live.* If Diminish destroys the dragon and Allegro makes it through the Crevice of Silence, then we'll need you to bring back the city of Aberdora."

He was an aberration, a threat to humankind. Didn't they realize that? Fear lanced him. Under no circumstances would he ever change into a panther again. He withdrew his sword, the rasp of the blade sounding obscene. "Then I will end it now."

That Tessa had also drawn her sword shouldn't have surprised him. Before he could inhale, she'd disarmed him. "You will not do something so foolish as to take your own life. You tried that before by setting up that ridiculous five-against-one duel and I stopped you then. Now that I know you ever so much better, do you think I won't hesitate to save you again?"

"You cannot watch me forever," he replied with brutal truth. "I cannot live among humans without endangering someone—and not just someone, but those I love. Therefore, I *will* do the deed eventually."

Blinking, she stared at him, startled. "Did you say in a roundabout way that you love me?"

"What does it matter how I feel? We cannot live together! Not without endangering your life."

Tessa bit her lower lip, her expression stricken.

He hardened his heart against her pain and turned to the troll. "Scaley, I'll have your word that you will kill me."

The troll stretched his rubbery lips into a grimace. "All right, but only if you threaten an innocent."

"Nolan," Tessa whispered, her face pale. "What has happened? Why are you willing to take your own life? You look . . . haunted. What is it?"

Bleakness draped his soul as he stared helplessly into her eyes, dark with concern. "I've recalled everything during the black spells of my past."

"Everything?"

He knew she was thinking of the one event that brought her into his life, the death of a woman they had both loved. "I distinctly remember slashing Selena's throat."

* * *

As Tessa anticipated, Nolan had locked the door.

Gritting her teeth against his stubbornness, she sighed. When would he realize that she loved him? That she accepted him, his whole shapeshifting self, just as he was? And not under any circumstances could she believe that he had killed Selena. No matter what form he took on, his honorable character shone through.

Perhaps it wasn't enough that she accepted him; he had to believe in himself.

Slipping the key from her pocket, she unlocked the door and stepped inside.

Through the open window the moon stroked silvery fingers over the sleek muscles of his back, the rounded masculine buttocks and those powerful legs as he lay asleep. Even in slumber he seemed taut, ready to pounce at the moon's command. Tessa ached, not only with the familiar passion that pooled down low as her body responded to him, but in her heart as she looked at him— so honorable, so beautiful.

Determination flowed through her. If she had to seduce him every night in order to make him understand that there was nothing that he could do to drive her away, then that was what she would do—gladly. Deliberately she took off her robe and folded it neatly on a chair. Then she reached for the hem of her gown.

"Tessa. How did you get in here?" He sat up on the bed.

She answered his question with a challenge of her own. "Did you think a locked door would keep me out?"

"A barred entrance would keep most women out," he retorted as he grabbed his breeches and pulled them on, his back to her.

"I'm not most women."

"So I've noticed."

Damnation, she'd known this confrontation would be

difficult. "Nolan, you can't escape me. I'm going to keep coming to you every night. Over and over again, with words, with written notes, with my body, I'm going to tell about your innate goodness, your heroic character, until you believe."

"Bloody hell, Tessa, I don't want you!"

His expression was so fierce, for a moment she faltered. No, he was lying. He had to be lying. He feared what happened to him when he shapeshifted.

With defiance, she jerked the nightgown over her head, baring herself with her head high, willing her chin not to tremble. "You do, too."

For a moment his eyes burned into her, his face tight with desire as he swept his gaze over her body.

Before she lost her nerve, she approached him and brazenly stroked his arousal, starting at its base, through fabric, and ending with its bared, engorged head.

With a low curse, he pulled her against him. "What am I going to do with you?"

"Love me," she replied.

"My God, Tessa, can't you leave me to my shame?" Neck corded, eyes shut and head thrown back, he was the epitome of agony. "I'm a freak of nature, an aberration. Leave me be."

"No." Throat burning as she experienced his self-torture, she ran her hands over his muscled chest, suckled his flat nipple and reveled in his resulting shudder. She moved to his other side, continuing to kiss him, then tasting him as she moved down his stomach. "You are so magnificent, my love. And I do love you so much."

She hooked her thumbs into his waistband and pulled down his breeches. The action caused him to spring free in all his male beauty. When she took him in her mouth, he groaned and shuddered again.

"Tessa," he whispered reverently before lifting her in

his arms and placing her on the bed. He adjusted her legs, widening them, plumbing her portal with erotic strokes of his fingers before taking the plunge, diving deep inside her.

She reveled in the sensation, feeling as if he were the part of her she'd always craved but never realized. He was her ultimate adventure; he was what she'd sought during her years of loneliness in the caravan, during her rejection in the abbey, then during her friendless travels for the Crown. She'd been searching all her life for the sense of belonging that he created in her now. As she met him stroke for stroke, she reached for stars in Nolan's arms . . . but found heaven instead in a kaleidoscope of brilliant colors.

As she lay sated and exhausted in his arms, a cold shadow crept over her heart.

A cloud of doom.

She shivered before sleep took over.

Chapter Nineteen

In the darkest part of night Nolan's sense of smell heightened again as he lay on the ticking, his arms cradling Tessa.

The click of small feet against stone warned him of the mouse. Instinctively, with his newfound skills, he knew it was the same mouse, and this time the small creature had found him in his bedchamber. Once more, the rodent communicated with him, then scurried away.

A disturbance filled the air, strong and alarming.

The thrumming had started up again, rolling across the lands—a drum pounding out the warning of death. Gasping, he glanced down at his body and saw that he had begun to shift. He stretched his will deep down into his mind even as he reached for Tessa's talisman around his neck, willing himself not to change. The Crystal Tuner heated and the sensation disappeared; the panther receded into its cave.

Tessa murmured something unintelligible and rolled away from him. The sense of loss was painful, for he knew that their time together was limited. He was a freak of nature. He didn't belong in this world, and he doubted he would survive the upcoming battle, one that promised to be fierce.

England, all of Europe, was in deep peril. The leaders of Europe were to be slain and because of the confusion and pandemonium, evil from the Underground would pour onto the lands and eventually enslave the entire continent. And because he communed with nature, he knew exactly where the assassins would strike.

The realization of Europe's complete and total destruction caused a film of perspiration to cover his bare body. Stealthily he rose from the bed, careful not to disturb Tessa, and pulled on his clothing. Just then the moon peeped out from behind the clouds. His warrior slept on her stomach, her arms embracing the ticking in complete abandon. Pain pierced him at the thought of their limited hours together. Then darkness enveloped the room again.

What he couldn't see, he imagined because he'd spent the last several days memorizing her—that beautiful body, the fire in her dark eyes, the manner in which her forehead creased when she was irritated, the arrogant twist of her sensuous mouth when she was challenged, the confidence and courage that oozed from her very being. He swallowed the bitter lump in his throat, left the chamber and walked out into the courtyard.

Scaley waited in the drive, his hulking form visible in the shadows. "You know the assassins are on their way."

"Yes."

Abruptly, a violet light appeared at the troll's nose. "Scaley? Largo? Why didn't you wake me?"

"Goddess, we need you to wait for Diminish and Allegro. If we don't make it, you must tell them what happened. Get help."

"Ridiculous. I'll get help now." Taking off one of her curly-toed shoes, she said a chant and flung the shoe into the night sky. A rainbow of colors arched and disappeared.

"Since when did you have a rainbow to save us?"

"Since I floated down to Earth. Why are you scowling? I was saving it until we really needed help."

"Oh? And the other sixty-two times our lives were in danger we didn't need help?"

"We're alive, aren't we?"

"Barely," Largo grouched. "I wish you would have confided in me instead of taking over like you have. I'm supposed to be the one in charge since I've been on plenty of missions before."

"Uh-huh. Well, for your information, I don't owe you any explanations since we're not affianced anymore." Dulce lifted her pert little nose and turned her back on the fat faerie to face Nolan. "Where is Tessa?"

Nolan checked the chamber of his pistol, then shoved the weapon in the waistband of his breeches. "She's not coming."

Dulce scowled in doubt. "No? From what I've learned, that doesn't sound like her. She's a warrior, like me."

"I don't want her in jeopardy." He didn't mention the fact that he also didn't want her around when he decided to leave and never look back. If he didn't leave on the sly, she would follow him, and he couldn't allow that. In fact, he feared he would never have the will to leave her if she was there to entice him. After she got over the shock of his abandonment, she would in time come to realize that his leaving was for the best.

The little female pixie gave him a penetrating look. Bathed in her light, he was certain she could see the remorse in his eyes. "And you stay away from Tessa. This is not her battle and I don't want her knowing about it."

Dulce raised her nose in the air. "All right, I understand everything perfectly now."

"You do?" He wondered if the little imp had read his mind.

"Yes, I did, so I know exactly what you're thinking," she answered, startling him. "And I've come to a conclusion."

"And what is that?"

"Simply this. Whether they are pixies or harmonics, it doesn't matter—all men are bastards." With a glare at him, then at the green light that hovered nearby, Dulce flew off in a huff.

"Goddess, wait," Scaley called to her.

When she hesitated he gave her something that resembled a miniature book. "Read this when you get the time. I believe it will explain a lot."

Frowning, she glanced down at the object. "About what?"

"I will say no more," Scaley replied and withdrew.

Shrugging, she flew off into the night.

Largo frowned after her, then looked at Scaley. "What was that about? What did you give her?"

"Never mind." Scaley turned toward Nolan. "So I want to know—are you still intent on not shapeshifting?"

"That's correct."

"You cannot go into a battle such as this one will be and not have magic to aid your fighting."

"I've managed to stay alive so far."

"Barely, Your Highness. We had to save you last night. You must survive in order for the royal city to survive."

Nolan didn't want to hear any more of that rubbish. "Surely you can use your magic to rescue a whole city."

"He will survive," Largo interrupted. He'd been staring after Dulce, so much so that Nolan hadn't thought the pixie had been listening. Obviously he had been. "Or at least he'll have a better chance at surviving with a little help from me. Allegro taught me how to use faerie dust to enchant swords. I can do this for Nolan's weapon." In his bass tone, he chanted a song. A shower of sparkles brightened the sheath where Nolan's sword was strapped around his waist.

"That will help ye kill shapeshifters and trolls. Scaley will use his own magic to get to the estate and I'll help ye travel by flying. It's much faster."

He touched the hilt. The energy that flowed through the sword should have reassured someone who wanted to live. The problem was that he didn't care whether he lived or died. All of his actions, who he was, who he represented, gave him shame.

That he'd locked his door against Tessa brought shame to his heart. As he was lifted from the ground, he realized he was a damned coward when it came to her. He didn't think he could ever resist her enticements. And that was the reason he would have to leave once this battle was over. Just like him, Tessa, too, wanted to belong. She wanted a home, someplace where she belonged. She probably wanted children. But he couldn't be her husband because he wasn't of her kind; their children wouldn't be human.

He had to leave because he was a freak of nature and he refused to shackle Tessa with an abomination.

Tessa reached for Nolan and touched cold bedclothes. Startled, she raised her head to look around. The indentation of Nolan's head was still on his pillow, but it was cold and she had no idea how long he'd been gone. Dread rippled through her. Something was significant about this weekend. Then she remembered. This was the weekend that Liverpool had arranged for the dignitaries from other countries to visit his hunting lodge in Sussex. He'd told her he would postpone the gathering. Then why this sudden feeling of impending doom? She remembered Liverpool's reluctance to do as she pleaded and she abruptly knew that he had not followed through.

She felt a frisson of fear. That was when she saw the violet star. The shimmering ball slowed in its spin to show Dulce's disgruntled features.

"Nolan left without you. Largo and Scaley left without me. Men! Can't live with them, can't live without them."

Tessa sighed. "Yes, it's a dilemma, isn't it? Has Largo courted you in the past? I get the impression that there's an affair of the heart going on between the two of you."

Dulce's piquant features twisted in remorse. "We were betrothed, but I called it off because I overheard something Largo said to his friends, something that wasn't very flattering. Anyway, I got the feeling that he enjoys life more without me." She pulled out a miniature book and gazed at it a moment before slipping it back in her reticule.

Tessa marveled, realizing problems with men were universal. "What is that?"

"Something Scaley gave me. It looks like Largo's journal."

"Aren't you going to read it?"

"Perhaps, although I feel as if I'm peeking into something personal."

"Scaley must have realized you two were at odds and decided to intervene. What better way to judge how someone feels than to read his personal journal? Perhaps you should read it."

The dainty pink faerie fidgeted. "Not now. There's no time. Nolan has gone to Sussex with Scaley and Largo to defeat the assassins."

"Good heavens!" Tessa cried, jumping out of bed, ignoring the cold wood under her bare feet.

"Curse a flat note! Don't they know they need *us*?"

"Evidently not," Tessa replied, her heart in her

throat. She'd always relied on her survival techniques, her fighting abilities, her skill at garnering information and getting people to confide in her, as measures of her self-worth. That Nolan had tossed her out, discarded her abilities like a sack of old potatoes, hurt her more than she could say.

Determination had her balling her fists. Plainer than words he had told her he didn't want her, didn't need her. Too bad because he was going to get her help. She marched down to her chambers and pulled out her breeches, stockings, waistcoat and shirt.

"What are you going to do?"

"Nolan isn't going to abandon me, not if I can help it. I'm going to dress like a man and be armed to the teeth so I can save his miserable life."

"Then so am I!" Dulce said with an emphatic nod. "You save Nolan and I'll save Largo, although he'll resent it. I think he's having a difficult time dealing with my newfound independence, and he doesn't much like the fact that I took over the mission and found the Shederin."

Tessa was immensely glad that Nolan didn't have a problem with her ability to protect herself, her ability to wield a sword. In fact, she'd seen the glint of admiration in his eyes more than once. She remembered their sensual challenge and she yearned for those days again. When he wanted her, when she was an equal, when she was cherished. But since he'd discovered he was a shapeshifter, he couldn't get over the notion that he was an atrocity. "Men and their insecurities."

Dulce sighed. Then she whipped out her wand and waved the stick all around Tessa as she sang in a high voice that sounded as lilting as a flute, the words indecipherable.

Warmth flowed through Tessa's blood, zinging down through her hands.

"Let's go!" Dulce cried. As had happened the night

before, Tessa felt her body rise from the floor. The ceiling disappeared and she was in the night air, lifted higher and higher. She swallowed a cry of fear. A wave of dizziness hit her as she stared at the dull street lamps becoming smaller with the distance. London was swallowed up in the dark and they were flying south. After a bug flew in her mouth, she learned to keep it shut as the night wind whipped her face, causing her hair to fly back and the long sleeves of her man's shirt to billow.

Soon they were flying over Grenfeld, passed the foreboding wrought-iron fence. Nobody guarded the gate and deep dread slithered through her. Just then, the moon peeked out from the clouds and she realized the ground was littered with lifeless bodies. The militia.

Dulce gasped. "Oh, my trumpets! Those poor, poor harmonics!"

Swallowing a lump of fear, Tessa forced herself to take advantage of her view and study the area. In the dark she couldn't see much, especially when a cloud slunk over the moon. Several stars shot sparks across the sky. Silvery moonlight shone once more and she saw the ground move with tens of wolves.

"Help has come but we are horribly outnumbered," Dulce whispered as she took in the scene.

Tessa narrowed her eyes, then realized the whole area around the mansion was writhing with wolves. On the west side of the mansion stood Scaley, his hulking form towering over a dozen trolls who shot blue streaks of fire at him. He knocked them down with the huge club he carried and shot a deep purple string of electricity in return. She couldn't see how he was able to hold off so many attacks and was amazed at how fast he moved.

A flash of green caught her eye and she realized that Nolan stood in front of the main entrance to the house, his sword glowing turquoise as he fought, cutting down three wolves before turning to kick out, thwarting an attack from behind. Something dark was on his face and his shirt was shredded with dark stains. She realized it was blood.

"Largo! Oh, my love is in trouble!"

A green star flashed, then dimmed. "Get us down from here," Tessa demanded, but she didn't have to because she was diving into the foray and already unsheathing her sword, the blade shimmering a bright pink. Before she had completely alighted behind Nolan, she'd cut down two wolves that had launched themselves at his back.

"Tessa! Stay away!" Nolan shot over his shoulder but was once again forced to fight.

Grimly determined, she concentrated on the snarling wolves, swallowing fear as two lunged from either side of her, causing her to duck even as she met a third attacker, catching the canine in the chest. The other two had collided. She swiveled and shoved her sword deep, stabbing them both at once. But now she'd been forced to step away from Nolan and the swarm of wolves broke them even farther apart.

As she fought her way back to his side, she despaired, wondering if this was the beginning of the end.

Allegro knew he was going to die. No faerie could survive a place without music, without sound.

The silence closed in on him, the buzz unbearable, bringing Allegro down to his knees. He forced his vocal chords to work but no sound came out of his mouth. Touching his throat, he could feel the vibrations rumbling beneath his skin. Then why couldn't he hear the sounds? Because the Crevice of Silence was feeding off the energy, sapping his strength.

Had Largo, Dulce and Scaley even been able to convince the Shederin of his powers and help him in his fight for survival? He hoped so because by now he knew that the Morthdones were most likely attacking the leaders of the harmonics. Soon they, along with their troll accomplices, would take over the world. Harmonics would become enslaved. Misery would dominate the earth. There would be no love among them, or happiness.

Then the faeries would perish. Evil would win.

Could he allow that to happen? But what was he to do? He could barely move and it was so dark, he feared he'd become blinded forever. Had he been down this tunnel before? There was no telling, for he couldn't even see his fingers as he waved them in front of his face. He couldn't give up, though.

He simply couldn't.

Forcing a swallow through his dry throat, he crawled forward on hands and knees. He swept his palms in wide arcs, not because he had any faith that he would find the Crystal Tuners, but because he simply had nothing else to do. If he stopped moving then he knew he was doomed.

Back and forth, back and forth his hands swept, first the left, then the right, then together in an arc along the earthen floor. Yet again he swept the left . . . and his fingers touched a smooth, cool surface. No, two long flat surfaces. He grasped the object and sat up on his haunches, examining it like a blind faerie.

One of the Crystal Tuners!

But where was the other one? Buoyed, excited, he searched the area several times, even extending his search several yards both ways. Nothing. He despaired.

But perhaps one would be enough. Even now he could see a miniature city shimmering like a mirage between the forks of the Tuner. He would leave the Crevice while he had the strength and play the Tuner. If nothing happened, if the crystal city of Aberdora didn't rise in the north, he would have to force himself to return to the Crevice. And if that happened, deep down in his heart he knew he wouldn't return. This was it.

He stumbled out of the Crevice and stood up, taking a deep breath, praying with all his might that this would work, that one Tuner would be enough to bring back the royal city of Aberdora. Then, with resolve, he struck the Crystal Tuner against his hand and held it up high. The sweet, clear note vibrated across the rocky hills of the Highlands. Would it work? Would the power released by the Tuner be enough to help the last Shederin bring back Aberdora? Was he still alive? He prayed that it would be enough, and that the Shederin had survived, because another trip into the Crevice wouldn't matter.

Earth would be doomed and Jubilant would be no more.

The wolves had breached the mansion.

Weariness dragged Tessa's arms down. Standing in the doorway to the drawing room in which the five leaders stood, she willed strength into her flagging muscles and swung the sword once more.

"What is happening?" Liverpool shouted, white-faced.

"Louis, you're behind this!" Tsar Alexander shouted at the fat King Louis, his voice shrill with panic as he pushed the French king.

"Not me! It's you . . . or Metternich," Louis replied, his chins quivering as he hit the tsar with his handkerchief.

Nolan growled as he skewered another wolf. "I'll explain later if I can. We don't need a fight among the sovereigns!"

Dulce hovered with Largo above Tessa's head. She

threw another deadly pink bolt at three wolves that charged the hallway. "Largo, do something! The harmonics are panicking and will only hinder our efforts."

"Got it," he replied and blew azure sparkles at all of them. The heads of states immediately lay down on the carpet.

Glancing back, Tessa gasped.

At the same time, Dulce laughed with delight. "What a clever idea, Largo! To put a sleeping spell on them, one in which they'll never remember any of this."

The green faerie blushed, then widened his eyes in horror. "Look out!"

Dulce just barely managed to block a bolt from a troll. Briefly, Tessa wondered what had happened to Scaley. The last time she'd seen him had been in the foyer; three trolls had jumped him at once. She could only hope that he'd survived.

Suddenly a beautiful hum filled the air, sweet and pure. The sound originated from far away and became louder. A minor key played, this one coming from Nolan . . . more specifically, from Nolan's chest.

Everyone froze. The trolls stood like salt pillars before caving into heaps of dust. The wolves began to shapeshift into their human forms, falling where they stood. Still the sounds of the notes grew.

Tessa followed Nolan's gaze down to his chest and realized that the Crystal Tuner was vibrating, the kaleidoscope of color a beauty to behold.

"The Tuner is calling the city of Aberdora," Nolan murmured, his silver eyes wide. His look turned to one of awe. "Look!"

She turned and saw the most amazing sight. A crystal ball with a miniature city inside floated down the hall toward Nolan. The buildings had turrets with long crystal spikes glittering at their tops. And people were waving.

Even though they were tiny, Tessa could tell that the older couple in front was related to Nolan. She stared at him and without words knew she was losing him.

"Those are my people, Tessa. That is my home," he said, his tone filled with marvel. For years he'd sensed he was different from others, and he hadn't understood himself. Now here was a chance to be with his kind, his people. Just by looking at them, she knew he felt a bond with them before he'd even met them; she could see the strong emotional pull in his silver eyes.

Her throat constricted in grief; she was losing him. *No!*

A clash of swords behind Tessa had her whirling to face this new danger. In horror she watched Perry and Carmichael locked in a deadly battle, their hilts locked, their swords pointed at each other's throat.

"Lady Ballard, help me!" Carmichael shouted.

"Get him away!" Perry cried.

Suddenly Nolan grasped her. "Tessa, be careful."

"You've got to stop them."

In an unexpected move, Perry stepped back, causing Carmichael's weight to thrust forward. Perry's sword skewered his chest.

Panting, Perry stared at Carmichael's inert form as the dying man gasped for breath, his life's blood leaking out on the carpet.

Bending down, Nolan pulled out a handkerchief and pressed it against the wound even as Carmichael's jaw worked. "Don't try to talk."

Grabbing a napkin from a nearby service tray, Tessa knelt down next to Nolan to help him stem the blood.

Perry shook his head. "Until I saw clearly with my own two eyes when McFearson changed from a panther into a human, I'd thought I'd drunk too much brandy."

"What are you talking about, sir?" Tessa asked, distractedly.

"A couple of nights ago, I saw Carmichael do the

same thing. That is, shapeshift. Only he changed into a wolf." Perry's expression became animated. "Carmichael must be the mole in the Special Committee. I suspected him, although I didn't know for sure until just now, when he snuck in through the servants' quarters and tried to kill Liverpool in his unconscious state. He would have murdered the others, too, if I hadn't stopped him. And obviously, since I saw him shapeshift, he's one of them," he exclaimed as he gestured toward the bodies of several wolves.

Once more Carmichael tried to say something but his chest stilled as his last breath escaped.

Nolan shook his head, his lips grim. "He's gone."

Sorrow pierced her heart as she stared down at the man who'd been her friend. A bitter taste rose in her mouth at the thought that he'd betrayed her. She would have never believed it. If anyone, she would have thought it was Tinsington.

Perry patted her on the shoulder. "I'm sorry, my dear. I know you were fond of him."

"The conspiracy is over," she whispered. She discovered herself being pulled into arms so familiar that she didn't have to look to see who held her.

Nolan.

Instinctively she knew this would be the last time he held her. She was breaking apart inside, knowing that she couldn't follow. But she wouldn't be selfish, she wouldn't deny him his heritage. If he wanted to go, she wouldn't hold him back.

And he wanted to go.

Nevertheless, when he kissed her she closed her eyes and savored the moment, knowing that this kiss would have to last her the rest of her life.

"I love you," he whispered.

She gave him a brave smile. "I know. I love you, too. But this is what you have to do."

Slowly nodding, he grasped the Crystal Tuner and withdrew the chain from around his neck. He pulled the trinket over her head. "If you are ever in trouble, or your life is in danger, play the Tuner and I'll come to you. Otherwise, this is farewell."

The beautiful stone was still warm from his skin.

A sense of strangeness surrounded her. She was vaguely aware of Edward Perry and the faeries in the room. The leaders on the floor were just beginning to stir. Scaley had just stepped into the chamber. But none of that mattered. Only Nolan mattered, and she was losing him.

To step back, to let him go, was the hardest thing she'd ever had to do. But she did it.

For a moment his eyes mirrored her anguish. Then he tore his gaze from hers and held up his arms to the magical city that glittered above him. "Take me!" he commanded.

His body lifted as twinkling stars blinked all around him. He spiraled, becoming smaller, smaller as he was sucked into Aberdora. Then the crystal ball floated out the window.

Chest so tight she could barely breathe, Tessa ran to the window and watched as the enchanted city blazed brightly, then disappeared into the north.

"So you both truly loved each other, so much so that he gave you the Crystal Tuner."

She hadn't realized that Perry was standing by her side, staring out the window with her.

Perry gave her a gentle hug. "I've been talking to your small friends. They told me how important the Tuners were to Nolan's and his kin's survival. You will always have your memories of him, and in the meantime you have me. I've always considered myself a father to you, you know."

"Thank you, Edward," she whispered.

His faded gray eyes held concern. "Come to my house tomorrow, my dear. I would like your company in my lonely old age."

She didn't want to see him—or anybody, for that matter.

"Please. My old battle wounds are flaring up and I would like some of your marvelous herbs to comfort me," he whispered, tears in his eyes.

"Oh, Edward, you are too kind to me," she replied, blinking the moisture away from her own eyes.

One more glance out the window confirmed that like a falling star, the love of her life, the whole meaning of her existence, had disappeared.

Chapter Twenty

"Largo, you were marvelous," Dulce enthused and stepped forward as if she were about to give him a hug.

Breath clogging at the thought, he stared at her.

She hesitated and self-consciously cleared her throat. "Uh, well, I mean, you were really, really brave. You were brave in your fighting and you kept the other diplomats from arguing and panicking by wiping out their memories. I would have never thought to do that, and I was so impressed."

His heart squeezed almost unbearably because she was so near, yet he couldn't nuzzle her ever again. After all, she'd jilted him. Not that he hadn't deserved it. He craved her nearness, yearned for what they'd had, but he'd carelessly thrown it away.

Dulce fidgeted, seeming unusually nervous. "Uh, Largo?"

"Yes?"

"I, uh, well, I . . . do you still love me?" she blurted.

He stared at her. "What?"

"Forget that I—"

"Yes! Dulce, I have never stopped loving you. I was a fool, a stupid flat note of a fool when I said those witless things to Allegro and Diminish."

"Oh, Largo, I love you, too. Always and forever!" She reached out and fluttered a delicate wing against him.

The caress made him shiver from head to foot. Something tumbled from her reticule and he glanced down. "My journal? You have my personal journal? That's what Scaley gave to you."

Lower lip between her teeth, she simply stared at him.

With a tilt to his head, he considered this. Then he laughed in a deep booming bass. "Why, that scheming hunk of a matchmaker. Scaley took my journal and gave it to you."

Dulce's eyes widened in amazement. "You're not angry?"

"How can I be angry? All this time I've tried to figure out how to convince you what is in my heart—that I love you with all my might—and Scaley showed you exactly how I felt by giving you my journal. *What a fine fellow he is.*"

"Aye, isn't he marvelous?" Dulce laughed and launched herself into his arms.

Largo treasured her closeness, the rediscovered admiration that he never thought to see again in his beloved's eyes. He cradled her in his arms on a pink cloud that hovered over London, a new cloud birthed from the stormy weather from the previous night, signifying that good had triumphed over evil.

Finally Largo had been able to break through the wall that she had formed around her heart. He knew that he'd hurt her terribly. In a heartfelt gesture, he dropped to his knees. "I vow to never take you for granted again. When I almost lost you, I felt as if my body would break in two. I love you, Dulce."

"Oh, pookie, I love you, too."

For awhile they fluttered their wings together, and Largo savored her brilliant touch.

"And I never knew you studied medieval magic. How did you remember the chant to return Scaley to his underground home?"

"I was so mad at Scaley because he had seemed to snag all your attention with that goddess stuff, I suffered a mind-block. But you know I always did fancy a trip to visit the podzol trolls."

"Well, I'm glad that you were able to return him to his home. Now that the Dingwols have been destroyed and the rest of the Runefyk have been freed, I hope he can rebuild his clan and find the happiness that he deserves."

"So do I." Largo sighed with content. "Now that we've conquered the last of the evil trolls and the Morthdones are no more, I do believe we need to attend to more serious matters."

"What matters are those?"

"Why, the matter of getting married."

"Uh, Largo, I don't know."

"Don't you want to be married to me?"

"M-married? Uh, well, that is . . . I just don't think our mission is completely over."

"What do you mean?"

"Well, there's Tessa and Nolan. They aren't together and it breaks my heart."

Largo gave her a tender smile. "I know, sweet cakes. But this wasn't a love-match mission, so we can't help them. They obviously weren't suited for each other anyway."

Dulce sat up, indignant. "How can you say that? Didn't you see the love in their eyes? Both of them are torn apart inside!"

"There's nothing we can do." Even as he said it, he saw that stubborn gleam in her violet eyes and knew there would be trouble. "Besides, don't you think we had better find Diminish and Allegro? They might need help."

She lifted her chin defiantly. "Go ahead and find them, then. I'm not about to abandon Tessa. She's my friend."

As he watched her fly back down to London, he had a sinking sensation that although she said she loved him, she wasn't about to give up her newfound independence.

He sighed, but realized it was a sigh of contentment. Although their courtship promised to be a long one, he didn't care. In fact, he was joyful. His little songbird enjoyed the same sense of adventure he cherished. Missions of excitement and adventure still loomed in the future, a future that was bright and so very promising.

Because his exciting Dulce would always be by his side.

"His lordship has given everything to you, Lady Ballard—all his funds, his estates, even his seat in Ardmaneth."

Sitting in her study with Nolan's solicitor, her heart seemed to break into a thousand pieces all over again. That she would never be able to share with him the Castle of Lorne in the Highlands, a place he loved so dearly, made her throat burn and her heart twist with unbearable pain. She didn't know if she could go there without him.

"Tell Mrs. Campbell and the rest of the staff that they will always have a position with me. I have decided to make Foxley into a wayward house for women to learn skills with which they can make decent livings. The funds will be used to help establish the women in whatever business they choose."

"Yes, my lady."

She stood, realizing that the hour was late in the day and that she must visit Edward Perry. "If you'll excuse me, I need to run an errand and will leave when you do."

"Of course, ma'am." The older man escorted her out of the townhouse. Addington had already had the carriage pulled around for her. After the butler handed her the basket of herbs she'd prepared for her friend, she walked outside. She was barely aware of stepping inside the coach, her movements as stiff as an old woman's.

Would she ever feel alive again? Would the sharp pain in her soul ever go away? Perhaps over time it would subside to a dull throb, but she instinctively knew it would always be there.

Time only marked the length of her empty days without him. When the coach stopped she was surprised that she hadn't noted the length of time it had taken. The butler showed her into the drawing room where Edward sat near the fire.

"Ah, my dear, I'm so glad you've finally arrived. Please sit." He stood and motioned to a high-backed Georgian chair across from him. She smiled but knew the effort was fruitless when he looked into her eyes. Sitting in the proffered chair, she felt a strange buzzing sensation around her wrists, her shoulders, her ankles. Glancing down, she saw nothing out of the ordinary.

"You look pale and so sad. I know you want your lover back. Shall we call him?"

"Oh, Edward, you have always been so attuned to my needs, but I'm sorry to say that you cannot help me in this. Nolan is gone and there's nothing I can do to entice him to return."

Rising, he walked behind her chair. "Ah, but there's something I can do." Giving her neck a gentle stroke, he brought a thin vine over her head and began to tie it around her neck.

"What are you doing?" Startled, she tried to sit forward but couldn't. Peering closely, she saw a slight shimmer in the air, like a heat wave, about two inches in thickness down the length of her body. Heart thudding in dread, she realized that somehow she'd been rendered immobile.

Perry threw her a menacing smile. "Threatening your life. I know the Shederin loves you. Since your life is in danger the Crystal Tuner will call him." The dead vine was a wisteria, which was stronger than rope. As he secured the garrote around her neck she realized it was wet. "I've tied it loosely, my dear. I figure the Shederin has about thirty minutes before it dries to the point of cutting off all your air. See? The Tuner is already calling him."

Indeed a soft note was beginning to sound. Bewildered, she contemplated the man she'd known for almost half of her life. "Why?" Suddenly it occurred to her. She stared at him, appalled. "Edward, *you're* the Shade Lord?"

Perry moved around to face her, and resumed his chair, leaning back and crossing one leg over the other. "Poor Tessa. I thought I had trained you to be a better spy. But I suppose I can't blame you. After all, how could you have guessed that the man who found you all those years ago is the enemy? It was I who discovered a way to ensconce a wild, half-breed Gypsy with outlandish fighting skills into the *haute ton*."

"Why did you even bother?" she asked. Bitter bile stung the back of her throat.

"I always hoped I could use you to further my plans. In addition, my benevolence helped with my ruse. Who would have guessed that I, your surrogate father, was the Shade Lord? A creature that's half-human, half-shapeshifter. My wizardry skills can only be equaled by the Royal Shederin, and only in his panther form."

Evil hatred shone from eyes that she thought she'd known, but now belonged to a stranger. How could she have been so blind to his true character? Had she been a child so lonely she could be this totally duped? Evidently so.

Testing the limits of her bondage, she realized she could move her hands to the side of her rib cage where one of her knives was sheathed.

In her state of misery, however, she hadn't brought any of her weapons. "But why are you doing this?"

"Because I hate all Shederins. Because I want to rule the world, and I can't do that as long as Nolan is alive."

Desperation clawed at her. "You're luring him here to kill him?"

"Cheer up, my sweet. You'll get to see him again after all, even though it will be the last time before he's gone forever."

She glared at him with a bravado she didn't feel. "Oh, he'll save me and we'll have a fine life together. But you won't even be around to witness anything because you'll be dead."

"Ah, don't be so sure. I doubt if he'll even shapeshift. He didn't last night. Too bad the Shederin fears the dark side of his character, for that is the only side that can save you . . . or kill you."

"What are you saying?"

"Why, that he can only survive the shield I've erected if he changes into a panther, and he can only save you if he can bite the garrote from your neck—which will be exceedingly difficult to do the more the garrote tightens."

Already the binding was getting tighter. "Why don't you think he'll want to bite the garrote off? I feel as if I'm missing something here."

"Ah, you're coming to understand me well, my dear. It's all quite clever, I believe. You see, I didn't know he was a Shederin until my half-brother, Giffen, saw you with him in the warehouse; I'd sent him to kill Chumley."

He motioned to Giffen, a man who posed as a butler

at the rendezvous house. Only Giffen wasn't a man—in horror she watched him shapeshift into a huge wolf. Snarling, saliva dripping from his mouth, he appeared ten times more vicious than any of the wolves they'd defeated last night.

"Why didn't Giffen die with the rest of the shapeshifters with the arrival of Aberdora?"

"Because, my dear, I have excellent hearing and I heard the Tuner from the north long before anyone else. I warned my brothers to change into their human forms, which protected them."

"Why couldn't you defeat us last night, then?"

"The podzol troll and the pixies ruined my plans. That's why I saved Giffen and the rest of my close relatives for later. In addition, I had you followed, especially once I saw your boy give you the note at the soiree."

"You were the one who stole the missive."

"But of course, and I had Giffen kill that traitor, Skeet. After that, I had you followed to Madam Chiartano's abode. The woman betrayed me by telling Nolan about his powers, so she had to die—after I tortured her to find out about Nolan, of course."

The memory of Madam's horrible grimace of pain after her death would be forever etched in Tessa's mind.

"But she did give me information that I'm going to enjoy using against the Shederin. You see, Nolan blamed himself for Selena's death, but little did he know that she was already dead, choked to death by my garrote. Honor and nobility are weaknesses."

"How can you say that?"

"You saw how devastated the Shederin was when he thought he'd killed his wife. Why, I discovered myself how he'd planned his own suicide with those ridiculous cutthroats. In fact, that's one of the main reasons he isn't claiming his love for you. He fears his dark side.

More than ever, he fears that he'll kill you. What will happen to his Shederin soul if he does? He'll die and we won't have to try very hard when we deal him the death blow."

"You won't succeed in this. The pixies will come."

With a shrug, he said, "They can't get in."

The garrote tightened more as her nervousness increased. "The other Shederins will come."

He merely smiled, a cold empty smile. Why hadn't she seen that emptiness in his eyes before?

"I'll tell him what you told me about how you choked Selena to death—that he's not to blame. That will give him confidence."

Shaking his head, Perry merely sighed in mock sympathy. "But he'll remember how he slashed her in his attempts to remove the garrote from her neck. By the time he arrives, the garrote will be so tight, he could very well rip your throat out. Do you want to remind him of that possibility?" Taking out his pocket watch, he flipped open the lid and glanced at the face. "Besides, I doubt if you will be capable of speech in another five minutes, which is when he'll get here."

Helplessness washed over Tessa, an emotion she hadn't felt since her early years with the caravan. As the rope became increasingly uncomfortable, she prayed that whatever happened to her, Nolan would be safe. He was the key to ending evil, which made him not only her hero, but the world's hero.

Vitality hummed around Nolan as he walked through the Passage of Kings in a alternative world that coexisted with Earth. He sensed Earth's energy, the ancient magic that fed the trees, surged in powerful rivers and sustained all creatures.

All his life, he had sensed his aloneness, his extreme

differences from the people around him. He hadn't understood himself, the internal code that was an innate part of his makeup.

He hadn't understood that he was supposed to be the steward of the lands, the warrior against evil forces that strived to tip the balance. According to the whispered legends that surrounded him as his people instructed him, he was the fulcrum—the balancing force that pushed against evil, the point that ensured the balance would tip toward goodness. But no matter how much knowledge was crammed into his mind by the lessons bombarding him about his warrior's strength, he worried.

Doubt crowded his senses because he couldn't reconcile the task of the steward of goodness with the memories of Selena's death. Slashing Selena's throat was too vivid in his mind. The cuts had been shallow, but obviously they had been deep enough to murder her.

How could he accept such a responsibility—to act as the steward of goodness—when he feared a black decay in his soul? How could he ever hope to overcome this evil side of him?

Then he knew. Only one advantage would conquer the evil that lurked inside him.

Love. Shared love for his soul mate.

Tessa.

She was the good part of him—the side that made him whole. He had made a colossal mistake. In leaving her, he had left the good side of himself. He must reclaim her. He needed her by his side.

The note floated in the hemisphere toward the plane that was now his world, the note from the Crystal Tuner that he'd given Tessa.

Her life's energy ebbed.

No! He couldn't lose her! My God, what had he done? His stupidity in leaving her might result in losing her forever, which would be his downfall—and the world's.

Fear shook him so much that he became weak-kneed. Desperately he searched through the atmospheric layers toward her dimly pulsating life light and found her, surrounded by black tar that no human could survive, which made him quake with renewed dread, for he knew what he must do if he were to save her . . . or kill her.

He must shapeshift.

Calling all his powers to him from Earth's magic, he closed his eyes and willed himself to materialize in front of Edward Perry's townhouse near Hanover Square.

Edward Perry?

The realization shocked him. For he knew that Perry was the Shade Lord. He reached for the Crystal Tuner but remembered that Tessa had the trinket. No matter, he must shapeshift and call upon the righteousness in his soul to guide him. *Dear God, could he do it? No.* He began to shake. Yes, he had to—he must. And in order to succeed, he must call upon Tessa's love as well as his love for her. Taking a deep breath, he opened his heart and his mind to her.

In her semiconscious state, with pain burning her throat, he felt her love and was liberated. His senses sharpened abruptly. The sound of a housecat's purr was just over the wall to his right. A cricket chirped to him before crawling into the groundcover by the front door. A mockingbird called a wish of goodwill before flying off. A sickly yarrow plant bloomed white.

The powers of love were with him.

Springing up the steps in his potent panther body, he willed the door to relent. He prowled inside.

Tessa's life energy throbbed weakly—to the right.

Perry lurked in the shadows. The Shade Lord. "Ah, you came," he said.

The wizard had hidden his true self, but now the cold grip of evil hovered in the air surrounding him. Nolan ignored him; his concern for Tessa was all that mattered. He found her trapped in the Georgian chair, her face turning purple as a slender but deadly garrote tightened around her neck. The strand of wisteria was so tight that Nolan had difficulty discerning the vine from her skin.

Suddenly he remembered that he'd discovered Selena also being choked to death. That had been the reason he'd bit her neck, slashed at her with his claws, slashes that had killed her in the end.

"You killed your wife. All those vicious teeth marks tearing into that delicate skin. Will you murder your lover, too?"

Fear rose to his heart. No, he couldn't bear the thought of hurting her delicate throat.

"You enjoyed tasting Selena's blood. Will you enjoy Tessa's sweet fluids as well?"

Shuddering, he discovered himself screaming a panther cry of agony at the doubts and terror that assailed him. Suddenly Tessa opened her eyes and gave him the sweetest, most loving smile he'd ever seen on her face.

She believed in him.

Gently he rubbed his nose, his black pelt against her, then bared his teeth and tried to slip a pointed tip under the garrote. A line of blood appeared. He growled in misery.

She arched her neck in return and went limp.

What could he do? How was this time different? Then he knew. She knew exactly what he was and she still loved him. Unconditionally. Licking her, this time he called on nature, on the powers of Mother Earth. The dormant speck of life that reminded the wisteria of the wonders of life responded by growing a sixteenth of an inch. It was enough slack for him to slip his tooth underneath the garrote and snap it.

As Tessa gasped a deep breath of life-sustaining air,

the Shade Lord pounded his staffs together, calling to lightning to strike Nolan dead. But the Shederin was already moving, calling the Earth's forces to battle. Power surged through him as he leapt toward the wizard, breaking through the barrier and sinking his teeth into his enemy's neck.

A ghostly howl was emitted by the Shade Lord as he exploded into the shadows of the universe, his particles turning to dust. Light poured over the townhouse, causing the dark spell to burn and wither in the sun. The remaining Morthdones barked in fear before they, too, detonated into nothing.

Bursting with love, Nolan nuzzled his cat's whiskers over Tessa's bruised neck, blowing his healing magic over her delicate skin. Her olive skin glowed, but not as brightly as her midnight eyes.

Hearty laughter peeled out of her as she threw her arms around his furry neck and kissed his panther's nose. In a flash he changed into his human form and returned her kiss, pouring into that embrace all the love from his heart, a love he knew would continue to grow.

"I can't live without you. Your love is a vital part of my goodness and I can't be the Royal Shederin warrior I was destined to be without you by my side."

She frowned. "What are you saying?"

"I'm trying to tell you that I need you with me to help me in the fight against evil. Just as the plants of the Earth will continue to grow, so will my love for you. I love you so much, but not as much as I will tomorrow."

Narrowing her eyes upon his face in suspicion, she seemed to consider. "What's your point?"

"Tessa, my love, the good part of me, will you be my wife and live with me forever in the city of Aberdora?"

Her dark eyes snapped with challenge. "I will consent only under one condition."

"Yes?"

"Only if we have grass before breakfast on a weekly basis." She mimicked a dueling stance without her sword.

A deep throaty laugh emitted from him. "Always, my dear warrior, my life mate."

With the power of their love surrounding them, they hugged each other tightly as they spiraled into the clouds toward Aberdora, their laughter causing flowers to bloom and the sun to shine brightly.

Kissed by Magic

Gloria Harchar

The faeries' mission—were Allegro and Largo to accept it—is to do the impossible: make the earl of Falconwood, "the Black Falcon," fall in love with Phaidra Moore, the incorrigible spinster of Nottingham. Never mind that the woman is a hoyden who makes the most atrocious hats and colors them with her own creation, the famous Nottingham Blue. And certainly forget that the earl is atoning for his brother's death, keeping himself at the fringes of the *ton*. Allegro and Largo have to make the twosome *fall in love*! But the Maestro wants it so, and thus the skinny faerie and the fat one make up their minds—very soon both Phaidra and Kain will be . . . *Kissed By Magic*.

TO KISS A FROG

ELLE JAMES

Craig Thibodeaux is cursed. Frog by day and man by night, he has until the next full moon to free himself—by finding someone to love him. Elaine Smith seems perfect. She is beautiful and smart, and even passionate about frogs. But while she came to Bayou Miste at just the right time, the sexy scientist needs a bodyguard—not a boyfriend. And truth be told, he was a bit more frog than Prince Charming even before he tangled with that Voodoo Queen. Elaine deserves more. She deserves to be the queen of someone's pad: a wife. But with a single kiss, Craig might start to believe in fairytale endings.

Dorchester Publishing Co., Inc.
P.O. Box 6640
Wayne, PA 19087-8640

___52620-4
$5.99 US/$7.99 CAN

KAREN WHIDDON
SOUL MAGIC

The ancient magic of Rune is fading, and legends speak of mortals and fae joining together to renew it. Thus to Thorncliff Keep the fae Alanna goes, to seek him: the mortal whom she left at the altar. Betrothed from childhood, she has always loved Darrick Tadhg. The knight's strong arms and mighty sword still cause her to shiver with desire. But a terrible wrong came between them, a terrible shame that she has no desire to reveal.

No, Darrick will not want Alanna, not now, with her secret, after his life has been darkened by tragedy and when his keep is besieged. He will not want to leave on the journey they must undertake. But Alanna will, for the sake of her life and the sake of her kingdom, and for the sake of their love, convince Darrick of the power of their joined souls—and of Fate, which never meant for them to be apart.

CHERYL STERLING

What Do You Say to a Naked Elf?

Apart from her being a TV and movie junkie and a saleswoman extraordinaire of adult lotions, potions and playthings, plain Jane Drysdale's life is nothing unusual. That is, until a moment of reckless driving catapults her into a fairytale world. From Walker, Michigan, to a place of wizards, elves and dwarves, Jane is suddenly fulfilling an epic destiny that holds certain death—and even more certain love. Everything starts with Jane on trial for her life and her Legolas-lookalike lawyer taking his shirt off, and the first thing she needs to know is…WHAT DO YOU SAY TO A NAKED ELF?

One or two things sprang to mind.

DIVINE FIRE
MELANIE JACKSON

In 1816, Lord Byron stayed at the castle of Dr. Johann Dippel, the inspiration for Mary Shelley's Baron von Frankenstein. The doctor promised a cure for his epilepsy. That "cure" changed him forever.

In the 21st century, Brice Ashton wrote a book. Like all biographies of famous persons, hers on Lord Byron was sent to critics in advance. One Damien Ruthven responded. He suggested her work contained two errors—and that only he could give her the truth. His words held hints of long-lost knowledge; were fraught with danger, deception…and desire. And his eyes showed the experience of centuries. Damien promised to share his secrets. But first, Brice knew, she would have to share herself with him.

Dream of Me
LISA CACH

Theron, undying creature of the Night World, knows everything about making love. But though he's an incubus, a bringer of carnal dreams to sleeping maids, he has grander ambition. He plots to step into the mortal world and rule as king.

The beautiful Lucia is imprisoned in a fortress atop a mountain. Her betrothed, Prince Vlad of Wallachia, wants her purity intact; but when the prince breaks his vow, nothing can keep her safe. In the name of vengeance, Lucia will be subjected to Theron's seduction; she will learn all his lips might teach.

A demon of lust and a sheltered princess: each dreams of what they've never had. They're about to get everything they wish…and more.